Skating the BLUE LINE

CHICAGO DARK KNIGHTS BOOK 1

JOCELYNE SOTO

Skating the
BLUE LINE
CHICAGO DARK KNIGHTS BOOK 1
JOCELYNE SOTO

PLAYLIST

Get You - Daniel Caesar, Kali Uchis

Happiness is a Butterfly - Lana del Rey

Für Elise - Beethoven Collection

Cherry - Harry Styles

Take Me To Church - Hozier

Still Don't Know My Name - Labrinth

Heather - Conan Gray

Give Me Love - Ed Sheeran

A Drop in the Ocean - Ron Pope

La Santa - Bad Bunny, Daddy Yankee

Mi Coranzoncito - Aventura

Suga Suga - Baby Bash, Frankie K

Nasty - Ariana Grande

My whole life, I have only dreamt of being one thing.
A ballerina.
From the age of three, I was obsessed with tutus, leotards, pointe shoes and everything that dancing had to offer.
After years of hard work, sweat and tears, I finally was able to make the dreams of the little girl in me come true.
Years later, I'm dancing for one of the most respected companies in the world, leaving out a dream and living the best life that I could have ever imagined.
Everything was going according to how I'd mapped it out.
Except…
I hadn't mapped out two little blue lines skating into my life after a one night stand.
Now, there's a possibility of me losing the dream I worked so hard to achieve.
And it's all thanks to a professional hockey player with pretty eyes and a nice smile.

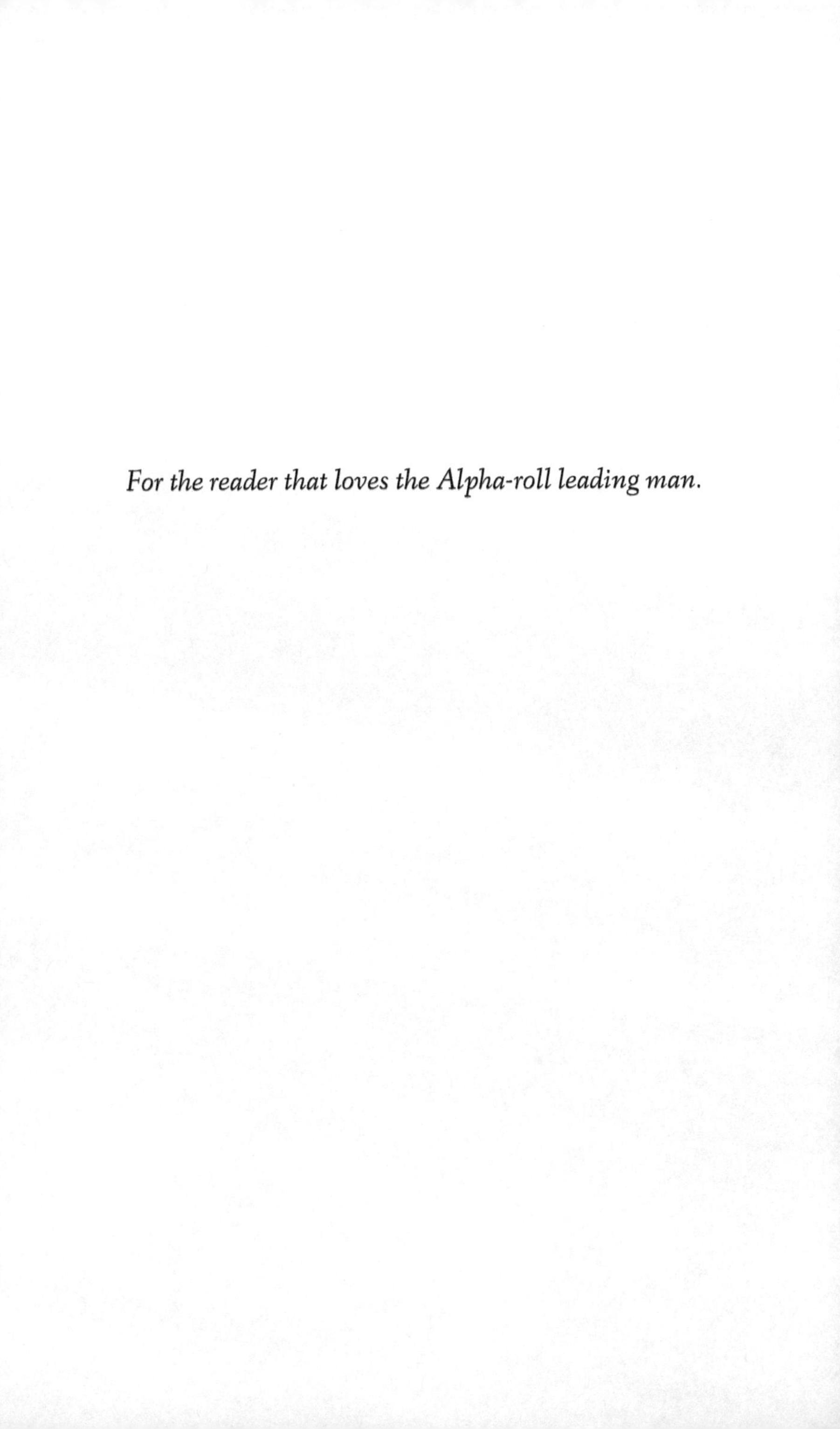

For the reader that loves the Alpha-roll leading man.

CHAPTER ONE

LIAM

SEPTEMBER

I LOOK DOWN at my phone screen and let out a sigh.

A text message stares back at me with a set of words that I honestly don't feel like hearing or seeing tonight.

Sorry. I can't make it.

Great. Now I have to go to this stupid event by myself.

I should have expected it given who I asked to go with me, but that didn't stop my mind from getting its hopes up just a little about not going to this thing alone.

These types of events are the kind of thing that make me want to stab my eyes and pull my hair out all at the same time just from boredom. I figured having someone there with me would stop me from doing that.

Guess not.

Grumbling, I pocket my phone and grab my tuxedo

jacket from where it lies on the bed, pulling it on before turning to look at myself in the mirror.

I don't usually hate wearing suits.

They've been a staple in my closet since I was eighteen, and I have fun with them. But there's something about wearing a tuxedo, with a bow tie no less, that makes my teeth grind. I'm sure that there are men out in the world who look for any excuse to wear a good tuxedo. I'm not one of those men.

Looking in the mirror right now, all I see is a fucking penguin in a bow tie chokehold staring back at me.

Don't get me wrong, I look good, but it's so damn constricting.

With another grumble, I shake my head and make my way out into the hallway.

If I hadn't committed to attending this event, I would stay home. Maybe order the one take-out meal that I allow myself each week and watch the San Francisco Gold's game.

But contractual obligations and all of that.

After grabbing the keys to my Aston Martin, one of my favorite babies, I lock up the place and start making my way down to the Chicago Opera house.

The city is alive tonight, and for a few miles I don't mind the fact that I have to drive through traffic. Seeing the city like this reminds me of why I was so excited to sign with Chicago at eighteen. It's times like this that my love for the city really shines through and I'm able to thank it for giving me the ability to do what I do.

That feeling doesn't last long, though.

Some asshole cuts me off ,and I'm quickly reminded that I could be at home right now instead of heading to this stupid thing.

There are things about being a professional athlete that I despise. Things that come with the professional part but have nothing to do with the athlete or the sport that is played whatsoever.

Those things make being a professional athlete unbearable at times.

You want to slap a C on my jersey? I'll wear it with pride and be the best damn captain you will ever see.

You want to make me the face of your team? I will smile proudly at the camera for any picture you want to take. I'll also happily take any picture next to any fan who asks.

Anything to do with hockey, and my team, or charity work, I will gladly do.

But if you want to put me in a monkey suit and make me a brand ambassador for your company? I will grumble and complain under my breath every chance that I get.

If I could go through my professional career without working as a spokesperson, ambassador, or whatever the fuck, for a clothing or watch company, I would.

But, of course, it's poor business for the captain of the Chicago Dark Knights, or any sports team, to turn down an endorsement deal with anyone with a respectable name.

Which is why I'm currently in a stupid tuxedo, driving through commuter traffic, to get to the opera house. At the very least, they tailored the tuxedo for my body, so I can't complain about that.

Tonight, one of the brands that I'm a spokesperson for is throwing an event. A night at the ballet.

That should have been my first sign to say no, and the second should have been the black-tie requirement at the bottom of the invitation.

Yet, I still RSVP'd and found a date.

Now I'm dateless and going to an event I really don't want to attend.

I don't usually complain about these types of things. Most of the time, I go to whatever event my agent tells me to and pretend that I want to be there. I may only do it for an hour or two, but I still do it.

Tonight, is a little different.

Ninety-nine percent of the time I usually have someone at my side to make these events a little more bearable. Whether it be a friend or a gorgeous woman, or hell, even my agent, I always have someone there. When I do attend an event all by myself, I make sure it's something that I enjoy.

Tonight, I would much rather do line drills without a break than sit in a theater for three hours watching ballet.

I'm sure whoever planned this wanted all their guests tonight to have a good nap because this is guaranteed to be a snooze fest.

Harsh, but the truth.

Shaking my head, I rein in my dislike for the night and pull into the valet station that is set up in front of the opera house.

My door opens, and I take a second to compose myself and my face.

I can't go out in public looking like I'm being tortured. That shit will hit social media platforms faster than I can slapshot a puck.

The second I step foot out of the car, I go from being Liam Crawford, the guy who doesn't want to be here, to Liam Crawford, the hockey captain with the charming smile who people pay big money to see.

"Sweet ride, Cap," the valet attending says the second my feet are planted firmly on the ground.

I look at the kid as I button up my tuxedo jacket and give him a smile. He can't be more than eighteen.

"Thanks." I give the kid my key and a hundred-dollar tip to go along with it. "Keep her safe, yeah?"

He gives me an eager nod and a smile so big it might rip his face in half. "Yes, Cap. Of course. Have a nice evening, Mr. Crawford, sir."

I give him a nod and start making my way toward the red carpet and the photographers and reporters who trying to make this event a lot larger than it needs to be.

With the amount of press here tonight, you would think it was an event put on by Chicago's richest family, when in fact it isn't.

It isn't even a charity event garnering this much attention.

It's a launch party for a new line of suits for Archwell, a suit company out of New York. I'm one of the many faces who the brand sponsors. Why they are having an event of this magnitude in Chicago instead of New York is beyond me.

But, here we are.

As I walk to the front of the theater, I try to avoid eye contact with anyone who might make me walk the small strip of red carpet.

I almost succeed but the head of marketing for Archwell spots me before I'm able to head inside and diverts me toward the flashing lights.

Grumbling, I slap a smile on my face, and take more pictures than necessary and answer mundane questions.

Am I excited about the new line of suits?

How excited am I for the ballet?

I want to roll my eyes at every single one of them, but somehow I'm able to answer all questions and make it believable.

Am I excited? Sure.

How excited am I about tonight? No scale can begin to measure how I feel about tonight.

Questions like this are just another one of those things about being an athlete that I despise.

Fifteen minutes after arriving, I'm finally able to make it inside.

The lobby of the theater is filled with people waiting for the doors to the auditorium to open so they can take their seats.

Every single person is dressed to the absolute nines.

It only takes a handful of seconds after I walk in for a few individuals to come up to me and shake my hand, all while telling me how they hope this is the season that the Dark Knights make it to the playoffs and possibly to the Stanley Cup finals.

Me and them both, I want to tell them, but I don't.

The Dark Knights haven't made it to the playoffs in six years. Our team is good, and I'm not just saying that because I'm the captain. We have the grit and strength to win the cup, but for some reason, when we come close, we always tend to fall apart. Both on and off the ice.

There are rumors flying around that the team is getting a new owner soon. Hopefully, if the rumors are true, it would be for the better of the team and not for the worse. Especially since the season starts in a few weeks. We need all the help that we can get to be able to bring that cup to Chicago.

New team owner or not, though, I'm going to make it my mission to get my team to the Finals. I'm promising myself that tonight.

No matter what, I will try everything to make it happen.

After some small talk with a few more hockey fans, I head to the bar and grab a drink. No way am I going to be sitting through three hours of this completely sober.

"Whiskey neat, please," I say to the bartender before he nods and goes to pour my drink and slides it over to me.

"Damn. Whiskey? And here I thought Liam Crawford was a vodka man."

I turn toward the voice and find Elliot Lane standing a few feet away, dressed exactly as I am in a penguin suit.

Elliot is a member of the richest family the city has to offer. The same family who would garner the amount of press coverage that's outside.

Having a professional athlete and company CEOs attend your event is a good draw for of media coverage. But having a

Lane family member here? Media coverage goes from being good to being fucking fantastic.

The family is known for their tech, their money, their good looks, their newsworthy charity work, and of course the bachelor status of the two oldest nephews.

Elliot Lane is Chicago royalty, its prince and heir to the family throne. Having him at your event is a surefire way of making big money.

I met the guy a few years ago during my rookie year. He's a cool guy, and from interacting with him, I know he hates these types of things just as much as I do.

Whereas I do it for my contract obligations, he does it for familial obligations.

"And I thought that Elliot Lane would be too big of a name for this type of thing." I throw a smirk in his direction.

"Yeah, well, everyone needs a good suit, right?" he says right before taking a sip from a drink that looks like mine.

The way he says the words, it's as if he doesn't want to be here anymore than I do.

"True, but I'm sure you can snap your fingers, and the new suit line will appear in your closet without the need to come here."

My comment earns me a shrug. "Sometimes it pays to show your face. Especially when it comes to a business deal."

Interesting. Knowing who his family is and what they do, he's no doubt here to see if he can get in someone's line of sight. Or buy a company or two.

"I hear the Knights might be getting new owners soon."

Elliot changes the subject quickly, not giving me a chance to respond to his comment.

The rumors of the Knights being sold aren't just rumors going around in the locker room or the team's group chat thread. The entire hockey world is talking about it.

It's no surprise that Elliot knows about it either, since at one point in time, his family owned the team before they selling it off to someone with better qualifications.

I give him a nod. "That's what's being said. You have any idea who it might be?"

"I've heard a few names being thrown around, but nothing concrete. Though you would know better than I would." He gives me a shrug.

Doubt that but I don't push it.

I'm about to change the subject again when it's announced that the audience should start taking their seats.

The show is about to start.

"I guess that's our cue," Elliot says, finishing up his drink before giving me a nod and heading into the theater.

Instead of following Lane and everyone else into the dark room, I stay behind to savor the rest of my drink.

The second the last drop of whiskey hits my tongue, I think about asking the bartender for another one but decide against it.

It would be bad form to get shitfaced at an event like this. Especially with the number of fans and press who are here. One bad picture or video and I can kiss my whole career goodbye.

Instead of asking for a second drink, I make my way into

the theater and take a seat in the back row. I'm in no way small. Being a two hundred-twenty pound, six foot four hockey player has some advantages but not in a theater like this. Sitting in the back doesn't have me blocking anyone's way of seeing the stage and it gives me a better opportunity to sneak away.

A few minutes after I take my seat, the theater fills up, and they close the doors, the lights above flickering to announce that the show is about to begin.

From where I'm sitting, I can see the whole room and every person in it. Apart from the select few individuals who I know from Archwell and Elliot Lane, the room is filled with stuffy rich people.

There is no doubt in my mind that not only am I one of the youngest people in the room, but I'm also probably the poorest.

I may have multiple multimillion dollar contracts in my name, but that isn't enough to reach the magnitude of wealth in the room.

Now I know why Archwell decided to have the event in Chicago. It will bring millions into their pockets.

The wealth in the room is forgotten when the lights dim.

Given the darkness that envelops me, maybe I will be able to take a nap during this thing.

I start to get comfortable in my seat, thanks to whatever stranger decided not to sit next to me, and start closing my eyes to take a quick cat nap. It's when my eyes are nearly closed when the spotlight on stage shines and takes all my attention.

The room is quiet as the light shines bright, as if everyone here is waiting to see what happens next even if they already know.

Even me, who was getting ready to sleep, is sitting here in anticipation.

I start counting in my head and it takes someone thirty seconds to step onto the stage and take their place at the center.

A woman from what I can tell even in the darkness.

Her back is to the audience, and we all watch as she gets into position.

She stands, facing away from us for another half minute before she turns.

The center stage light shines bright and illuminates her up beautifully. Everything about this woman, this dancer, glows, especially her eyes.

Even though I'm sitting far away, I can still make out a twinkle in them. A twinkle that tells me that she might be her happiest while on stage.

She's beautiful, and when she gives the audience a smile, even more so.

Music starts to fill the room and soon the curtains are pulled back, and others join the first dancer.

For the remainder of the show, I forget about my nap or feeling any type of boredom for the full three hours.

I forget about not wanting to be here and how I wanted to stab my eyes out at the beginning of the night.

I forget about my distaste for penguin suits and being in a room filled with rich, old people.

Everything I thought this night would be, is completely forgotten, and I spend three hours being captivated by what is happening on stage.

Not only by what is happening on stage but also by one person.

For three hours, I follow the first female dancer and everything she does. Smiling, cheering her on, and admiring her as if she is the one and only star of the show.

And in my eyes, she is, and I don't even know her.

Three hours of her having my whole, undivided attention.

For the first time ever, I enjoy a night at the ballet.

CHAPTER TWO

CHLOE

I GIVE my lips one final swipe with my favorite lip gloss and when they look exactly how I want them to, I give my reflection a smile.

Damn, do I always look this good after a performance? Because right now, my reflection is smoking hot, and I'm loving it.

Performances should feel like this more often.

Moving past the mirror, I go to the small clothing rack with my name on it in the corner of the room and grab the garment bag that I brought with me tonight.

Usually after a performance of any magnitude, I'm all for taking off every ounce of makeup on my face and slapping on some sweats and a sweatshirt that covers the majority of my body. Then spend the rest of the night eating Chinese food and watching crappy rom-coms.

I'm not one to join the after-parties very often.

Tonight, though, our director is having all us dancers stay

and mingle a bit with the guests who were invited here by a suit company.

Who this suit company is, I have no idea. All I know is that they are becoming one of the dance company's sponsors, so it means we have to stay and show our appreciation.

I would much rather head out and grab a slice of a deep-dish pizza, but I'm getting paid to talk to a few people, so I won't complain all that much.

Pulling down the zipper of the garment bag, I look at the dress I bought a few days ago specifically for this.

Usually, our busiest time of year is around the holidays, so if I ever attend an event like this, I always tend to be in the holiday spirit or wear something black.

For some reason, though, I wanted to wear something different tonight, something more Chloe the person than Chloe the ballerina.

The blue satin material looks amazing on the hanger, and I have no doubt it will look the same on my body.

With a smile, I take the dress off the hanger and slide it on.

The fabric feels like absolute butter against my skin.

I turn to look at myself in the mirror, and I absolutely love the reflection staring back at me.

This dress is from a small boutique in Austin. I had been home visiting my parents for a few days and went to go look for a dress for tonight. The baby blue color caught my atten-tion from outside the shop. I hadn't even stepped foot in the boutique, and I already knew that I wanted whatever piece of clothing that was in that color.

Walking into the boutique, I went straight to the color and silently hoped that it was at least a decent design.

When I pulled it from the racks, I smiled instantly. Not only was the color gorgeous from outside, but the dress the fabric and the dress it was made into were equally as beautiful.

It was the only piece in that color, and it was my size, so I saw it as fate and had to get it. Even if I was going to be eating spam and eggs for the next two weeks given the price.

As I was paying, the woman behind the counter smiled at me when she saw the dress I was buying. I guess the dress was designed by someone who used to work there before she branched out the year before to design on her own. They carry all her new designs, she told me.

I told her that the dress was gorgeous, and she agreed.

Leaving that boutique, I was happy, and now as I look at my reflection, happiness returns.

The dress might have cost me a pretty penny, but damn, it was worth it.

Once the dress is sitting perfectly against my body, I slide into the strappy heels that I bought to go with the dress and give myself one last look.

Everything is sitting exactly how I want it, and adding to how I performed tonight, I look and feel like a million bucks.

Satisfied with everything, I start making my way to the front of the theater where the cocktail hour is being held.

Along the way, I pass a few of my fellow dancers, who throw compliments my way as I pass them. But it's one dancer who has my smile of the night growing even more.

"Damn, Chlo. You look hot! I would definitely leave my husband for you," Betty, a fellow dancer, and my best friend, says as I walk toward her in the hallway.

I give her a twirl so she can get the whole effect. "Isn't the dress gorgeous?"

"The dress? Girl, I wasn't talking about the dress. I was talking about you! You're looking smoking hot right now," she tells me, and I can't help but beam.

Betty always tells me that I look good. I can be wearing my most raggedy sweats, and she will tell me that I look gorgeous. For some reason, hearing those words tonight, enhances the high I'm on.

I had an amazing night on stage. I feel gorgeous and my best friend telling me so makes me feel like I'm on the moon or something.

"Thanks," I say, giving her a kiss on the cheek. "Aren't you heading to the party?" I ask, taking notice that she's in sweatpants and still has stage makeup on.

Betty lets out a sigh. "I got a call from Cole. One of the kids is throwing up, and he's freaking out. I have to go rescue him."

My best friend is about three years older than me and has been by my side ever since I signed on with the company. That was almost eight years ago, and we have been joined at the hip ever since. We're very much alike, but while we are both professional dancers for the Chicago Dance Company, we're in different stages of our lives.

Betty is married and a mom to two adorable kids, and while she loves dancing just as much as I do, she has decided that this will be her last year. She is putting up her pointe shoes and retiring as a dancer.

All the while, I'm here at the peak of my career, nowhere near calling it quits or even close to thinking about having kids or getting married.

"That sucks. Who's supposed to rescue me when I get approached by creepy old men?" I tease, knowing that her kids are more important than some silly party.

"Oh, please. You can handle them on your own." She rolls her eyes. All the while a smile plays on her lips.

I can't help but laugh. She's right. I can handle any creep who comes my way.

"I guess. Go take care of your babies." I wave her off.

Betty closes the distance between us and plants a sloppy kiss on my cheek.

"Call me tomorrow with all the gossip," she says when she pulls away.

"What gossip? I doubt anything is going to happen at a function put on by a suit company," I say, laughing a little.

Betty lets out a gasp like she can't believe what I just said. "Hello. Half of Chicago's elite is in that room. Anything could happen. Especially when everyone sees you walk in with that dress on. Not only will you be the talk of the town, you'll probably also have more than a handful of offers from old men begging to be your sugar daddy."

I roll my eyes at her dancing eyebrows and at the smirk that is currently forming on her face.

"Don't you have a husband to go rescue or something?" I ask, giving her a shove.

She laughs before leaning in again and giving me another kiss. "I'm not kidding. Text me all the details. I bet a coffee tomorrow that you go home with a hottie tonight. You look worthy of some toe sucking."

"So gross. Go," I say through a laugh, shaking my head at my best friend.

Betty lets out a laugh to match mine before giving me a wave and walking away.

Toe sucking worthy.

I knew I was looking hot tonight, but damn, that's another level. One that I really don't want to reach.

Nobody, and I mean nobody, is putting their mouth on my toes. I have ballerina feet, and half the time, *I* don't even want to touch them.

Just thinking about it makes me cringe.

So gross.

Getting the image of toe sucking out of my mind, I continue to make my way down the hall toward the front of the theater.

The music that's playing gets louder, and as soon as I open the door and cross the threshold, I'm enthralled by the magnitude of this event.

I knew it was a packed house the second that I stepped foot onto the stage earlier, but I didn't expect this.

The room, it's more like a ballroom really, is jammed packed with people and photographers.

Betty was right when she said that this event was full of Chicago's elite. If I had to guess, the majority of the city's one percenters were here enjoying the night.

The more I look around, though, I notice that the place is filled with older people.

For some reason, I thought an event like this would be attended by social media stars and young celebrities. Given what our dance director told us about the brand, I would have thought they would be marketing to that demographic.

Guess not.

As I take in all the aspects of the room, I see a few of my fellow dancers having conversations with some of the attendees.

We were told to interact with guests and get them interested in coming to another one of our performances in the next few months.

As much as I don't want to network, I abandon my place by the back door and make my way through the sea of people.

I throw smiles in the direction of men who look at me as if I'm food and nod toward the women who look me up and down as if I were their competition. I'm not, but that doesn't stop them from giving me looks of judgment.

If I have to deal with getting predatory or judgmental looks all night, I'm going to need a drink to get me through it.

It doesn't take long for me to get a glass of wine from the bartender, an expensive one at that, and start making my way around the room again.

I throw out a few more smiles and nods as I make my way around. I'm about to head over to where some of my dance mates are when I catch a glimpse of something.

Well, not something, but someone.

A big someone. Someone whose face I've seen around the city.

Liam Crawford.

Liam Crawford, who is one of the few professional hockey players whose name I actually know.

Do I know anything else about hockey? No.

My knowledge of the sport is limited to a few things. Knowing that the puck has to make it into the net to score, that Chicago has a team, and knowing some of the players' names on said team.

Being a dancer for this particular dance company, you sometimes have to interact with the athletes and celebrities the city has to offer. Chicago is a city that takes its sports seriously. When you live in a sports city like Chicago, you come to know athletes' names and faces without having to follow their teams.

Which is how I know of Liam Crawford.

His face and name are plastered all over the place. There isn't a day that goes by or a corner you can turn, where you won't see his face.

He's on billboards and buses, and every pub and sports bar in the city has at least one poster of him or his jersey hanging on their walls.

Mr. Crawford is everywhere.

Seeing him here should be a little surprising, but it isn't.

He's exactly who should be at an event like this. He's who Archwell should be marketing toward, since I know athletes tend to wear a lot of suits.

Him being here isn't surprising, but seeing him alone is.

From the pictures that I've seen online and the rumors that I've heard, Liam isn't one to attend an event like this alone.

He always has someone at his side.

Seeing him here by himself, nursing a drink, has my interest piqued.

I have to network and he's not currently talking to anyone, so he might be a good person to start mingling with.

The man in question must be a mind reader or something because a few seconds after I decide to head over and talk to the guy, he looks up and meets my gaze.

I've never spoken to him. Never been anywhere within five feet of him, so he doesn't know who I am, but from the way he is looking at me, it's as if he does.

His gaze is full of with something that I can't name. It's like curiosity and admiration all wrapped into one, but I'm not sure. Whatever it is, though, it's causing small flutters in my stomach.

Flutters that I sure as hell don't get when I see his face on a giant billboard.

Feeling them now has to be because I know he's famous and I've never made eye contact with someone famous. At least not someone who's plastered all over town.

Besides, he has to look at everyone like that.

Right? Right. I'm not so special to warrant that kind of look.

Maybe it's the dress.

It has to be the dress. Why else would Liam Crawford be looking at me like I'm his next meal?

Whatever it may be is causing this serious stare down, I push it aside and make my way over to the man.

I wonder if he's this intense up close as he is from across the room.

He must be, because his gaze doesn't waver as I make my way over to him. We both watch each other, and unlike what I've experienced with most men tonight, his eyes stay on my face and don't move down my body.

His eyes stay on my face. Mine stay on his. I try to register as many details as about him as I can, but it's a little difficult with the distance between us. The only thing that I can pinpoint is the fact that he has tattoos covering both of his hands.

In all the pictures that I've seen of this man, I never noticed he has hand tattoos.

There is definitely something sexy about that, especially when he's wearing a tuxedo.

Great, I just thought that the guy I'm about to approach is sexy. It's not a lie, but it's definitely not something that I should be thinking about.

Feeling a bit awkward, I throw a small smile in his direction, expecting for him to just continue to stare at me, but he doesn't.

A closed-lip smile forms on his face in return. He looks almost boyish wearing that smile instead of the professional hockey player with hand tattoos that he is.

I like it. Maybe a little more than I actually should.

Pushing down the feeling of wanting to see this guy smile some more, I continue my path toward him. I'm a few feet away, when someone else comes into my line of sight and stops me in my tracks.

"Oh, I'm sorry. I didn't see you there," I say to the older gentleman I bumped into, even though he walked right in front of me.

"It's alright," he says with a head nod, as if it was truly my fault he stepped in front of me. "You're one of the ballet girls who was on stage earlier, aren't you?"

I give the older man a smile. "I am."

"I thought so. You were great."

My smile grows slightly bigger. "Thank you. I'm glad that you enjoyed the performance."

He gives me a curt nod. "Absolutely. I do have one question. Do you do private performances?"

Umm. What?

"Private performances?" I ask as I feel my eyebrows bunching up. I try to keep a smile on my face, but I have no idea if I'm succeeding or not.

Is he asking what I think he's asking?

There is no fucking way. I have to be imagining this conversation or something.

"Yes, private performances," he states. "I host a poker night for me and a few friends once a month, and I would love to add some entertainment to it. Given your dancing skills, I think that you would be perfect for what I'm thinking."

Perfect for what he's thinking.

So many images run through my head of what that could

be. Especially given that it would be for a poker night filled with men. At least I assume it's men.

For all I know, he's thinking about having me at one of his poker games in my leotard, dancing around and having me strip for him and his friends.

I'm not a strip ballerina, even though the idea does seem like a good one if it is for someone I'm seeing, but not with a group of men I know nothing about.

Red flags everywhere.

I give the guy the sweetest customer service smile that I can muster. "Unfortunately, I'm not allowed to do any performance not put on by the dance company per my contract. I'm sorry."

That's a complete lie, but he doesn't know that.

"I'll pay you whatever your contract is for you to do it," he offers, his face stoic.

Enticing, but no.

I'm about to tell this man no once again, but I'm stopped when a figure approaches us.

My eyes go slightly wide at the person who just joined us.

Liam Crawford.

He is a lot bigger up close than he is across the room or on a TV screen. Not as big as the billboards, though.

What is he doing over here?

"Can we help you with something?" The older man's voice takes me out of the small cloud that having Liam close by has put me in.

"Sorry, I didn't mean to interrupt," Liam tells the man, turning slightly to give him a gleaming smile before turning his attention to me. "I was just wondering if I can borrow my girlfriend for a bit. I have yet to congratulate her on her performance tonight."

If I was drinking my wine right about now, it would be all over the old man's fancy suit.

Girlfriend?

Did he just call me his *girlfriend*?

I'm not hearing things, am I?

From the wink he throws in my direction, I certainly heard him correctly.

He must have seen how awkward my interaction with this guy was and decided to step in.

He's pretending, and the wink he threw in my direction was him asking me to play along.

I'm here for it.

I wipe whatever surprised expression is on my face and give Liam a bright smile.

"You did promise me a slice of deep-dish pizza if I was able to take your breath away," I say, fluttering my eyelashes at him for effect.

Liam lets out a chuckle and gives me a nod. "I did, and since you took more than just my breath away, I think I owe you the whole pie."

The butterflies I was feeling a few minutes ago are back and a hell of a lot stronger.

Not only are the butterflies in full effect, but I can also feel a blush creep up my cheeks.

For a second, I get lost in his gaze, one that I'm positive he uses on everyone, before I remember we have company.

I move my smile from Liam to the older gentleman and give him a nod. "I do apologize for not being able to accept your offer. I hope you find someone," I say as politely as I possibly can. "Have a great rest of your night."

At the last few words, Liam holds out a hand for me to take, and without question, I place my hand in his.

The second my hand is wrapped around his, a feeling of normalcy starts swimming through me. A feeling that I shouldn't have with a stranger.

We both give the older guy one final smile before Liam pulls me away and walks us over to a door that leads us to the second ballroom the theater has to offer. Thankfully, it's empty.

The second we're behind closed doors, Liam drops my hand. I don't know why, but the second that my skin isn't touching his, I miss it.

I push that feeling aside and give this practical stranger a smile.

"Thank you for saving me," I say through a small laugh feeling awkward.

Liam matches it. "You looked a little uncomfortable from where I was standing, so I walked over there to see if you needed some rescuing. Then I heard his offer and decided to step in."

"Well, I appreciate it. I don't want to know what else he would have proposed."

We both let out another small laugh, and then we go silent, just looking at each other with smiles on our faces.

After what feels like a long minute or two, I shake my head and nod toward the party.

"I should get back in there," I tell him, not wanting to leave but turning to do so anyway.

Liam doesn't say anything until my hand is close to wrapping around the doorknob.

"Or you can let me buy you that deep dish."

I turn to find him looking at me, standing in a relaxed stance with his hands in his pants pockets.

"And why would you want to do that?" I ask curiously.

Liam shrugs, throwing yet another boyish grin in my direction. "I wasn't lying when I said you took more than my breath away during your performance. Seems fitting that I repay you."

"Shouldn't you know my name before you buy me pizza?"

The smile he wears grows, and he closes the distance between us and holds out a hand. "Hi, I'm Liam, and I was captivated by your performance tonight. Every damn minute of it."

I might have blushed earlier, but that blush sure as hell won't compare to the one that is currently coating my face. There is no doubt that I'm red beyond belief because of his words.

Not wanting to waste any time, I place my hand back in his.

"Hi, Liam. I'm Chloe and I would love to take you up on that deep dish offer."

CHAPTER THREE

LIAM

I DIDN'T LIE.

From the second she went on stage until the lights inside the theater turned on, she had my attention.

Every single one of her movements captivated me, and a part of me wished that I could witness the beauty that was this woman whenever I wanted.

I told myself that the only reason that I was feeling that way was because her performance was just that good. Every little thing that she did was, in fact, breathtaking. I had never liked watching a performance like that until I saw Chloe.

She is a spectacular dancer and every single person in that theater bore witness to it.

When the lights came on and everyone started making their way out of the theater and into the reception area, I continued to think about her.

Every single one of her movements continued to play through my mind as I talked to fellow attendees.

For a good thirty minutes, I thought that I was going crazy because she kept creeping into my mind.

Somehow though, I was able to think about something other than her. All thanks to someone who mentioned hockey.

That lasted a whole thirty minutes.

My mind and attention were back on her as soon as she walked into the room.

It was as if my mind could sense her and immediately sought her out as she was coming through the door.

The second I saw her, it was as if the image I had of her on stage was heightened.

I thought that she was beautiful and captivating as she was dancing and moving from one position to the other but sitting at the back of the theater and watching her didn't compare to seeing the beauty a few feet away. My eyes followed her as she made her way through the room, and when I caught her gaze, I felt like a complete creeper.

I had spent the majority of my time tonight watching this woman, and she was heading in my direction.

For some reason, I felt like a teenage boy, freaking out because the popular girl was coming over to talk to him.

I studied her as she closed the distance between us. The way that blue satin dress sat against her body had me picturing her curves in ways I shouldn't be. The way her curls sat high on her head and framed her face had me wanting to dig my fingers through them and pull her mouth to mine. Then my thoughts shifted even more, and I started to think what it would feel like to slide that dress off her.

How would that blue dress look discarded on the floor of my apartment?

My thoughts surprised me. Then the old guy approached her and took her line of sight away from me and all I wanted to do was interrupt.

I wanted every ounce of her attention on me and me alone.

When I heard him ask her to dance at one of his poker nights for his buddies, I decided that interrupting was the best decision.

Did I have to call this girl whom I had never met or seen before tonight, my girlfriend?

No, but hey, she went along with it.

Now we're in the back of a pizza place eating the deep dish I fake promised her as if this was planned all along.

We left the opera house soon after she accepted my invitation. She quickly went to grab her things, and soon we were walking down the busy Chicago street, heading to a pizza parlor a few blocks away.

Our walk here was quiet.

We exchanged a few words about the weather and our favorite pizza toppings but nothing too deep.

Which felt nice.

Other than when I was watching the performance, I spent most of the night talking about the hockey season coming up or business stuff. It was nice to talk to someone about mundane things.

Especially when it was with a beautiful woman. A beautiful woman who has had my attention from the first second I laid eyes on her.

Even in the fluorescent lighting of this pizza joint, I can't help but stare at the beauty in front of me.

"Did you really mean what you said?" Chloe asks, taking a drink from her iced tea.

Who drinks iced tea with pizza?

It's beer or pop, nothing else.

"You're going to have to refresh my memory. What did I say?" I ask, bunching up my eyebrows for effect.

I know what she's talking about. I just want her to say it. A blush crept up her cheeks when the words left my mouth back at the opera house. It's something I want to see again.

Chloe gives me an eye roll, and a smile starts to play on her lips as she answers my question.

"About me taking your breath away with my performance. I know you told me you weren't lying, but a part of me is having a hard time believing it."

The little laugh she lets out at the end has me smirking at her.

"And why is that?" I ask, trying to keep the smirk contained.

"Because," she says, giving me a shrug.

I laugh a little at the impending dance we are about to do.

"Because why?" I ask like a little kid trying to get on her nerves.

Chloe playfully rolls her eyes again before answering my question. "Because of who you are."

A small blush starts to color her cheeks, making her look absolutely adorable.

"And who am I?" I ask, taking a bite of my slice. I'm trying my hardest not to laugh, but as I swallow down the bite of cheese and dough, it's becoming hard.

The blush on Chloe's cheeks gets deeper, and there is almost a look of embarrassment on her face.

Given what I do for a living and the fact that my face is plastered all over the city, I had a small inkling that this girl knew who I was from the start.

The blush that is coating her cheeks tells me that I was right.

Do I care that she knows who I am? Not really. There is no way for me to go incognito, even if she isn't a hockey fan.

When someone's face is on billboards and buses, it's a little hard to not know that person's name.

I just have to keep my fingers crossed and hope that she's not an overly obsessed fan or something. That wouldn't be good.

"You know," she says, trying to brush it off.

The laugh that I've been trying to hold in slips a little, but I control myself before giving her the best serious look that I can right now.

"I have no idea what you're talking about."

Chloe narrows her eyes at me. "You're going to make me say it, aren't you?"

I answer her with a shrug instead of words.

She lets out what sounds like an annoyed sigh, but the

smile she gives me tells me that she's anything but. She looks like she is having as much fun with this as I am.

"Because you're Liam Crawford," she finally answers. "A professional athlete who has women falling at his feet. Telling a woman that her performance took more than your breath away is a surefire way of getting a pair of panties handed to you with a promise of more later."

There is no more controlling of my emotions with that statement.

I burst out laughing, and Chloe quickly joins me. If we weren't at the back of the restaurant, we'd for sure draw attention to ourselves.

But it's just the two of us and a half-eaten pizza in between.

And all I can do is laugh and take in the beauty of the woman who is sitting across from me.

She really is a sight, and I don't know if only seeing it tonight will be enough.

The laughter quiets down and I give the gorgeous dancer in front of me a smile.

"I can one hundred percent guarantee you that you are the first and only woman who I have ever that to."

I watch as her eyes go slightly wide and the blush coating her cheeks spreads. Chloe tries to hide the smile that my words bring to her lips but I'm able to catch a glimpse of it as she bows her head and tries to hide herself in her food.

My attraction to this woman is increasing with every single minute.

"I guess I should feel special then, huh?" she says, her

voice barely a whisper as she looks at me through her long, dark eyelashes.

That look alone has me shifting a bit in my seat to rearrange a few things.

"You really should," I throw in her direction. "Before you went on stage, I was planning on sleeping through the whole thing. The second you came out of the shadows; you were all that my eyes could see."

Okay, Liam. You are laying it on way too thick. Bring it down a notch.

It's the truth, though, and I'm not one to spew out lies.

"Deciding not to nap is huge," she says, still slightly embarrassed.

"It really is. Especially when you had a crazy workout a few hours before. Naps are a necessity. You're lucky you captured my attention."

The sweet laugh she releases has me shifting once more.

"What was so breathtaking about it?" she asks, a piece of hair falling from its place on top of her head and framing her face.

I want to reach over and tuck it behind her ear so that it doesn't block me from looking into her hazel eyes.

"Everything," I say to her, completely forgetting about the pizza in front of me and shifting my mind back to her performance. "I don't know what it was, but from the first second, my eyes were following you. Not in a creepy way, of course."

"Of course," she says with a smirk.

I lean back in my chair and continue. "I may sound like a

total dweeb here, but from the second you stepped onto that stage, it was as if you were in your element. Even from the last row, it was as if each one of your movements was effortless and you could do that whole routine in your sleep. You literally had me on the edge of my seat, waiting to see what you would do next. You made me follow the damn story. I know how hard ballet is, and you made it seem like it was the simplest thing in the world. Every single thing you did had a grip on me, and when the lights came on, I wanted more, because, damn. What you did tonight, was fucking amazing."

I didn't realize I was rambling until I finished talking and saw the expression on Chloe's face. She's looking at me with the widest eyes, and her mouth slightly open, like I took her by surprise.

I took myself by surprise too.

Sure, I'm the type of person that tells the truth, but even I'm surprised by everything I just told her.

It was as if I had verbal diarrhea.

That's something one of my teammates would do. Not me.

"Sorry," I say, picking up my beer and taking a drink before giving her an easy smile. "I guess the performance affected me a hell of a lot more than I thought."

It takes Chloe a second to snap out of the stupor that I apparently put her in. Eventually she shakes her head and reaches across the table to place a hand against my forearm.

My tuxedo jacket and bowtie were discarded the second we got here; I couldn't wait to get rid of the constricted feeling that the tux was giving me.

Stupid-ass penguin suits.

Her hand lands directly on skin, and it sits warm against me in the best way.

I can't help but look down and like the way her hand looks against my tattooed skin.

"It's okay. I'm glad it looked as good as it felt," she says, her small smile growing into a full grin. "You just took me by surprise is all. Usually, the only thing people tell me is that I did great. They never really go into detail as to what was so great about it. My family are the only people who say more." She pauses for a second, looking down at her food before looking back up again. "You really think it was a great performance?"

I give her a nod. "I wouldn't have said it if I didn't. You were amazing tonight, Chloe. And that's coming from someone who has never seen you dance before."

I don't know how it's possible, but her grin grows even more, causing her eyes to shine just like they did on stage.

"It felt amazing. Even afterwards, it was as if I was on a cloud, and I never wanted to get off." She is absolutely beaming as she speaks the words.

"I'm guessing by the look on your face that the feeling is new," I let out, giving her a smile of my own.

"There have been both good and great performances, of course, but none of them have felt like tonight. Tonight felt as if everything was on a different level."

I nod in agreement. "That is definitely a feeling I am familiar with."

"I bet you've had quite a few of those moments in your career, haven't you?" she asks, giving me all her attention.

I like having her attention on me a lot more than I should.

There is no doubt in my mind that I'll be heading home tonight with a set of blue balls that I won't be able to get rid of for a while.

I move my thoughts from my aching balls and answer her question.

"A few times."

"And do you wish that you were in that state of mind every single time?" she asks, but I'm not concentrating on her words.

Her hand is still on my forearm, her thumb moving along my skin. Either she's not aware that she is doing it, or she is, and she doesn't care.

I don't care either.

I clear my throat, definitely not thinking of her hand on another body part.

"All the time. Sometimes I even beat myself up over it because I have a team depending on my performance. But that type of thing isn't something that you can force. Not every performance—or every game—is going to be like the last, and that's okay."

Her thumb stops the back-and-forth motions against my forearm, and when she pulls her hand back and is no longer touching me, I miss it. It takes a lot of control to not reach across the table, grab her hand and place it back where it was.

"I didn't think that my night would turn into some inspirational insight with a hockey player while eating pizza," she states with a chuckle.

"Hockey players know how to do more than just move a puck along the ice, you know. We make great counselors."

Another sweet laugh fills the air. "I'll keep that in mind whenever I go to a game."

"Let me know when, and I'll get you tickets," I offer.

"Just like that?" She gives me a smirk.

"Just like that. Best seats in the house, too. We can't have the best ballerina in Chicago sitting up in the nose bleeds. It's right behind the glass or nothing."

"That sounds like fun. I've never been to a hockey game," she says, and I can't contain the fake gasp that leaves my mouth.

"Damn, and here I thought that you were the biggest Liam Crawford fan in the world and have gone to every single one of my games." I clutch my chest for effect.

"Sorry, but I only know who you are from the thousands of billboards around the city that have your face plastered on them."

I figured.

"I don't know what hurts more; The fact that you've never been to a hockey game or that seeing my handsome face everywhere isn't enough to convince you to buy tickets and go to one." I grin at her as she rolls her eyes.

"I never said that you were handsome."

"No, but I know you thought it."

The way she bites down on her lip tells me that I'm right.

I decide to move the conversation back to her attending a game instead of teasing her some more.

"So, what do you say about attending a game?" I ask, already going through the season schedule in my head.

"I'd say, why not? If it's anything like tonight, I'm all for it," she says, pushing her food away, signaling that she's done.

Anything like tonight.

She's as affected by all this as I am.

I can't help but give her a charming smile. "I'll give you the complete Liam Crawford experience," I tell her as I get up from my chair and hold out a hand for her to take.

"And what does that experience entail?" she asks, taking my hand and not letting it go once she's settled on her feet.

"Oh, I don't know." I try to think of something that will make it worth her while. "Seats behind the glass, a jersey with my name on it, a picture with our mascot, and without a doubt, dinner afterward."

"Dinner, huh?" Her eyes sparkle.

"Definitely dinner."

"Does everyone who takes part in the Liam Crawford experience always get dinner afterward?" Her perfectly sculpted eyebrow raises in a challenging way and I fucking love it.

"Only those who I want to see more of," I say, closing the distance between us and finally tucking that loose strand of hair behind her ear.

A small gasps leaves her lips when my hand doesn't drop and rests against her neck, softly caressing her jawline.

"And you want to see more of me?" she asks, her eyes moving from my eyes to my mouth.

Given how close we are, all I would have to do is lean in an inch or two, and I would be able to taste her.

"More than you know," I say to her, leaning in closer, feeling her breath against my lips. "Do you want to see more of me?"

Chloe doesn't say anything right away, but she doesn't have to say any words because the way she moves her body closer to mine tells me everything I need to know.

Eventually, she breaks her silence.

"More than you know," she says, repeating my words to me, sounding almost breathless.

"So, you will come to one of my games?" I ask, my hand making its way into her curls, giving her a slight tug to angle her mouth perfectly for me to be able to claim her mouth.

"Yes, but that seems so far away. I may need something sooner." Her hands land against my chest, and her mouth forms into a delicious pout.

What would that pout look like wrapped around my cock?

"How much sooner are we talking about?"

"I was thinking tonight," she says, her words a literal whisper against my lips.

I don't hesitate with my next question.

"Your place or mine?"

She doesn't even get to answer before my lips are on hers, and I'm getting a taste of just how sweet she really is.

CHAPTER FOUR

CHLOE

THE SECOND HIS lips met mine, I was a goner.

Actually no, that's not true. I was a goner the second he smiled at me back at the opera house and rescued me from the old man and his invitation.

I was a goner then, but the second his mouth touched mine, I was obliterated into a million pieces.

That's when I learned that I was a sucker for a handsome guy with a pretty smile.

His kiss was hungry, and when he slid his tongue along my bottom lip, asking to be let in, I let out a moan that I'm sure was heard all the way to the front of the restaurant.

I didn't care though, his kiss made me feel something that I hadn't felt in a very long time. All that mattered was that this gorgeous man was kissing me and had his hands on my body.

Nothing else but the two of us existed in that moment.

We eventually pulled apart, and when we did, the same hunger that I was getting from his mouth was filling his eyes.

The way he looked at me had me wishing that I had something between my legs helping me relieve the pressure I was holding.

The butterflies I felt earlier in the night were in full swing. He wanted me just as much as I wanted him.

And he showed me as much because as soon as we pulled apart, he grabbed my hand, and we ran out of the restaurant.

We laughed the whole way back to the theater to get his car and head to my place after I had finally answered his question.

Now I'm sitting in a car that is probably worth four times more than I make in a year, with Liam's hand on my lap and a smile on my face.

"Promise me that when we get to my place, you won't judge me," I say to him, feeling slightly embarrassed.

"Why would I judge you?" he asks, quickly looking at me before turning back to the road.

"Because I don't make hockey player money. My apartment is nice, but it's probably not as nice as what you're used to." I can feel a blush start to coat my cheeks with embarrassment just saying the words.

"Chloe, that's not something to judge you over," he says, giving my hand a reassuring squeeze.

"I know, but it will still be a clear sign that I don't make as much as you."

"I honestly don't give a shit about that. Would it make

you feel better if I told you I lived in a shoebox of an apartment up until two years ago?"

His comment takes me by surprise.

I'm not much of a hockey fan. Hell, I don't even know what position Liam plays. What I do know, is that Liam has been one of the many faces of the Dark Knights these last few years. Surely that pays enough to not live in a tiny apartment.

"Why? Don't you make millions?" I ask curiously.

"I do, and for a few years, I would spend money on things I wanted. Like this car, but I didn't feel the need to spend a few grand a month on a place I was just going to spend a few days a month in. I travel too much."

That's not a bad way of thinking.

"That's smart. What made you finally move?"

Liam shrugs as he turns into my neighborhood like I told him to. "I wanted to get a dog and needed more space. Now I have the space but no dog."

I can picture Liam running around a golden retriever puppy and naming said puppy Princess or something cutesy and spoiling the hell out of it.

The image alone is enough to make the smile on my face even bigger.

As we make the last turn toward my apartment, I can't help but to wonder why it feels so easy between us.

It shouldn't feel that way.

I only met Liam less than three hours ago and it already feels like I've known him my whole life.

Is that normal? Out of all the one-night stands I've had in my life, no one has ever felt like this before.

I wonder why.

What's so damn special about this guy?

Liam is lucky enough to find a parking spot close to my building while I'm having a mental crisis, but instead of getting out of the car, he turns to face me.

The hand that is currently on my lap squeezes around mine.

"You okay with me going up to your place? I can leave right now and call it a night."

Is he this sweet and caring with everyone or just me?

I don't bother answering his question with words.

Taking note from my onstage persona, I let go of Liam's hand and lean over the center console and bring his face to mine.

There is nothing sweet or slow about the way my mouth lands against his.

My body has been on the brink of explosion from the second I caught his gaze. The kiss back at the pizza place was just the spark, and now I'm letting the fire burn and taking what I want.

Liam has to feel the same way because he digs his hand into my hair as if he can't pull himself close enough to me.

He's just as starved for me as I am for him.

I slide my tongue along his bottom lip, asking for entry, and all it takes is one swipe, and my tongue is dancing along his.

His hold on my hair becomes tighter, and I can't help but let out a moan.

The pulling and the grabbing feel so damn good.

"We should head inside," Liam lets out as his mouth travels down to my jaw and then down my neck.

I'm already a panting mess, and all this man is doing is kissing me and pulling my hair.

I fucking live for it.

"We should," I state, but don't make the move to pull away from him and get out of the car.

My panting gets heavier as I feel Liam's tongue slide against the length of my neck and stop to suck on the skin above my collarbone.

I'm loving my dress so much right now. It's exposed in all the right places.

I shift a bit in my seat but not to open the car door. No, I shift so that my body is leaning over the console with one hand threading itself through his hair to hold me up and the other landing onto his lap. My mouth doesn't waste any time landing back on his.

"Chloe," Liam growls against me the second I start massaging his dick through his tuxedo pants.

I let out a hum against his mouth, continuing with my movements.

"You don't want to keep doing that," Liam tells me, pulling away slightly only to take my bottom lip between his teeth and nipping me.

A small giggle escapes me followed by yet another moan when the hand that was in my hair, slides down my body and rests along my hip.

"And why is that?" I ask, pulling from him to give him a smirk.

Liam gives me his own smirk and before I know it, he's pulling me fully onto his lap so that I'm straddling him.

For being in such a small space, it still doesn't feel like I'm close enough to him.

Strong hands land against my exposed thighs, and I can't help but marvel at the feeling.

"Because if you keep touching me like that, I may start doing things that may not be suitable to do in a car or in public," he tells me, his hands moving closer and closer to the throbbing between my legs.

"Maybe that's what I want," I say, moving my hips in small circles to rub against him.

"You're trouble, aren't you?" he asks, his fingers digging deeper into my skin.

"Only when I want to be." I lean in and give him a small nip along his neck, my hips continuing to move back and forth.

Liam looks at me with hooded eyes, and all I can do is continue to smirk at him and let my hips move.

By the way I'm sitting on him, I can feel him getting harder underneath me. I can't help but wonder how much more I have to move in order for him to say fuck it and make me come.

I'm about to suggest it, when one of his hands leaves my thighs and makes its way back up to my hair.

The way he pulls my hair and brings me closer to him has me filling the car with moans that I didn't know I was capable of.

"As much as I want to fuck you in this car, someone can

see us and plaster it all over social media," he says, his mouth barely touching mine.

He has a point.

Given who he is and how this city views him, getting caught having sex in public would be bad. For him and for me.

As enticing as it is, I have to think about the bigger picture.

"You're right," I admit, my body sagging in the process.

Liam lets out a small laugh, planting a few kisses along my lips and my nose. "Don't look so disappointed. Just because we can't do anything in the car doesn't mean we can't do anything upstairs. So be a good girl and get out so I can do to your body what your mouth has been silently begging me to do."

"Only if you call me a good girl again," I let out, thrusting my hips for good measure.

"Whenever you want." With one last kiss filled with hunger, we make our way out of the car and up to my apartment.

Never have I disliked the fact that my building was a walk-up more than I do now.

Running up stairs when all you can think about is sex is no fun.

But we make it up the four flights, and the second we step foot into my apartment the hunger we have for each other is on a whole different level.

The second that we are behind the locked door, it's

mouths, and hands everywhere. It's as if both of us need more of each other, and we're the last two people on earth.

"You in this dress is going to haunt me for a long time," Liam says, pushing me against the front door.

His hand lands on my thigh and travels up, pushing up the blue silk.

"That right there makes the price tag on it worth it," I say, arching my body back to give him better access.

A growl leaves Liam's mouth right before he slams his mouth back on mine, and his hand finally touches me where I need him to.

His touch is gentle at first, but then it becomes more aggressive, causing me to come closer to an orgasm than I expected.

He doesn't even have a finger in me, he's just teasing my most sensitive areas, and I'm ready to explode for him.

"You're so wet already," Liam lets out, his fingers sliding my panties to the side and moving along my pussy.

"Since our first kiss."

That must have flipped a switch in him because he presses his body against mine, letting me feel every single hard inch of him.

This man is still fully clothed, and I'm already salivating at what is underneath all the material.

I want my hands on everything.

Letting my boldness take over once more, I give Liam a little push to give me some room.

When he steps back, he gives me a look of panic, like I changed my mind about us potentially hooking up tonight.

Giving him a smile, I silently reassure him and slide down to my knees in front of him.

The smirk that takes over his face fuels me even more.

"You don't have to do that," he says, brushing a few strands of hair out of my face.

He's sweet, and I like it, but right now I don't want sweet. I want him hungry and losing his mind.

"I want to. I really, *really* want to," I answer, looking up at him through my lashes.

My eyes stay on his as I undo his belt and then pop open the button holding his slacks together. My eyes still don't move as I push his slacks down just enough to pull him out.

The second his cock is out and in my hands, I give him one final smile before taking him in my mouth.

One lick and the whole place fills with Liam's moans.

I take him deeper and give him a few swipes of my tongue just so that I'm able to hear him lose it again.

"Fuck, Chloe." He lets out after a minute, throwing his head back, his hands slapping against the wood of the door. "Your mouth feels so good."

I let out a hum and continue working him as best as I can with his length and girth.

Looking up at him, I find his eyes open and looking down at me. They're hooded and filled with lust, and if I wasn't concentrating on him right now, I would slide a hand down to my pussy and make myself come. But for the moment, I want to concentrate on him.

"You look so fucking gorgeous taking my cock in your

mouth like that," Liam praises, caressing my face. "Such a good girl."

He must see how much those two little words affect me because his gaze grows even more heated.

"You really do like me calling you a good girl, don't you?" he asks.

I just nod, taking him deeper into my mouth until he's hitting the back of my throat.

"Show me, then," he orders. "Show me just how much of a good girl you are."

A hum leaves my lips and I do as I'm told.

Right now, I will do anything he tells me to.

CHAPTER FIVE

LIAM

THE SIGHT before me is one that will stay in my mind for a very, *very* long time.

Never did I think that going to the ballet tonight would end like this. I had no idea, or expectation, that it would end with the dancer who made me like ballet—at least while she was dancing—on her knees in front of me with my cock in her mouth.

It hadn't been a thought, but now it's the only thing I can think about, and I'm not mad about it.

Chloe takes me out of her mouth, only to lick my length from base to tip, all the while a sexy smirk plays on her lips.

I could have this girl on her knees in front of me every single day for the rest of my life and not get tired of it.

This might be my only night with her, though, even if a part of me doesn't want it to be, so we might as well make the most of it.

My cock slides in between her lips again and for a minute or two, I lose myself in the way her mouth feels.

It's hot, and the way she is working me is absolute perfection. It's as if we have done this before, and she knows exactly how I like it.

One of her fingernails drags along my balls as she takes me deeper in her mouth, and when she gives me a hardy squeeze, I about lose it.

A loud groan leaves my mouth, and when a little giggle leaves Chloe's lips, I swear I see stars.

"Such a perfect mouth. Look at you, being such a good girl for me."

She licks my cock one more time before sliding me back into her mouth.

If this is how good her mouth feels, her pussy is going to feel ten times better.

Not wanting to waste a second, I pull away from her, letting my cock fall from her lips, having other things in mind.

Chloe looks up at me with wide eyes, as is she is wondering why there was such a sudden change in direction.

The look doesn't stay long because as soon as I bend down and pick her up, she automatically knows what I'm doing.

She wraps her long legs around my waist as soon as she gets the chance. If my cock wasn't hard already from her mouth, it would be now. In this position, I'm able to feel the heat that is radiating from her pussy. She's all ready for me.

"I'm going to need a bed for what I have in mind," I say into her neck, my hands digging into her ass.

How I wish I could rip this dress apart right now and have her naked in my arms. But I will save her dress from destruction and take my time with this woman.

"Down the hall to the left," Chloe directs me, and I quickly follow her orders.

The second that I step over the threshold of her bedroom, I don't think twice about tossing her onto the bed as soon as I'm able to.

Her sweet laugh fills the surrounding space, driving me even crazier for her and what's coming.

"You okay there, Mr. Crawford? You look a little hungry," Chloe teases, and the only thing that I can do is watch her.

As she says the words, she leans back on the mattress and opens her legs ever so slightly, letting her dress rise, and giving me a view of her barley covered pussy.

Fuck, this woman is so damn sexy.

So damn sexy that I fall to my knees before her, just to have a taste of her.

"Very hungry," I say, grabbing her legs and dragging her to the edge of the bed, her pussy in a perfect location for my mouth. "I think it's time I have my dessert."

Chloe starts to say something, but whatever words are about to come out of her mouth disappear the second my mouth makes contact with her panty covered core.

I slide my tongue along the fabric, causing Chloe to not only let out a moan but to squirm under me.

Continuing the motions of licking her, I slide one hand under her dress and grab on to one of her breasts.

Her tits are a little less than a handful, but I already know that they will be perfect for me.

"Liam, I need more. Please," Chloe pants out, squirming and grinding against my face to get more friction.

Wanting to give her what she wants, I use my free hand and start tearing off her panties.

Could I have slid them off? Yes, but where's the fun in that? Besides, the way that Chloe gasps makes my cock twitch.

"Whatever you need. Whatever you fucking need," I say against her folds.

A groan fills the room the second I take her clit in my mouth and start to suck on her.

Chloe is a mixture of vanilla and something else that makes my mouth water. Like the rest of her, I'm going to be thinking about it every time I jerk off for the next few months.

Thoughts like that are dangerous, and I have no idea where the hell they are coming from.

For right now, I'll keep them there and continue to lose myself in this beautiful woman.

I tweak Chloe's nipple and slide my hand down her body until I have two fingers teasing her entrance.

My name is on her lips, and when I slide my fingers into her, she lets out the most delicious sound. So delicious that I want to embed it in my mind.

"You take my fingers so well. Makes me wonder how you

will take my cock," I say against her, feeling her tighten around my fingers.

"Maybe you should find out," she pants out, moving her hips, looking for the climax that is trying to escape.

"Don't worry, baby, I will. I just need you to do something for me." I give her one long lick, before meeting her gaze.

"And what is that?" she asks, her eyes so beautifully hooded.

"You're going to come on my tongue like the good girl I know you are, and as a reward, I will fuck you with my cock in ways that will have you feeling me for a whole damn week."

She bites down on her bottom lip, trying to suppress either a smile or a moan. "I like the sound of that."

I throw a wink in her direction, ignoring my cock as it throbs and continues to beg for attention. "Good. Now, come. Beg for it, and I will reward you even more."

"Yes," is all Chloe is able to get out before I intensify my movements.

My fingers slide in and out of her, all the while my mouth never leaves her clit.

One of her hands settles in my hair, and she pulls at the strands as tight as she can. It's moments like this one when I'm fucking glad I keep my hair this long.

Her pussy continues to tighten around my fingers and hold them as if they were in a vise.

"Liam, please. I need to come. I'm right there. Please."

"You want it, sweetheart?" I nip at her inner thigh, my fingers not relenting.

"Yes. Please," she pants out, her back arching in the process.

"I like hearing you beg."

My lips stay on her, as I bite down on her clit and stroke her inner walls. All it takes is one swipe at her G-spot and Chloe is unraveling, screaming, and begging for more.

"Oh my god. Yes!"

She explodes on my tongue, and even though she tries to push me off, my mouth stays on her even as her body starts to calm down. I lick up every single drop of her release, and as soon as I'm done, I want more.

I give her pussy one last kiss before standing up to full height and ridding myself of my clothes.

Chloe's eyes stay on me the whole time, watching my every move as her breathing continues to settle. As she watches me, studying my body, one of her hands moves to her pussy and starts rubbing at her clit as if it wasn't in my mouth just a minute ago. Each one of her movements tells me that she is ready for more.

Watching her touch herself and looking at me with lust-filled eyes has me reaching for my cock as soon as my boxer briefs are discarded.

Being the little vixen that she is, Chloe sits up and reaches for me, getting close enough to run her tongue along my length.

The image of my cock in her mouth and swallowing me whole is still in my mind from earlier, but I'm on the brink of a fucking explosion. I need a hell of a lot more than her mouth.

I slide my hand into her hair and pull her mouth away from me as gently as possible, tilting her head enough to look up at me.

"As much as I like watching you suck me off, I have other plans."

I reach for her, grabbing the fabric that is pooling at her thighs and pulling it over her head until she is sitting in front of me in nothing but torn panties.

She is sexy as fuck, more so with the smile she gives me.

I can't help but to reach out and slide the back of my finger along her face.

Just like she did while she was on stage, she has captured my attention, and I don't want to let it drift away.

My finger makes its way under her chin, and I bring her mouth to mine and give her a kiss.

All our kisses tonight have been hungry and desperate, but this one is slow and sensual. This kiss is filled with a lot more emotion than a kiss between strangers is supposed to have.

That isn't normal.

I should push it away.

I should keep all emotions out of this, especially if I don't see her again after tonight.

But I can't.

Chloe is bringing everything out of me tonight, and whatever it is that I'm feeling when it comes to her, I want to feel it as much as I can. It's like a never ending high, and she's only been in my life for a handful of hours.

I end the kiss with one last swipe at her tongue. When I pull away, she gives me a smile that messes up my mind even more.

Ignoring whatever thoughts are happening in my mind right now, I do what I promised this girl I would do. Reward her.

"Get on all fours," I order.

With a lick of her lips, Chloe does what she is told and when she's in position, I can't help but let out a groan.

This woman may be a dancer, but she has curves in all the right places.

Her ass is facing me, and it wouldn't take a lot to lean down and to take a bite of her. To mark her.

But I ignore the urge, instead I rip the remainder of her panties off her and caress the exposed skin.

"You look so damn sexy," I say, giving in and placing a kiss on her lower back.

"I'm thinking the same thing about you. Tattoos every-where," she tells me, looking over her shoulder and giving me a smirk.

I give her one back.

If I don't get inside of her soon, I'm going to embarrass myself and come all over her back.

Grabbing a condom from my wallet, I slide it on, and within a few seconds, I'm sliding into Chloe's pussy, groaning at her tightness.

"Holy fuck," she lets out, her upper body falling onto the mattress.

"You feel so damn good. I don't know if I will be able to get enough of you," I say, my head tilting back and my eyes closing at the feeling of her as I move in and out of her.

She lets out a moan, and hearing it is music to my fucking ears.

I fuck her slowly at first, letting her get used to my size, but soon enough, she is begging me for more, to give her everything that I have.

So, I do just that.

I give her every little thing that I have.

The sound of our bodies slapping together, mixed with our moans, and panting, on top of all the sexual tension that has been swimming between us all night is enough to bring me close to the edge.

I almost came in her mouth earlier, and now sliding into her like this is becoming torturous. I don't know how much more I can handle.

"Are you close, sweetheart? I don't know how much more I can handle." I try to think of anything that will stop the inevitable, but the only thing that I can picture is Chloe touching her pussy for me.

"I'm right there," Chloe pants out, her head falling back.

I grab her hair and pull her back until she is on her knees and her back is pressed against my front.

I press my face to her neck and pepper her skin with kisses just as I release her hair and slide my hand down to her pussy.

A moan sounds in my ear.

"You like that, don't you? You like having my cock sliding into you while I rub your clit," I say into her ear.

"Yes," she lets out, almost in a desperate cry.

I feel her tighten around me, telling me that she's close.

"Come on my cock, sweetheart. Come all over my cock and milk me dry. I know you want to. Take it. Take everything that you need. I'm yours all damn night."

"Yes. Yes. Yes," Chloe yells out, her body starting to shake.

Her pussy tightens around my cock, and that is the last thing I'm able to handle before my own release shoots out.

I grunt into Chloe's neck, tightening my hold on her.

"Fuck," I say against her skin, not wanting to move from this position.

"Fuck is right. Holy shit," the woman in my arms pants out.

From the way she sounds, I'm going to make a wild guess that what we just did took a lot out of her. I know it took a lot out of me.

"If you want to do that again, I'm going to need a break," she chuckles, relaxing into my arms.

"We can take as long of a break as you want."

And for the rest of the night, that's what we do until sleep finally takes over.

Sleep that is filled with dreams of Chloe and everything she made me feel tonight.

Dreams that a part of me, a small part at that, wish had the possibility of coming true.

Dreams that may mean that I've taken one or too many hits to the head.

CHAPTER SIX

LIAM

THERE'S a heaviness against my body that isn't usually there.

For a few minutes, I try to ignore it, but eventually my eyes pop open as if it wasn't the middle of the night. Given the minimal amount of light shining through the room, I'm going to say it's not even dawn yet.

I lay there for a few seconds, trying to get my head on straight and trying to figure out where I woke up.

When I feel something shift next to me, every single memory from last night and the last few hours comes rushing back.

The ballet.

The dancer.

The blue dress.

Chloe moaning out my name.

Every last detail of the past few hours replays in my head like a movie. Every single, glorious second of it.

Just thinking about it has my cock twitching.

But I can't stay.

I look at the woman next to me, and every part of me is telling me to stay.

To skip the morning workout and the team skate that are scheduled for today to stay here in bed so I can get lost in her body all over again. If I stay, I can make her scream my name out even more, both in bed and in the shower, and then make her breakfast.

It's so fucking tempting, but since the season starts in a few short weeks, practice and ice time are a necessity.

I look at the time on my phone and let out a sigh, knowing that I have to go. I promised Christian, my team-mate and best friend, we would hit the team gym before getting on the ice.

I've never hated my best friend more than I do right now. I should have texted him last night to cancel, but I was so enthralled with Chloe, I completely forgot.

Now, I have to leave her when I really don't want to.

Reluctantly, I untangle myself from Chloe and start looking for my clothes, trying my hardest to not wake her.

As much as I try, though, I don't succeed, because when I step out of her en suite, I find her awake, curled up under her sheets.

"Do you always get up this early?" she asks, her voice having a rasp to it from the minimal sleep she got.

"Only when I need to," I say to her, sliding on my dress shirt.

"And today you need to?" she asks, and I give her a nod as my answer.

Her eyes shine bright with the moonlight that is floating through the room.

I can't help but abandon buttoning up the rest of my shirt and going over to sit on the edge of the bed, just to place a kiss on her lips as I take her face between my hands.

Her lips are so fucking soft and full that, as soon as my tongue glides along her bottom lip, I want more of her.

Chloe lets out a moan when our tongues meet, and all I can do is keep my hands on her face so that they don't travel down her body and make me late for my workout.

It's easy to get lost in her, and if I had canceled on Christian last night, I would be doing a lot more than getting lost.

But I'm an idiot, so as I yell at myself to not stop kissing this woman, I pull away from her.

A sleep -illed smile forms on her lips, and I have to force myself to not lean forward and take her mouth again.

"And here I thought that you would at least stay for breakfast," she says, lying back down, her eyes falling closed.

I reach over to her face and brush a few loose curls away. "Any other day, I would, but I promised one of my teammates a few workouts before we hit the ice."

She hums at my response, and I smile down at her, even though she can't see it.

"I'll make it up to you. I promise."

"With the Liam Crawford experience?" she asks, reaching up and taking my hand from where it's sliding along her face and bringing it to her lips.

Every single one of our actions is not something you do with a one-night stand.

If someone was looking at us right now, they would think that we've been in each other's lives for a lot longer than seven hours.

"Definitely, but I was thinking sometime in the next few days."

Chloe's eyes pop open right away, as if she wasn't expecting those words to come out of my mouth.

"You really want to see a one-night stand more than once?" she asks, her tone full of wonder.

She's cute if she thought this was really a one-time thing. I thought I made it clear last night that it wasn't, no matter how much my brain wanted me to keep it that way.

I should keep it that way. This should only be for one night, especially with the season starting soon, but I sure as hell don't want it to be.

"You're hell of a lot more than a one-night stand, Chloe," I say, sweeping my thumb along her lower lip.

She is silent for a few seconds, just looking at me with those hazel eyes of hers, not giving me a single clue as to what she might be thinking.

For a small moment or two, I think that I'm possibly reading too much into all of this. I've only spent a handful of hours with this woman, and I'm planning ahead, and thinking, and getting excited about when I'm going to see her after this.

I'm usually the guy who is completely fine with spending the night with someone and leaving without a word.

One and done, that's it. Not seeing Chloe after tonight, though, feels wrong.

But maybe I'm the only one who feels that way.

Chloe pushes herself up into a sitting position and places a hand against my bare chest, the movements of her fingers gentle.

"I was thinking the same thing," she says, her hand making its way up to my neck and sliding into my hair, bringing my face closer to hers.

This girl isn't shy about what she wants, and it's such a fucking turn on.

A smirk lands on my face as we close the distance between us, and my mouth is almost on hers, almost tasting her sweetness one more time, when my phone goes off.

I would ignore it but given the song that's blaring from the stupid thing, I know it's Christian. The asshole always finds a way into my phone and to change my ringtone, no matter the passcode.

If I ignore the fucker, he's just going to keep calling.

"You have Bad Bunny as your ringtone?" Chloe asks, sounding like she wants to laugh.

"My friend's doing," I grumble, getting up from the bed and finishing getting dressed.

"Your friend?" A small chuckle leaves her like she doesn't believe me.

I wouldn't believe me either if I hadn't met the guy.

"Yup, I'll tell you more about him over dinner," I say, throwing on my jacket, followed by my socks.

"Sounds like a plan to me," she answers, giving me a sexy smile when I turn back to look at her.

"It's a date then," I say, leaning down and giving her one more kiss. "I wrote my number down and left it on top of your phone. I expect you to use it."

"And if I don't?" Her voice is filled with mischief.

"I know where you live."

"Darn, I didn't think that through," she says, her smile growing.

"You definitely did not." One more kiss for the road. "I'll see you later."

With a giggle from Chloe and one final look, I walk out of her apartment with a high that I haven't felt in my personal life in a while.

I've only gotten this feeling in the last couple of years from hockey.

It feels fucking amazing.

That feeling stays with me all the way to our practice facility, and it continues to stay as I make my way into the locker room and for Christian takes notice.

"You get arrested or something?" my best friend asks in place of a greeting as I walk into the locker room.

"The fuck? No," I throw at him, as I walk over to my locker.

"So, there's a reason you're wearing a tux at five in the morning. I'm assuming it's the same one from that event you went to."

I grab the spare workout clothes I keep here and start to undress before answering him.

"Yeah, asshole. There's a reason why I'm still in a tux," I grumble. I can feel my high fading away.

"You going to tell me? Or do I have to continue pulling it from you?"

For a broody motherfucker, Christian loves gossip a little too fucking much. If I don't tell him, he's going to continue to hound me for details.

"I haven't been home," I tell him, throwing the clothes from last night in a gym bag. I should hang them up, but they've already spent half the night on the floor, so what's a few more hours in a gym bag?

"And why is that?" Is he always this annoying, or am I just now noticing?

Might as well give him some details so that he can shut up.

"Because I spent the night with a woman, and I came straight from her place," I say, turning to him and flipping him off.

"Since when do you spend the whole night with a woman?" he asks as he ties his running shoes.

"I spend nights with women," I argue back.

"You spend a few hours with women. Usually, you are out of there before two in the morning, not giving a shit. If you're coming here from her place, this one must be special."

He's...not wrong.

I honestly can't remember the last time I woke up at a woman's place and came to practice right after. No matter the circumstances, I always head home. It was an unspoken rule that I broke for Chloe and one I would break for her again.

Is it possible to be pussywhipped after one night? Because the way my mind is thinking, I'm certainly heading in that direction.

"She definitely is," I answer, my mind instantly filling with thoughts of her and our night together.

"Given that dumb smile on your face, she must be."

Dumb smile? He has a dumb smile.

"Are we going to spend the whole morning talking about how I spent my night or are we going to work out?" I throw out, not wanting to add more fuel to his fire.

"Touchy," he says, giving me a grin.

If he were anyone else, I would punch him in the face just to wipe it off.

"Shut up," I say back.

Christian lets out a laugh, and I'm tempted to drop him as my best friend. Childish, I know.

"I can't wait to meet this woman," he states, standing up from the bench and starting to make his way out of the locker room.

"Why?" I ask as I follow behind him.

"Because in all the years I've known you, you have never had a woman light a fire under your ass. And from the sound of things, this one has."

"You don't know what you're even talking about," I throw out, shoving the asshole and walking into the gym.

For the rest of my work out, I think about what he said and as much as I don't want to admit it, he's right.

One night, a handful of hours, and Chloe lit something in me that nobody else has before. And I fucking like it.

The question is, though, am I going to try to make more out of it, or let it be?

Right now, I have no idea.

CHAPTER SEVEN

CHLOE

I SIP my tea as I look at the note with a neatly written phone number on it.

After Liam left, I went back to sleep only to wake up about half an hour ago, and the first thing I did was reach for my phone.

The piece of paper fell to the floor, and I instantly reached for it, afraid that if I didn't, it would get lost in the abyss that is the mess under my bed.

773-210-1210

I'M EXPECTING A TEXT FROM YOU.

LIAM.

For five minutes, I stared at the note. I memorized the number and studied his writing. I looked at it until I forced myself to do something besides obsess over it.

I decided that making myself breakfast would be distraction. For the most part it was, but now that I'm finished eating and just sipping on my tea, his number is the only thing that I can think about.

Should I use it?

I know I agreed to go to one of his games and dinner in the next few days but texting or calling him seems like we are stepping into uncharted territory.

In the last ten years, I've had one serious relationship, and that was while I still lived in Texas trying to decide if I should take a shot and audition to become a dancer.

My relationship with Marc lasted about a year, and when I decided to pursue dancing professionally, we ended things.

Last I heard, he married his high school sweetheart and is living in San Diego, and I became the ballerina that I am today.

Since then, dating has always taken a back seat. Sure, I've gone on dates here and there but nothing that lasted more than a night or two.

That's how I thought it would go with Liam. I thought we were going to have one night of fun, and then I wouldn't hear from him ever again.

He's a professional hockey player whose season is about to start and I'm about to enter the busiest time of year for us dancers. I thought that he would leave this morning and tell me that we should hang out sometime when our schedules lined up, but we would never actually do it.

I thought that Liam was a "never stay in contact with a woman" type of man.

But from everything that he told me before he left and then leaving his number, I'm starting to think that I was wrong for even thinking that.

It's just a number. It doesn't mean anything. Use it or don't.

Right.

It's just a number. Having Liam's number doesn't mean that he's going to be my next boyfriend or anything. For all I know, we could go to dinner again and spend more time together and become friends and nothing more.

Would it even be possible to become friends with someone that made me beg for an orgasm and made every single inch of my body weep?

It might be hard, but it's possible.

God, why am I overthinking this so much?

The guy I slept with last night gave me his number, that's it. There is no need to think about all the things that can possibly happen.

I doubt Liam is thinking this hard about what our night together could turn into, so I shouldn't either.

Besides, I have other things to worry about, like going to the grocery store and breaking in a new set of pointe shoes for the week.

Something that they don't tell you about being a ballerina, or any professional dancer for that matter, is the number of dance shoes you go through in such a short period.

During the offseason, I go through ten pairs of shoes in about three months and that's only with one dance class and two or three practices a week. When performance season comes around, I'm going through double, if not triple, the amount in any given month. It's nuts.

If it weren't for the dance company giving its dancers free shoes whenever they needed them, I would go broke buying new ones every few days.

But I'm exactly where I want to be.

I've dreamed about being a professional dancer, a ballerina, for as long as I can remember. From the day my mom took me to my first dance class, I knew that that's what I wanted to do for the rest of my life.

Being on stage, with a spotlight on me, called my name and for years I did everything in my power to achieve it.

It kicked my ass on more than a handful of occasions, and there were more than a few times that I wanted to quit, but I didn't.

And good thing, too, because if I had, I wouldn't be where I am today— part of one of the most well-known and respected dance companies in the world, being the ballerina I wanted to be when I was three years old.

I'm at the height of my career and climbing higher is the only option I see fit.

Three-year-old Chloe would be very proud.

Sure, dancing has taken up a lot of my time the last ten years. I've lost friendships because of it. I don't get to see my family as often as I want, and it hurts, but I'm doing something for myself. I dance because I love it, and it's what *I* want to do. I'm not forcing myself to do it, and in a few years, when I finally decide to hang up my pointe shoes, I know I will be happy about it.

Well, hopefully. Things can change.

But fingers crossed things stay how they are for a little while longer.

For now, I ignore the phone number sitting on my counter and go do what I had planned.

As much as I try, though, I can't seem to think about anything else other than Liam.

Thoughts of our night together and how he controlled my body invaded every single square inch of my mind.

Nobody has made my body sing the way he did, and as I think about it, I can't help but want more.

I almost give in and text him exactly that as I get back to my apartment, but I don't. Thank God.

If Liam and I become friends, those are not things I should be thinking about. No matter how good they feel.

By mid-afternoon, I have somewhat succeeded in keeping Liam out of my head. He only crept in a few times, and I see that as a win.

Around dinner, all that goes down the drain, and it's all thanks to a text message from Betty.

Betty: So, how was the party? Any sugar daddies that I need to know about?

. . .

Should I tell her?

A part of me wants to keep Liam and our short time together to myself, but the other part really wants to tell my best friend. I had a professional hockey player in my bed, for crying out loud, that's worth sharing with her.

Besides, Liam didn't say I couldn't.

I text her back.

Me: Well... I owe you a coffee...

The message barely says read when my phone starts to ring with my best friend's name dancing across the screen.

"Tell me everything!" Betty yells out as soon as I answer the phone.

I can't help but giggle like a schoolgirl at her excitement.

"There's not much to tell," I say to her, a smile forming on my face.

"Not much to tell? Chloe, you just giggled like a little girl on Christmas! There's so much to tell!"

Another giggle escapes me, and the second it does I know that I won't be able to hold anything back.

"What do you want to know?" I ask, shyly.

"Everything!"

"Well, his name is Liam..." I start, and the second I do,

Betty is screaming every thirty seconds, enjoying everything I tell her.

I tell her everything from meeting his gaze at the opera house to us grabbing a bite to eat together to us coming back to my place. I don't tell her all the lovely details of course, but I do say enough to get her by.

"Did he really say that?" Betty asks, after I told her what Liam said about me being more than a one-night stand.

"Yeah, he really said it, and trust me I was just as shocked as you are."

She lets out another shriek that has me pulling the phone away from my ear.

"So, are you really going to see him again?" she asks, and I'm sure if she were standing in front of me right now, she would jump up and down.

"I don't know," I answer, telling her the truth.

"What's not to know? A hot hockey player wants to take you out to dinner again. It's a simple yes or no answer."

"I know it is, but I don't want it to turn into anything." As soon as the words leave my mouth, I know it's a shit reason.

"Who says it has to turn into anything? You can have fun, Chlo, and it doesn't have to be more than that. If the guy wants to wine and dine you, then make you scream out his name afterward, let him. It won't hurt."

I roll my eyes even though she can't see me.

She's right, I know she is. Going to dinner again with Liam isn't going to hurt, and it doesn't mean that something more has to happen between us.

But why does a part of me want something to happen?

Why does a part of me want to go on a date with him and see if we have a chance of working out?

Why is it that, after only one night with him, I want more?

Maybe I should just say yes and see where it goes. If it does head in the direction of a relationship, it wouldn't be so bad, would it?

No, it wouldn't, but as much as a part of me wants to see where this could go, the other part is telling me that I don't have time for a relationship.

Fun, yes. Relationship, no.

I'm at the peak of my career, and I have to concentrate on that.

Nothing else.

"I say, call him and set something up, because after next week you won't have a whole lot of time," Betty tells me, not waiting for me to respond.

What she says, though, catches me off guard.

"Next week? Why won't I have time after next week?" I try to rack my brain for what she might be talking about, but I don't come up with anything.

"Because rehearsals for *The Nutcracker* and *The Little Match Girl* start up the following week. Haven't you checked your email? They sent the schedule out this morning."

I mentally slap myself.

For weeks, we've been told to be on the lookout for the rehearsal schedule for our winter shows.

I knew it was coming, so I shouldn't be surprised, but it's still a little shocking that rehearsals are starting so soon.

It's only September.

"No, I haven't checked my email," I concede.

Putting the phone on speaker, I reach for my laptop and start looking for said email.

Sure enough, sitting between two department store coupons is my rehearsal schedule for the next two months and the show schedule from November to January.

I guess I won't have a personal life until after New Year's. But it will be worth it, I know it will.

"It's a lot," Betty says after a minute. "So do as I say, and text or call the guy. Get some fun in before dance takes over your life."

She's right yet again. This might be the only chance I get to have some fun for the next few months. Might as well take my shot.

"Alright. I'll call him," I say into my phone, a smile spreading across my face.

"Attagirl. Get that hockey dick," she says with a giggle.

The call ends quickly after that and as soon as I get off the phone with Betty, I open my messages and start typing out a message to the number I memorized this morning.

I promised him that I would contact him.

This is me doing that.

I'll just send one text message. We will go out to dinner, have some fun and then I will concentrate on dancing for the foreseeable future.

Nothing, and I mean nothing, will come out of a little text.

I'm sure of it.

CHAPTER EIGHT

LIAM

SWEAT DRIPS down my face as I make my way off the ice.

I don't usually feel this exhausted after a morning of skating drills, especially before the season officially starts, but my late night with Chloe is coming back to bite me in the ass. Spending the night with her was worth the body exhaustion, though. And no matter how tired I am be on the ice, I would do it again in a heartbeat.

Grabbing a towel from one of the equipment assistants, I wipe my face and head down the tunnel to the locker room.

It's been a day so far, and right now all I want to do is grab a shower and head home for a long ass nap.

Also to check my phone to see if a certain ballerina actually did use my number like I told her to.

I walk into the locker room and head straight to my small section of the room.

The second I sit down, my whole body groans like it's been waiting to sit down for days.

Damn.

Either my body is giving up on me at twenty-nine or my night with Chloe put me through the wringer more than I thought.

It was all of the sexual gymnastics.

The image of Chloe's flexible body and the positions we were in before falling asleep invade my mind.

Her body was beautifully fluid, and mine tried to do its best to keep up. I can move, but there is only so much that a man my size can do.

But damn, now the only thing I want to do is have a repeat and thinking about that right now is not a good idea.

Especially when I'm about to get naked in a room filled with men to hop in the shower.

"Hey, Cap?" A voice comes from in front of me as I'm untying my skates.

I don't have to look up to see that it's our newest rookie standing in front of me.

The Knights drafted Blake Jacobi at the age of eighteen, fresh out of high school. He went to college, decided to leave school early, and officially signed and reported to the team last summer.

The kid is good, and with time, I know that he will be great. And that doesn't have anything to do with the fact that he has a Super Bowl-winning older brother.

I can't think of anything bad to say about him. The only thing that might be a little off-putting is that he has the personality of a golden retriever.

"What's up, Jacobi?" I ask, sliding my skate off.

"Do you think I can get an invite to your next early morning workout session?" he asks, his nervous tone making me look up at him.

"Why do you look terrified?" I ask him, feeling my eyebrows bunch up as I take in his facial expression.

Blake looks down at me like I caught him off guard with my question. He takes a few seconds to compose himself.

After what feels like forever he finally answers. "Because even though this is my second year here, I'm still a rookie and there is a good chance you don't want me in your space."

That's not what I expected him to tell me.

I first met Blake back when he was drafted.

The captain at the time thought it would be good to show the young hockey players that we would share the ice with, a warm welcome. We invited them to the arena and took them out to dinner a week or two after the team called their names.

I personally didn't keep in touch with him while he was in college, but since he was signed last year, I've been trying to make him feel welcome.

At least I thought I was.

Jacobi shouldn't be terrified to ask if he can join a workout session.

I don't know if that makes me a bad person or a bad captain.

I'm going with both.

"You don't need to be invited invite, Jacobi. You can join us whenever you want," I say to him. I'm not going to isolate the kid. "The only thing is that you will have to deal with that asshole at five in the morning," I say, nodding toward Christian, who's in front of me looking pissed off as always.

"He can't be any worse than Volkov. We worked out two mornings ago, and the dude only said one word the whole time."

We both turn to look over at our teammate, Logan Volkov. He's one of our top enforcers, right next to Christian, and he can be just as scary off the ice as he is on it, but from what I've seen throughout the years, he's a good guy. He just keeps to himself a lot and can come off as an asshole at times, but if he's working out with Blake, it's a good thing.

Logan doesn't do that with a lot of people. There must be something about Blake that he likes.

"Logan is Logan. But if you can handle a workout with him, you can handle the moody bastard. Just don't let him get his hands on your phone."

Blake gives me a confused look. "Why?"

I slide my other skate off and stand up to start getting rid of all the sweaty gear that is covering my body.

The shower is desperately calling my name.

"Because the man knows no boundaries when it comes to switching your ringtone."

The rookie looks at me like I'm pulling his leg, but I just give him a shrug and head for the shower. The sooner I get out of this locker room, the closer I am to heading home and taking that nap.

Right after I check my phone, of course.

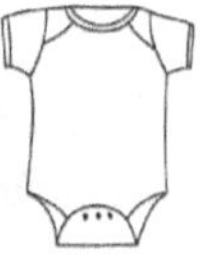

No text message.

When I finally got a chance to check my phone after leaving the arena, I was a bit disappointed there hadn't been a text from Chloe waiting for me.

Had I hoped that she would use my number like I told her to? Yeah, of course, but whether she used it or not, wasn't up to me. Us seeing each other again is her choice, and if she doesn't want that to happen, I will respect it.

I'm a grown ass man. I can handle a woman not texting me back.

So, I tried to forget about my night with Chloe as best I could and went about the rest of my day. A few thoughts of Chloe slip through, but I'm able to push them aside for the most par and get things done.

A grocery run, a dry-cleaning pickup, and a takeout order later, I'm back at my place watching the football game I missed yesterday.

I don't usually have the time to watch other sports live or even on TV, so when I do get a chance, it's a good night.

The next hour or so is spent watching Hunter, Blake's older brother, and his team go into halftime with a twenty-point lead.

From the looks of things, it looks like the reigning Super Bowl champs are going to fight hard to stay on top.

Maybe I can ask Blake if his brother can come talk to our team and give us some words of encouragement.

We're good, but we are going to need all the help we can get if we want to make it past round one in the playoffs.

A captain will gladly accept help from another captain.

Liking my idea way too much to wait until morning practice to ask him, I reach for my phone and pull up his message thread.

I'm about to send what I just typed when a message notification pops up at the top of the screen.

Usually receiving messages doesn't cause me to freeze, but this one does.

Why?

Because an unknown number sent a message with three simple words that instantly puts me back on the high I was feeling this morning.

Unknown: Hi, it's Chloe.

She texted.

Forgetting all about Blake, I tap on her message and don't bother texting her back. Instead, I hit call button instead.

The high this woman brings to me, is causing me to do stupid shit, but I don't care. All I want is to hear her voice and feel her body in my hands again.

The phone rings for a while. My guess is that my call surprised her, and she has no idea whether to answer or to send me to voicemail. After what feels like the hundredth ring, she finally answers.

"Hello?" Her voice comes through, and it's as if my cock remembers all the sweet moans that she let out not even twenty-four hours ago.

"And here I thought that you wouldn't use the number," I say in place of a greeting.

"You told me to," she answers, a small laugh following.

"I did, but you don't seem like the kind of woman who takes orders very well," I say, a smile spreading across my face.

"If I remember correctly, I followed orders pretty well last night. I even got praised for it."

Her tone has turned breathy, and my cock picks up on it right away.

"That you did," I say, remembering everything we did last night for the tenth time today. I need to get myself together. "Why did you text, Chloe?"

I've spent time around enough women to know that a majority of the time, they overthink things.

A big one is what they are going to say, followed by when they are going to say it.

Chloe not using my number right away tells me that she probably spent all day thinking about it. Her texting me most likely came after she had talked herself into it.

"I told you, because you said to," she answers a little too quickly.

"There's more to it," I say, leaning my head back against the sofa cushion.

There's a long pause on Chloe's side, and as much as I want to break the silence, I don't.

It's after sixty-three seconds—I counted in my head—that she finally speaks.

"Because I want to see you again." Her answer causes my smile to grow even more.

"I want to see you again, too, sweetheart, but why do I hear a but at the end of that sentence?" The fact that I can read this woman after just one day is surprising and impressive.

Chloe lets out a sigh, one that I can't really decipher. "Your season is about to start, right?"

I nod even though she can't see it. "It is."

"In a way, so is mine. Rehearsals for the winter shows start up next week. Usually from the first rehearsal to the last performance, all I think about is dance. I become like a dancing zombie."

"You're committed," I state, not questioning her devotion to her craft.

"I am. But before I get into that head space, I want to see you and maybe get to know you a little in some capacity. I have a whole week of free time before the craziness hits."

If she's suggesting what I think she is, I'm here for it.

"And what do you have planned during this free time?" I ask, my smile turning into a smirk.

"Well, I texted to see if maybe you wanted to help me with said planning." Her voice gets low, and I bet anything that she is biting her bottom lip right now holding back a smile.

"You have one whole week?" I ask.

"I do."

"I might have a few ideas as to what you can do with your time," I throw out, my mind already filled with ideas.

"Why don't you come over and share those ideas with me. That is if you have time tonight, of course," she says in that same sexy voice that my cock loved so much last night.

I'm already getting up from the couch before she even finishes her sentence.

"I'm free. I can be there in twenty minutes." I slide on my shoes and grab my keys all while Chloe's laugh sings in my ears.

I waste no time making my way over to Chloe's and running up the four flights of stairs up to her apartment.

The second that she opens the door for me, I walk in, and take her face between my hands, and kiss the ever-living shit out of her.

My attraction and my thought processes when it comes to this woman are probably not the healthiest thing, especially after only knowing her for a day, but I don't give a damn.

Chloe can drive me crazy as long as she fucking wants. I'm not going to say no.

My tongue slides against hers, and she lets out a moan. A moan that tells me that she doesn't want me to stop, but I do anyway.

"I didn't mean to attack you like that," I say, leaning my forehead against hers.

A lazy smile forms on her lips as she looks up at me and wraps her arms around my neck.

"It's okay, it's all part of the Liam Crawford experience, right?" she asks, her eyes shining through her eyelashes.

"Yes, it is. Now the question is, do you want to experience it for a whole week?" I ask, moving my hands from her face and sliding them down her delicious body.

"If I say yes?" She gives me a teasing smile.

"Then you will get it."

She looks up at me for a few seconds smiling, inching her body closer to mine.

"Okay then, Mr. Crawford. You have one week to give me the Liam Crawford experience. You better not disappoint."

"Sweetheart, you weren't disappointed last night, and you sure as hell won't be disappointed seven days from now."

She lets out a laugh. "Alright then. One last question."

"And what is that?"

A hand slides through my hair and gives it a good pull. "Is that hockey game still on the table?"

"Damn right it is."

"Okay then, give me everything you got. I need something to keep me busy until the game." Chloe leans up and gives me a kiss.

It's slow at first, but then it's as hungry as mine was.

"You're going to have to beg, sweetheart," I say against her lips, lifting her up into my arms and walking us to her bedroom.

A sweet laugh fills the room.

A laugh that I get to hear for the four out of the next seven days.

For four glorious days, I get to hear Chloe laugh in my ear every single night and get to feel the softness of her body against mine.

Every single time my fingers, my tongue, and my cock slide through her lips, both sets of them, I'm in fucking heaven. Every minute and late night I spend with her is worth getting my ass kicked the next morning at practice.

One night wasn't enough for either of us, and I doubt four more days will be either.

For now, I will take everything I can get from this woman.

On the bright side of things, I got her tickets to the first home game of the season. That means I will be experiencing her again in no time.

Something I know is that we will both be counting the days until.

CHAPTER NINE

CHLOE

OCTOBER

TODAY'S THE DAY.

After four long weeks of rehearsals, trying to drink enough water, eat enough food, and avoid all thoughts of a certain hockey player, today is the day I've been waiting for. The day I even set a reminder for in my calendar.

This lovely Tuesday is the day I finally get to see Liam again for the first time since he left my apartment the day before rehearsals started.

I've been excited for this day. I've been looking forward to this day so that I can have the Liam Crawford experience for the second time.

Today is the day, and I feel like absolute shit.

My first warning sign today wasn't going to go as I had planned should have been getting a reminder that I have a gyno appointment this afternoon. But of course, I just swiped away the notification and went to my morning dance class.

Now I feel like I'm going to puke, and it has nothing to do with the fact that I'm on my way to get a pap smear on top of getting my birth control shot.

Though, I do hope it has something to do with it because I do not want to feel pukey when I see Liam later tonight and pass whatever bug I have on to him.

That would make me a bad...friend?

What do you call the person you spent one night with, then proceeded to spend the next four consecutive nights with as well, and are now going out to dinner with four weeks later after his hockey game?

Friend with benefits?

Occasional hookup?

Just a friend?

Definitely not girlfriend or partner, I know that for sure.

Whatever I am to him, I can't get him sick.

The universe must have told him I was thinking about him, because as soon as I press the button for the crosswalk, my phone beeps with a message from him.

We've stayed in touch since we last saw each other almost four weeks ago.

It has mostly been us trying to decide which game I wanted to attend, since I won't be able to make the first game of the season, and mundane things like how our days have been going. Friendly, platonic things that people talk about when they are getting to know a new person who has come into their lives.

The platonic stuff may be a big reason why I feel nauseous today.

Liam and I went from being complete strangers to giving each other orgasm after orgasm for five nights straight back to strangers again.

I know this is what I wanted. I know I wanted to concentrate on dancing and not dive into anything serious, but I have a feeling that tonight is going to be weird.

How do we act?

Do I kiss him as soon as I see him? Do I hug him, or do I just give him a small wave and have an awkward dinner?

I don't know.

I'm excited for tonight, but I'm also nervous about how it's going to play out and how I am going to come out of this after the night is over.

Both Liam and I have things that we need to concentrate on. Things that have nothing to do with having sex day in and day out. I'm going to make the most out of tonight because come tomorrow, we really need to set our foot down as to what we are. Whether that is just friends or the occasional hookup, we're going to have to be put on hold until the new year.

It's not something I want to do after getting to know him during our days together. But if I want this to be my best season yet, I have to.

Shaking the nervousness away and drowning out the city noise, I open his text message.

Liam: I left two tickets for you at the box office. Right behind the glass like I promised.

I smile at his words. He had asked me if I wanted to bring anyone with me to the game a few days ago. I had said yes, because there was no way Betty was going to let me go alone. She wants in on all the drama.

Me: Thank you so much! Can't wait to see you!

The second I hit send, regret starts flowing in.

Can't wait to see you?

God, that sounds so desperate. He's probably going to think that I can't stop thinking about his dick.

I'm about to throw my phone into the street so that it can get run over by oncoming traffic when it beeps again.

Liam: I can't wait to see you either. I left you something with the tickets. See you tonight!

I guess I didn't sound desperate after all.

That right there makes the remainder of my walk to my appointment a bit lighter. Even with whatever is going on in my stomach still disturbing me.

I try to push all the feelings of puking, uncomfortableness, and nervousness down and head into the doctor's office.

It's weird that walking into the familiar office calms me. I might be the only one.

Since I'm here every four months, the check-in process is easy and within ten minutes, I'm getting called back.

"Are we doing any testing today?" the nurse asks me after getting my weight and blood pressure.

"Please," I say, giving her a nod.

It's not that I don't trust Liam, I do, but we never had that discussion, so I would rather be safe than sorry. Besides, a few tests never hurt anyone.

"Okay," she says, writing something down on my chart. "I'm going to have you head to the bathroom and pee in this cup. When you are done, you can put it in the little door."

She hands me the little plastic cup and sends me down the hall to the restroom.

Peeing in a cup never gets easier, no matter how many times you do it. You always get your pee in places where you don't want it to go.

But I finish and leave the cup in the little door like instructed and head back into the hall before heading into the sterile room.

"Okay, the doctor will be with you shortly," the nurse

tells me after she went through an extensive list of questions about my health and hands me a paper gown.

"Thank you," I say to her with a smile.

As I pull on the gown and sit on the table completely naked waiting for the doctor to come in, the uneasiness in my stomach doesn't go away. I feel like puking even more sitting in this room.

"It's just a pap. It's not going to hurt too much. She's going to do it, and then I can go home. That's it."

My pep talk doesn't help. My stomach still feels like it's going to explode all over the room.

I need to eat some saltines or something. With my stomach turning, there is no way I'm going to be able to enjoy the nachos I was looking forward to at the game.

Maybe I should just cancel on Liam.

No.

No canceling. It's just nerves about the pap. That is it. This stomach thing will go away as soon as I leave here.

Thankfully, I don't have to wait for the doctor much longer because five minutes later she walks in.

"Hi Chloe, how are you?" Dr. Long asks as she walks into the room, closing the door behind her.

"Good, just trying to get over this bug I caught on," I say, giving her a small smile.

"Bug?" she asks, taking a seat on the stool in front of me.

"Yeah, it's just a stomach thing. I'm sure it's nerves about the pap smear or something."

Dr. Long looks at me with bunched up eyebrows, like she doesn't believe it's just nerves.

"What exactly are you feeling?" She starts taking out a pen to start writing on my chart.

"Like I want to throw up," I answer.

"Have you?"

I shake my head. "No, but I have gagged a few times today. That's about it."

"Do you feel tired at all?" she asks, writing something down on the piece of paper.

I take a second to think about her question. Rehearsals and dance class have been kicking my ass lately, but that's nothing out of the ordinary. I did go to sleep early last night, which isn't unheard of for me.

"Usually after a dance rehearsal, but that's a normal thing."

The doctor gives me a nod as she continues to write.

"It says here your last period was two months ago."

I nod even though she's looking down. "Yeah, it's been irregular for years."

Dancing changes your body in a lot of ways. One thing it can do is affect your menstrual cycle. For me, not only did I get my first period in high school, but it comes whenever it wants to, not when it's scheduled to.

"Okay, let me check your urine sample. I will get a better idea of what is going on."

Shouldn't she have done that before she came in here? Also why is she so worried about a stomach issue? That's something for a regular doctor, not the gyno.

Oh my god, what if Liam gave me something?

We used a condom.

So? You can get an STI through oral.

Oh my god, if he gave me something, I'm going to kill him. I'll use his hockey stick for all I care. I'm sure Betty will help me get rid of the body.

"When were you last sexually active?" the doctor asks as she looks at the computer screen to her left.

"A month ago," I answer.

She gives me a nod, and all I want to do is grab the computer monitor and see what she is looking at.

After what feels like a million minutes, she turns back to me and gives me a small smile. I can't tell if it's a happy one or a sad one.

Liam gave me something, I know it. That bastard.

"From the looks of things, we won't be able to administer your Depo shot today," she states, standing from her stool.

"What? Why?" Instantly, I start to worry.

What kind of STI did this asshole give me?

"Because you're pregnant, Chloe," Dr. Long states, looking me in the eye.

This must be my stomach issues traveling to my brain because no way in hell did she just tell me I'm pregnant.

"I'm sorry? I'm what?" I ask, feeling the nausea I've been feeling all day travel up my throat.

"You're pregnant," the doctor states and all I can do is stare at her in disbelief.

Pregnant.

I'm *pregnant*.

I'm pregnant.

What the actual hell? Am I dreaming? Is today even real?

"Um," I start, stuttering a bit as I try to find my words. "How? How is that possible? We used a condom, an-and I'm on birth control. I thought that the shot was like ninety-six percent effective."

I'm trying really hard not to spiral right now, but it's becoming impossible.

No way she's right. She can't be.

Sure, I want kids, but not right now! And not with a guy I've only seen for a total of five days!

"It is ninety-nine percent effective, but only if it's taken on time and correctly. Even then there is still a chance. A one in one hundred chance."

And I had to be that *one*?

Oh my god.

"Are you sure?" I ask her, trying to get it straight in my mind.

"I will need to do a vaginal ultrasound to confirm, but your urine test is coming back positive," she tells me, but then her expression changes. "Given your reaction, I'm going to say that this is both a surprise and unplanned."

My head nods. "Very unplanned," I whisper to her.

"Okay, then let's do an ultrasound to confirm, and after we can talk about your options."

She gives me another smile, but I can't seem to find it in me to give her one back.

The whole time she is getting everything ready for the ultrasound, I feel like I'm having an out-of-body experience.

I can see and feel everything that is happening around me, but it's as if I'm just someone seeing it from the outside.

It feels like a dream, like nothing is real.

I don't know how to feel or how to even react. This was not the news that I was expecting today, and I sure as hell don't know how to wrap my head around it.

So many damn questions run through my head as Dr. Long conducts the most uncomfortable ultrasound known to man, with the wand sliding into a place I wasn't expecting today.

And those questions double when she turns the screen to face me and confirms that I am indeed pregnant.

I am pregnant.

What am I going to do? I'm not ready to be a mom. I had plans. I *have* plans.

But most importantly, what the hell am I going to tell Liam?

CHAPTER TEN

LIAM

"HEY, Crawford. Those jerseys you asked for are up in the box office. We put them with your tickets," Gage, the team's equipment manager, tells me as he walks into the busy locker room.

"Thanks, man," I say, giving him a nod.

I promised Chloe a jersey with her tickets, and since I haven't seen her, I thought it would be a good idea for her to get it when she gets here.

Hopefully, she puts it on, and I get a glimpse of my name across her back. I also wouldn't mind seeing her in it while I slide into her tight core if the night takes us in that direction.

A man can only dream.

"How come he was able to get jerseys? When I asked you, you told me no," Blake asks Gage before he leaves the room.

Gage looks from me back to Blake before answering.

"Because he only asked me for two. You asked for four. I can't give every single one of your flavors of the week a jersey."

I look over at Blake's expression, and the dude looks like a damn puppy dog.

"They weren't for my flavors of the week. I have women in my life that are important," Blake answers, sounding a bit offended.

"Yeah, who?" Gage asks, crossing his arms.

I don't know why, but this whole interaction is entertaining.

"My mom, my sister, my sister-in-law, and my best friend," Blake answers, copying Gage's stance.

The whole room can tell Gage realizes that he messed up. He seriously thought that Blake was giving these jerseys away to random girls.

I would think the same thing, too, if I hadn't gotten to know the guy a lot more these last few weeks.

The guy either spends time with his teammates or his best friend, Sophia. According to him, he doesn't have time for anyone he doesn't already know.

"I'll have the jerseys ready by the end of the game," Gage concedes.

"Thank you," Blake gives him a nod and heads back to his bench.

I can't help but be nosy. "I didn't know your brother was married already," I say, sliding on my hockey pants.

You would figure the wedding of the number one quarterback in the NFL would be all over social media.

Blake gives me a shrug, pulling on his jersey.

"He hasn't. Last I heard, they were thinking about next year. I just call Lennie my sister-in-law because she is a lot more than just my brother's girlfriend."

I've met his brother's girlfriend once, and from what I saw, she's shy but it seems like both Jacobi men are enthralled by her.

"It's nice that you already include her in things," I say, grabbing my jersey.

"Oh, the jersey is to piss off my brother. He hates it when she wears someone else's name on her back. You should have seen it when she wore a Maddox Bauer jersey to a game. So, I'm making it my mission to fill Lennie's closet with so many Blake jerseys that the vein in his forehead pops. She and I are in on it together."

"But you have the same last name." Surely that would be okay.

"You would figure that would be fine, but the asshole has this weird possessive thing going on. His name, team and number or nothing." Blake rolls his eyes.

Damn, that's a little insane.

"Sounds like a smart man," Christian says, joining the conversation from god knows where.

The dude is serious about his superstitions, and before every game, preseason and beyond, he disappears to do one of his rituals.

What that ritual is, I have no idea. All I know is that he comes to the arena, disappears for a good twenty minutes, and then reappears again ready for the game.

I have asked him about it more than a few times, but he

always just says don't worry about it, it's his superstition not mine.

Whatever. I'll find out eventually.

"Sounds like an asshole," Blake replies.

Chris snorts back at him. "You're going to tell me that if Sophia walked into this arena with my jersey on, you would be okay with it?"

In the last few weeks, Chris and I have gotten to know Blake a lot better. We've not only included him in our workouts, but we've also asked him to hang out with us a handful of times.

We've come to learn that wherever Blake is, his best friend Sophia is not far behind. It's as if the two of them are attached at the hip.

Blake has told us that there isn't anything going on between them, but we both think that is a complete lie. There might not be something going on physically, but there is something going on deep down. They just don't want to open their eyes to it.

From the few times that I've been around them, Blake can be very possessive of Sophia. They call it brotherly love; Chris and I call it he's secretly in love with her.

She came to every single one of our home games last year, and every single time she wore a Jacobi jersey.

No doubt if she wore anything else, Blakey here would not like it one bit. Even if he wouldn't tell her. She is his best friend after all.

From where I'm standing, it looks like Hunter isn't the only Jacobi with a vein that could pop with anger.

"Of course, I'm not her keeper. She can wear whatever she wants," Blake says, but I bet a hundred bucks that he had to try really hard to get those words out.

"Cool, so you wouldn't mind if I send her one? Bet she'd look good with the number ninety-three on her back." Christian claps him on the back and heads over to his locker.

I try not to laugh at Blake's face, but I can't help it. The kid has it bad and can't even admit it to himself.

"Ignore him. We got a game to play. He's just trying to get under your skin," I say to him making my way to the tunnel now that I'm all set to go.

Tonight, is the last preseason game and come Friday, every game starts to count.

Eighty-two games to show the hockey world that the Dark Knights have what it takes to make it to the top.

And we will. This is our year; I can feel it in my fucking bones.

It doesn't matter that we are getting new owners or that our team didn't succeed in years past. This year is different, and we will win the Cup.

We just have to play this last exhibition game, and we'll hold nothing back.

The team makes its way out to the ice for our warm-up, causing the fans who are here early to raise the energy level a bit.

I skate around the rink, but instead of warming up like I'm supposed to, I look out over the stands. Usually I interact with fans, throw them a puck or two, but tonight, I have something else occupying my mind.

Chloe.

She said that she would come tonight. She's been saying it for weeks, even earlier today, but a part of me still thinks that she will skip out.

I wouldn't fault her for it, but it will hurt a bit, I'm not going to lie.

We're not together, we're more friends than anything but I can see us becoming more in due time. Possibly once she's done with her busy season we can revisit the topic.

For now, though, I would be happy if she attends one of my games.

Catching a glimpse of her becomes an obsession during the majority of my warmup. I spend most of my time looking over at her two empty seats rather than stretching or hitting a few slapshots.

I'm about to give up and head to the other side of the ice when I spot her.

The seats aren't filled, so I'm able to find her. She must have shown up when I wasn't looking.

From my spot on the ice, I can see her giving her friend a small smile and tucking some hair behind her ear. Not only can I see her smile but also the fact that she is wearing my jersey.

As I watch her, I now understand what Blake was talking about when he mentioned possessiveness.

Seeing this woman with my name on her back is something I like seeing a little too much, and I don't want her wearing anything else.

Women wear my name on their back all the time, so seeing Chloe with it shouldn't be any different, but it is.

She's different in the best kind of way.

It's times like this one when I know for a fact that the attraction I have to this woman is way too fucking strong.

I take a break from my wannabe warm-up and skate over to Chloe and her friend.

The friend is the first to notice me, giving Chloe a nod in my direction.

The woman who has taken every moments of my thoughts, turns to look at me and gives me a smile.

But it's not the same smile that in ingrained in my mind from our days together. It doesn't reach her eyes, and there is no sparkle to it, which right away tells me something is wrong.

I give her a wave, and she gives me one back, the small smile not going anywhere.

This woman may not have been a part of my life for long, but I've come to learn how to read her.

I nod over to where there's an opening between the stands and the ice, and both women walk over.

The closer Chloe gets to me, the more I can see that something is off.

But what, I don't know.

"Hi," I say to Chloe, wanting to reach over the barrier and kiss her, but I don't.

She's already freaked out about something. I don't want to add to it.

"Hi," she says back, but her voice is so small I barely hear it.

What's up with her?

"Are you okay?" I ask, my curiosity getting the best of me.

She doesn't answer me with words. She just gives me a closed-mouth smile and a head nod before turning to her friend.

"This is my friend, Betty," Chloe waves to the blonde next to her.

The friend doesn't look as freaked out as Chloe does. *She* looks excited to be here.

"It's nice to finally meet you! Been a fan for years," she tells me, a huge smile on her face.

I give her one back. "It's nice to meet you, too. Glad you were able to make it."

"Oh, I wouldn't have missed it for anything. Even if my husband almost cried because I was going out and he wasn't."

I like this woman. "Next time I'll make sure to invite him as well."

"That would be great," Betty answers before turning to look at Chloe.

She looks uncomfortable, looking down at the floor instead of up at me.

Betty must see the same thing that I am because she clears her throat and gives me a smile.

"I'm going to go take pictures from our seats to send to Cole," she says right before walking away.

I don't know who Cole is, but I couldn't care less. Right now, my focus is on the woman in front of me, not her friend.

It's not even on the hockey warm-ups that are happening behind me.

"Are you okay?" I ask Chloe again, sliding a bit closer to her.

Again, she gives me a nod and a tight smile.

"Yeah, I'm fine." She's lying.

"It's okay if you don't want to be here. There won't be any hard feelings if you want to leave."

I like having her here. I like seeing her with my name on her back, but if this is all too much for her, then I'm not going to force her to stay.

Chloe's face drops at my suggestion.

"What? No. I want to watch you play," she states, nervously biting her bottom lip.

"There are going to be other games," I remind her, bending my knees a bit to be able to look into her eyes.

The extra height that my skates give me doesn't help.

Chloe looks up at me for a long minute, chewing on her lip and with an expression that looks both sad and angry if that's even possible.

I want to reach for her and take her in my arms so that I can comfort her, but a million things are stopping me. One of them being that I'm technically at work, and two, I'm nothing besides a hookup to her. I shouldn't care. I shouldn't want to offer her comfort, but I do.

After a bit, she finally lets out a sigh and shakes her head.

"It's just been a long day, both physically and mentally. I do really want to be here," she says, giving me yet another small smile.

This one at least looks a little more sincere.

"Are you sure?" I ask.

She gives me a head nod. "Yeah, it's just..." she pauses, looking around like she is debating if she should say what she wants to say or hold it in. "Do you think we can talk tonight? I have something I really need to tell you."

If I didn't have a game that was about to start in a bit, I would say fuck it and offer to talk right now.

But again, I can't.

"Yeah, I'll have someone come get you when the game is over, and we can talk."

"Okay." She gives me a nod, and before I know it, I'm getting a wave and she's walking away.

I don't know what is going on with her, but I have a feeling that I'm not going to like whatever she wants to talk about.

I'm getting friend-zoned. I just fucking know it.

Who knew that could happen to the captain of a professional sports team?

CHAPTER ELEVEN

CHLOE

"WHY DO YOU LOOK SO PALE?" Betty asks as she hands me a plate of nachos that were brought to us. The same nachos that I was thinking about this morning, but now I can't even look at them.

It's as if the whole nausea thing intensified the second Dr. Long told me I was pregnant. It has to be a mind trick or something.

Just thinking about them has me gagging.

I debated not coming.

I debated staying home and thinking about everything that Dr. Long had told me. Not only thinking, but also reading through all the information that was handed to me as I was leaving. Or possibly stare at the five pregnancy tests that I took when I got home because even though Dr. Long confirmed it, I still had my doubts. But sure enough, every test had a little blue line staring back at me confirming what I was told earlier.

For a solid three hours, I just sat on my bed and told myself that I shouldn't come to the game. What would coming to the game accomplish? I wasn't going to be able to tell Liam right away. There sure as hell wasn't going to be any decisions being made while I sat in the stands.

But no matter how much my brain screamed to not come, I still got up, changed into my good jeans, and came to the game.

At the very least, being at the game serves as a distraction from the hurricane that my life has turned into in just a short amount of time.

"My stomach just feels a little queasy, that's all," I say to my best friend.

"What did you eat today?" she asks, taking a bite of her hot dog.

Has eating at a sporting event always looked and smelled so gross?

Dr. Long did say that my sense of smell might be heightened, but I didn't think it would happen on day one of me finding out.

"Papas con huevo for breakfast and a chicken wrap for lunch," I lie.

If I tell her that the only thing I've eaten has been some saltines, and I sucked on a lemon or two, she will question me beyond measure.

But of course, my best friend knows me better than anyone else.

"Why are you lying?" She looks at me with narrowed eyes.

I have two options here. Tell her the truth, or continue to lie, which she will properly see right through. I decided on option two.

"I'm not lying."

Right away, she gives me a look that tells me that she doesn't believe me.

"Fine, don't tell me, but something is seriously up with you. I thought you would be more excited to be here. Especially since you are getting laid afterwards."

I cringe a little at the getting laid part.

That was something I was looking forward to, but now, with my situation, it's the last thing I want to think about. Sex is what got us here.

"I'm excited to be here," I say in return.

Betty gives me an uh-huh sound and takes another bite of her hot dog.

God, I wish I could eat one.

Hot dogs are one of my guilty pleasures, but right now, all I can think about is how disgusting they are.

Will I get my love for hot dogs back?

"I thought you wanted nachos," my friend interrupts my hot dog-filled thoughts, and nods at the paper plate I have in my hands.

Looking at the staple food, if I wasn't pregnant, I would have devoured them the second that they were handed to me. But they look gross, and my stomach does not like what it's seeing.

"They smell funny," I say, not looking away from the plate. I'm sure my face is contorting in all different ways.

"They smell funny?" Betty asks, a little worried.

She takes the plate from my hand and takes a whiff of them, checking to see if they gave me bad cheese. She sniffs them once and then twice, and gives me a weird look.

I give her a nod hopefully not giving anything away.

But Betty is Betty. She can read through every single little thing even if she doesn't know it.

"Upset stomach and nachos smelling funny. If you'd asked me, I would say you might be pregnant."

My whole body goes stiff, and I can feel my expression shift in shock of her figuring out. I try to compose myself quickly, but of course, I don't have enough time before Betty notices.

I watch her, and after a whole minute it all clicks for her and the second it does, she gives me the expression that I probably gave Dr. Long.

Betty's eyes look like saucers when she finally speaks.

"You're pregnant?" my best friend asks in a whisper.

Given where we're at, it's surprising that I can even hear her.

But I can, so I give her a nod.

Admitting it makes it feel all that more real, and I still can't wrap my head around it. I have no idea how I'm supposed to feel. Not only that, what the hell am I supposed to do?

"And the father is..." Betty asks, her eyes moving over toward where Liam is skating on the ice.

The game officially started a while ago with the scoreboard telling me that they are in the second period with the Knights in the lead.

I haven't paid a whole lot of attention the game, what with my body in crisis mode.

I give Betty a nod.

Of course, Liam is the father. Of course, five nights with a professional athlete turned into a future of shared holidays and alternating days.

"Holy shit," she states, her mouth forming an 'O.'

"Yup," I say, because what else can I say? I can't believe it myself.

"I'm guessing you haven't told him," she says, her eyes on the game.

I shake my head. "I found out this morning at my regular check-up. I wasn't going to tell him before the game. Hearing 'hey, you knocked me up,' while he had skates on would have been bad."

Even though all I wanted to do was tell him. The second that he asked if I was okay, I wanted to yell it out.

"But you are planning on telling him, right?" Betty turns to look at me, a worried look on her face.

I've been asking myself the same question all day.

When I pictured myself having kids, I always thought that I would be in a committed relationship with someone I've known for years. In that scenario, we would be excited about the news and jumping for joy. I would be so excited that I wouldn't waste any time calling my parents and telling them that they were going to have the title of abuela and abuelo.

In that scenario, I would also be in the next phase of my career and no longer dancing. I would be teaching ballet instead of spending countless hours practicing for a performance.

I pictured this whole thing so differently.

Now here I am at a hockey game, pregnant with the captain's baby, in the middle of my career, not knowing what to do.

But one thing is for sure—that even though the scenario is different, even though Liam and I have only spent five days with each other, I'm still going to tell him.

I can control that much.

His reaction to the news is a whole different story. I don't know him well enough to know how he will take it, and if I'm being honest with myself, I'm a little scared to do it. I shouldn't be, but I am.

"I am. After the game, I'm going to tell him, and then I'll decide what to do."

"Whatever you decide, I will be there for you no matter what."

Years ago, Betty and I had a similar conversation. Except our roles were reversed. She thought about it long and hard because she didn't want to give up dancing. She and Cole talked about it and decided that they wanted to keep the pregnancy. I was there for emotional support.

I know that with whatever I decide to do, Betty will be there to support me too, no matter what. Both physically and emotionally.

"I know, and I love you because of it. I'm just freaking out right now, and my mind is running a thousand miles a minute." Tears start to form in my eyes, and even though I try so hard to keep things at bay, I fail, and a sob escapes me in the middle of a hockey game.

Fingers crossed that TV cameras aren't pointing in my direction because I sure as hell don't need my breakdown to be all over the place.

Betty abandons her hot dog and wraps her arms around me, pulling me in closer and comforting me.

"Everything is going to be okay," she says into my hair.

"What if it isn't?" I hiccup back to her.

"It will be."

"What if I make the wrong decision and then later regret it?" I ask her the one question that has been plaguing me all day.

I want to dance. I want to be the best damn dancer that the company has ever seen, but I also want to be a mom. I want to do both, but I wasn't expecting to have to choose one or the other.

What happens if I decide and later down the line, I not only regret it but also resent it? What happens then?

Would I hate myself?

Betty?

What about Liam? Will I hate him, too?

Or will he walk away and want nothing to do with any of it and leave all the heavy decision-making to me?

So many damn questions.

"That won't happen. I won't let that happen. You will

make the decision that's best for you right now, and there will be no regrets about it. I promise."

I let out another sob, but it's drowned out by the siren going off signaling a goal.

Lifting my head just enough off Betty's shoulder, I watch the replay on the jumbotron and see that it was Liam who scored.

My eyes shift to where he is on the ice, and the urge to puke comes back stronger than ever.

This pregnancy isn't only going to affect my life, but it will also affect Liam's.

If I decide to keep the baby, what is his life going to look like? Will it look the same, or will it make a complete one-eighty?

I don't know, but I think that's what terrifies me the most.

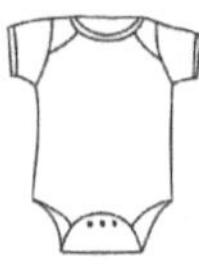

Liam was true to his word when he said that someone was going to come get me after the game.

Almost as soon as the last player left the ice, a security guard came to where Betty and I were sitting and offered to escort us back.

As much as she wanted to join me, Betty decided to head home. She said something about not wanting to impose on my conversation with Liam and called an Uber.

A part of me wishes that she would have stayed, but a

bigger part knows that if Betty were here, I would chicken out and not say anything to Liam. I would hold in the words and continue acting like absolutely nothing is wrong.

Right now, though, as I wait in a sea of wives, girlfriends, parents, children, and fans, I'm in the wishing stage of wanting Betty here.

I have to be a big girl and do this, even if I do want to puke.

Players start coming out and walking over to their loved ones. The whole time, I try to make myself appear small and hide within the crowd as best as I can.

Eventually, I come out of hiding when there are only a few people left waiting for their players.

Liam is one of the last ones out with two guys following behind him.

All three men look like they belong in a fashion magazine with how they're dressed. Seeing them like this gives me a clue as to why there were so many women in the stands tonight. They all want a piece of a sexy hockey player in a suit.

If I wasn't in the middle of an existential crisis, I would be one of them.

The Chloe of just yesterday would take Liam home this very second and peel off that suit bit by bit until each one of his tattoos was showing. Then I would map each one out with my tongue.

The Chloe of today is trying really hard not to cry as the man in question looks up and meets my gaze.

What the hell have I gotten myself into? How did we even get here?

A handsome man and lots and lots of sex. That's how.

Liam sends a smile in my direction, but the smile that I send back must have been too tight because his expression quickly shifts.

He looks worried, just like he did earlier when he came to talk to me during his warm-up.

And just like when I saw that expression earlier, I want to yell out my secret to him, but I hold it in.

The three men approach me. Well Liam approaches me, and the two other guys follow. When they are about a foot away, I can't help but stare at them with my mouth wide open.

They are seriously gorgeous.

Are hockey players always this hot?

I thought the majority of them had broken noses and missing teeth.

"Hi," I say, my eyes dancing between the three men.

Liam gives me an intense look, his eyes not moving from my face. His friends, on the other hand, are looking at me like I appeared out of nowhere.

Eventually they both compose themselves. One of them gives me a smirk, and the other keeps looking between me and Liam, trying to figure out who I am to him.

The one who is smirking, looks over at Liam and throws a nod in my direction.

"Are you going to introduce us?" he asks, his smirk getting bigger.

Liam doesn't even look at his teammate. "No."

The intensity in his stare is enough for me to shift on my feet.

Is he always like this, or is it only when he is trying to figure something out?

The dark-haired teammate gives Liam an eye roll and turns back to me.

This time the smirk is gone, and in its place is a smile that I'm sure has helped land a woman or two in his bed.

"I'm Christian, this ill-mannered idiot's best friend," the dark-haired man says, nodding toward my baby daddy.

I give Christian a smile. "It's nice to meet you. I'm Chloe, the idiot's..." I pause. What the hell am I to him? There aren't many things I can call myself, so I settle with what is easiest. "Friend."

The way Liam flinches at the word friend doesn't go unnoticed.

Does he want us to be more?

Well, little does he know we will be, if I decide to go through with this.

"I'm Blake," the other teammate says, holding out a hand for me to shake.

He looks younger than Christian and Liam and has a boyish charm to him that seems sweet.

"Nice to meet you, Blake," I say, shaking his hand.

"You, too, Chloe." He gives me another smile, but it quickly turns into a smirk that matching Christian's from a few moments ago. "How do you and Liam know each other?"

It's a simple question, it really is. I just don't know if I want to tell two complete strangers that I'm Liam's one-night stand from a few weeks ago.

I guess Liam noticed the predicament I'm in because he finally stops his staring contest with my face and turns to his teammates.

"It's none of your business how we know each other. Don't you two have shit to do or something?"

Blake and Christian look at each other before they both shrug and start walking away.

"It was nice meeting you, Chloe."

"Bye, Chloe."

I watch both men leave, and once their backs disappear, I turn back to Liam.

His intense stare is back.

He looks both hungry for me and confused, and I'm sure once I tell him my little secret, that expression is going to shift into something else.

What, I don't know.

"Hi," I say again, my voice a lot smaller.

"Hi," he responds, his gaze not wavering.

This is going to be an interesting conversation, to say the least.

"You played a good game, and that's coming from someone that doesn't know much about hockey," I say, trying to give him a big smile.

The small smile he gives me tells me that my smile wasn't big enough.

"Thanks," he says. "Where's Betty?"

"She went home," I answer, wishing again that she was here as a buffer.

He nods, finally taking his eyes off me and looking around. "Want to get out of here and have that conversation?"

I give him a nod, and he starts guiding me away from the remaining friends and family.

His hand lands on my lower back, and for a long minute, I wish we weren't in this position. I wish that life hadn't changed this morning, and that he was leading me back to his place to have his way with my body.

But life did change, and now we have to have a conversation that will possibly change us forever.

I haven't said a single word about what I want to talk about, so I can't help but wonder what Liam thinks this is all about.

From the way he flinched at me calling myself his friend, he no doubt thinks I'm friend-zoning him.

And in a way I am.

I need to figure my shit out, and I can't do that and figure out how to start a new relationship.

That will just add to the chaos.

Liam and I make it out of the arena and to the parking lot, where he leads me to the fancy car he drove the night of the ballet.

It's like we've come full circle.

When we make it to the car, I think that Liam is going to open the door for me to get it, but he doesn't.

He just lets out a sigh and leans against the passenger side door.

I guess we're having this conversation in the parking lot.

Great.

We're both silent for a minute, both just looking at each other, waiting for the other to speak.

I should start.

I should break the silence and just let it spill out that I'm pregnant. I should do that.

So why the hell am I terrified to do it?

It's two simple words. Just two. I can say them. I can say them right now.

Just say them, Chloe.

SAY. THEM.

"Look, Chloe. We're both adults. If you no longer want to see me or just want to be friends, just tell me and—"

"I'm pregnant!"

CHAPTER TWELVE

LIAM

GROWING UP, my parents always told me I was a talker.

My dad has even told me that from the ages of two to six, I was like a parrot that wouldn't shut up. I always had something to say.

That extended into my teenage years, and into adulthood. As I got older, I learned to only talk when I wanted to add something to the conversation, but I still always still had something to say.

I can't remember the last time where I was rendered speechless.

Not until just now when Chloe spits out two little words.

I'm pregnant.

Two words, and I have no idea what to say.

My mind is blank, my mouth doesn't move. All I keep hearing are those two words coming out of her mouth.

No other sounds make it through my ears. Not even the

sounds of the busy city surrounding us. I don't hear anything besides what she just said.

She's pregnant.

Chloe is pregnant.

And here I thought she was going to friend-zone me.

Right now, I have no idea which would have been better.

I don't know how long I stand there not saying a word, but eventually Chloe steps closer and places a hand on my forearm taking me out of my trance.

"Say something, please," she begs, her voice having a shake to it.

She's scared. I don't have to know her for longer than I have to know that.

Even knowing that she's scared, though, doesn't stop me from asking a stupid question,.

"Is it mine?"

I don't have time to think about the question. It's out of my mouth before I know it.

But it has to be asked.

I haven't been with anyone since we started our time together, but that doesn't mean that she can say the same. For all I know, she was with someone either before me or right after me and is trying to pawn this off on me.

"Before you, I hadn't been with anyone for four months and I haven't been with anyone since. It's yours," she states, a bite to her tone.

I can see it in her eyes that she's telling the truth.

Now I feel like a dick.

"I'm sorry," I say to her, not knowing what else to tell her. My thoughts and words are all jumbled up.

Chloe lets out a long sigh and gives me the same small smile she gave me before the game.

"It's fine. I would have asked the same thing if I was in your shoes. I just didn't expect the question to sting like that." Her voice shakes even more, like she wants to cry but is holding it in.

I think about my next question carefully.

"When did you find out?"

"Right before the game. I had an appointment for my birth control shot, and well, I left without my shot and in its place a positive pregnancy test. According to the doctor, she puts the date of conception around the night we met."

Fuck.

That's why she was acting weird during warm-ups. She had just found out and then had to act like nothing had happened.

"We were careful," I say absentmindedly, trying to digest everything.

"Apparently, even with double protection, there's still a chance. It's small, but it's there."

"Fuck."

I run a hand across my face. This is definitely not how I thought this night was going to go. Just like our first night together.

"Trust me, I feel the same way," she says, her voice cracking.

My hand drops immediately, and my eyes find hers. They're filled with tears and her bottom lip starts to quiver.

She is trying to keep it together, but the second that I reach for her, she breaks.

Her whole body shakes as I wrap my arms around her and hold her tightly against my chest.

Hearing her sob does something to me. It's as if it's breaking something in me. I may not know this woman very well, but I do know that I want to take her pain away and make every single thing better.

"I don't know what to do." Chloe grabs onto my suit jacket, pulling herself to me as tightly as she can.

I don't have to ask to know what she is talking about.

"We can figure it out together," I tell her, tightening my hold on her.

"I don't want to make the wrong choice."

"You won't," I reassure her even though I have no idea what I'm talking about.

"I want to be a mom. I really do, but I don't want to give up dancing. Not right now. I don't know what to do." She pauses, taking in shallow breaths. "Please don't hate me."

It's her last four words that have me pulling back from her and placing a finger under her chin so that she can look up at me.

"I don't hate you now, and I won't hate you whenever you make your choice."

"You say that now, but things could change," she says through a shaky breath.

"They won't. It's your body, Chloe. You may not know

me very well yet, but know this, I will never, ever, hate you for making whatever choice is best for you."

Chloe looks up at me with tear-filled eyes and all I want to do is slide my hand up just a little and wipe her tears away.

I want to take away all the uncertainty and pain that she is feeling and make everything easier for her.

But she's not mine to wipe the tears away. She's not mine to protect from the bad and the pain.

Even if she is pregnant with my baby.

I have no claim on her, and I doubt that I ever will.

Things are silent between us for a few seconds until she breaks it.

"Do you want kids?" she whispers, new tears springing to her eyes.

Her question takes me a bit by surprise.

Do I?

I answer her question as truthfully as I can.

"I never really thought about it. Kids are part of life, sure, but they haven't been something that I've actively thought about. I never really thought about the when of it all."

My mom has been asking me for grandchildren for the last four years. Every time I go home, she tells me to meet a nice girl and to at least give her one grandkid to spoil.

I brushed her off every single time.

"And if the 'when' of it all isn't right now?" One of her tears escapes, and I don't bother holding and stop it away with my thumb.

"Then that would be okay. I would be okay as long as you are. I'm not going to stand in front of you and force you to do something because the time isn't right for you, but it is for me. No matter what, you'll have my support."

And it's the truth.

I'm not the type of man who is going to force a woman to do anything that she doesn't want to. And I'm not one to walk away when he is needed the most. Baby or no baby.

"You mean that?" she asks, wiping at her face.

"Yeah, I do," I say, brushing away of hair.

Chloe gives me a nod before stepping back into my arms and letting out another sob.

We stand like that for what feels like a long time but in the end, it only turns out to be ten minutes.

Eventually, we break apart, and I offer her a ride home.

The whole way to her apartment, we don't say a single word, both of us deep in our thoughts about how quickly our lives have changed.

This morning, the only thing I was thinking about was seeing Chloe and possibly having a repeat of our nights together.

Now, all I can think about is the fact that the one night that started it all between us might bring a new life into the world, and I have no idea how the hell to feel about it.

Do I want her to keep the baby? Do I want the opposite?

With all the honesty I can muster, I can safely say that I don't know the answer to either question.

So many things are up in the air that my emotions and thoughts are all jumbled up.

When we get to Chloe's apartment, I walk up with her,

not wanting her to be alone. It's when we reach her door that she finally breaks the silence.

"I haven't decided anything yet, but are you okay if I take a few days to think about things, and if I need anything, I can call you?" she asks, fidgeting with her fingers as she does.

I give her a nod. "Take all the time that you need. I'm not going to go anywhere."

Chloe closes the distance between us, wrapping her arms around my waist.

"Thank you, Liam," she whispers, her words followed by a sniffle.

"Don't cry. We will figure it out. Whatever decision you make, we will figure it out. Together." I wrap my arms around her for the second time tonight.

She nods her head against my chest and pulls away quickly after.

Chloe surprises me when she leans up and places a kiss on my cheek before giving me a quiet goodbye and walks into her apartment.

On the drive home, all I'm left with is my thoughts.

Thoughts of what it would be like if Chloe and I went through this. Thoughts of how our lives would look, what we would both look like in a few years' time.

Thoughts of if we chose to do this, would the baby have her curls and eyes? Or would they look like me?

Thought after thought starts flowing in, and I just let them.

Even if they are dangerous with everything up in the air.

But that doesn't stop me from thinking them.

CHAPTER THIRTEEN

CHLOE

I'M ninety-seven percent sure that I've figured out what I want to do.

For the past week, I've been thinking about every single thing, coming up with every scenario that I could to help me make my decision.

I tried to go through life as if nothing had changed, and I wasn't fighting with myself to make the biggest decision of my life. For the most part, I was able to, but whenever I wasn't busy, more thoughts and scenarios popped up.

Liam checked in on me. So did Betty. Both asked if I needed anything, including company. As much as I wanted to take both of them up on their offers, I needed to be alone.

I did occasionally text Liam here and there, asking him questions like I did the night of the hockey game. Even though I wanted to be alone, I did want to include Liam in the decision making in some way.

Me being pregnant not only affects my life, it also affects his.

Even though he told me it was my choice, it feels wrong not including him.

So, I did.

Now, a whole week later, I'm ninety-seven percent sure I have made my decision.

I'm not one hundred percent because there is still some doubt getting sprinkled in.

Stupid three percent of doubt.

Today, though, I'm going to push away that doubt and get through that three percent and be confident in my decision.

I will.

The only thing in my way is a phone call to my mom.

In all my life, I have never been afraid to tell my mom anything. As a teenager, she was the first one to know whenever I had problems with my friends or a boy. She knows almost every single secret that I hold.

But just because I wasn't afraid of telling her everything as a teenager, doesn't mean that I'm not to tell her this.

Leticia Vega may be my best friend at times, but she is still a woman who holds strong values, especially when it comes to getting pregnant out of wedlock.

It was ingrained into my brain from an early age to not have kids unless I was married or in a long-term committed relationship.

I'm neither.

Once I tell her the predicament I'm in, she might freak

out, and act like I'm still a kid and the fact that I'm twenty-nine years old won't even matter.

I can't keep avoiding calling her, though. I've already waited this long. If I wait any longer to call her, she's going to know something is wrong and possibly hop on the first flight out of Austin to come see me.

So with my hand shaking, I reach for my phone, sending a quick text to Liam to call me when he gets a chance and then start dialing my mom's number.

Might as well tell her and get my lecture over with.

I'm barely able to take a few calming breaths before my mom's voice comes through the speaker.

"Hola, hija. You finally remembered to call your mother," my mom says, guilt-tripping me for not calling her.

I nervously start biting my thumbnail. "Sorry, rehearsals have taken a lot out of me."

It's not a complete lie.

"I was looking at the performance schedule to plan a visit, and it's a lot of shows," she says jumping straight into the conversation, not wasting any time with pleasantries.

One thing about my family is that they are incredibly supportive. They will take time out of their lives to attend as many of my shows as they possibly can. I love them for that.

"Yeah, it's a lot, but I'm going to make every performance count, especially if I want to take next year off," I tell her, cringing a bit as I do.

Slowly, I'm going to do it slowly.

"Why would you want to take next year off? Are you going to dance with a traveling company?" she asks, excitedly.

Being a traveling dancer was something I have looked into this past year, but I never did anything with it. I told my mom about it, so I know where she got that idea.

I shake my head even though she can't see.

"No. I'm not going to go with a traveling company. I just think that given my situation. I'm going to need to take some time off."

I bite down on my nail. After this conversation is over, I'm not going to have a nail left.

"Situation? What situation? Estas bien? I can see if I can fly in later this week if you need me to." She starts, getting worried. I can hear her shuffling around, probably getting ready to call my dad to book her a flight out.

"Ma, estoy bien," I say, trying to reassure her. "I just..." I pause. I have to tell her. If I continue to keep it in, she's going to worry even more. "I just have something to tell you."

"¿Que?"

So much for doing this slowly.

"I'm pregnant, and I'm going to keep the baby." That's the first time I've said what I've decided to do out loud and it feels like a weight has been lifted off me. I didn't have to tell her I was keeping the baby. She probably already assumed it, but I needed to say it for myself.

Saying it made it all the more real.

Saying it made me one hundred percent confident in my decision.

There's silence on the other side.

She's probably still thinking of jumping on a plane and yelling at me in person.

"You're pregnant?" my mother asks, her voice a bit shaky.

I nod as if she were in the room with me. "Yeah, I found out last week."

"Why didn't you tell me sooner?" she asks, the shake that was just there gone, and in its place is something else. It's probably anger.

"Because I was scared," I admit.

"Why would you be scared of telling me something like this?"

Is she serious? Both my sister and I heard the same lecture every single day when we started dating.

No babies. Not until you have a ring on your finger.

"Because you always told us to not get pregnant unless we had a ring on our finger, that's why."

"Oh, mija. I only did that so that you and your sister would be safe in your choices. Not to scare you when you were older. You're almost thirty. Telling me that you're pregnant shouldn't terrify you."

Safe in our choices?

Is this woman for real?

I didn't lose my virginity until I was twenty-two because I was afraid to get pregnant and have my mother hate me.

Hell, I felt that way now.

"So you're not going to lecture me?" I ask, dumbfounded.

"Why would I lecture you? You're an adult, you don't need me to lecture you for this."

I guess I was scared about nothing.

"I'm sorry I didn't tell you sooner," I say to her, feeling relieved.

"It's okay. If I had to guess, I would say that you didn't call me because you were trying to figure out what the best choice was for you, and when you made that decision you decided to call."

My mom knows me so damn well.

"Yeah," I whisper.

"Are you happy with this decision?" she asks, her question taking me by surprise.

I pause, but I don't even think about my answer.

"Yeah, I think so," I admit.

I don't even have to ask to know that she is trying to dissect my answer. "Tell me your thought process," my mom suggests.

She will forever be the counselor.

I let out a sigh and go through my entire catalog of thoughts and dilemmas I've had over the last week.

"It's a lot," I say, throwing myself onto my couch.

"I have time. Your dad is still at work," she tells me. "Tell me."

Why do I feel like I took a trip to my therapist's office instead of calling my mom?

Either way, I tell her everything.

"When the doctor told me, I got scared. You know how important dance is to me. You know all the hard work I put in to get where I am. All the sweat, tears, and injuries I suffered so that I could even be considered for any dance company. I have wanted to be a ballerina for so long that the second she told me I was pregnant, I saw everything I worked so hard for start to vanish. It didn't help that I had told myself that I wasn't going to get involved in a relationship, that I was going to concentrate on dance and dance alone. So when she told me, I started to freak out."

I sink deeper into the couch, feeling an urge to cry as I tell my mom everything.

"You thought that if you were pregnant, you would have to give up dancing and possibly never be able to wear your pointe shoes again."

I nod.

Ding, ding, ding. We have a winner.

"Yeah. I knew I wanted to be a mom, but there were moments during the last week where I wanted to be a dancer more. I kept telling myself that I was at my peak, and I couldn't give that up. I couldn't walk away weeks after having the best performance of my life. I needed to choose dancing and then maybe in a few years I could revisit the whole mom thing."

Stupid tears betray me and escape. If my mom and I were on FaceTime, she would be seeing my snot go everywhere.

"What changed? Did something happen that made you shift your perspective?" she asks.

Now I really am in a therapy session.

I sniffle. "Yeah."

"What?"

Without even trying, my mind goes to two days ago.

I was at my morning rehearsal with a few other company dancers, going through a small number that was added to our Christmas program. The routine itself was simple and something that most of us could do in our sleep. What wasn't simple was one of the lifts our choreographer decided to add that day.

It was an overhead lift, something we do all the time, but for some reason that day, the lift was off.

Someone's hand placement was off, and the choreographer lost control, causing both him and the female dancer he was lifting to fall to the ground.

The girl ended up going to the ER with a broken collarbone, two broken ribs, and a broken arm.

She's out for at least the first half of the winter season.

"Someone got hurt a few days ago. She's out until at least December," I say, remembering the way her arm was bent.

"And seeing her like that, scared you, too." I can practically hear my mom nodding on the other side.

"It did. It reminded me that I can get hurt tomorrow and never be able to wear my pointe shoes again. That's when I started to think that maybe I can keep the baby and still dance. Betty does it, so do a number of other girls at the company. If they can do it, I can too."

Saying everything out loud cements my decision.

I'm really going to do it.

I'm really going to be a mom and a dancer.

"And the dad? Is he going to be involved? Does he know?"

My mom loves to ask the hard questions, doesn't she?

"He knows I'm pregnant, but not that I'm keeping it. I haven't told him yet. We have a lot to figure out."

I have to keep my fingers crossed that Liam is okay with my decision. If he's not, that's on him. I would really like for him to be involved, though. He seems like the type of man who would be a great dad.

"Are you two together?" my mom asks, and I should have expected it.

"No," I answer way too quickly.

If things were different, I totally can see myself being in a relationship with Liam. But I'm not going to force it with the guy just because he got me pregnant.

A baby does not make a relationship.

I know my mom wants to add something else regarding Liam, but thankfully she doesn't.

"I'm happy for you, Chloe. I can't wait to meet mi niñito."

"Thank you, Mami," I say, smiling into the phone.

"Ahora, mi pregunta para ti, who's going to tell your papi that he's going to be a grandpa?" she asks.

By the way that she sounds asking the question, I know that not only is she smiling at the thought of becoming a grandma, but she's also excited.

"I'll call him and Anabella later today," I promise.

My dad will probably have a calm reaction to the news whereas my sister... she's probably going to go crazy the second the words are out of my mouth.

Soon after I promise to make that call, I end the call with my mom ends.

I didn't realize how much I needed one of her talks until I pressed the end button.

Talking to her made me believe in and accept my decision wholeheartedly.

That three percent of doubt is no longer trying to get through.

All I need to do is let Liam know what I finally decided and hope that he's on board.

And if he is, maybe we can figure out a type of relationship—a platonic one because there is no way am I capable of being someone's girlfriend right now—will work for us.

Fingers crossed.

I'm about to get up from my place on the couch to look for something to eat when my phone starts to ring.

For a second, I completely forgot that I texted Liam to call me when he had a chance. I guess he had a chance, and not even a few seconds after he popped into my head.

A small smile forms on my lips as I answer.

"Hey," I say, feeling nervous all the sudden.

"Hey, you okay? You said to call," Liam says, sounding out of breath like he was just running or something.

"Are you at practice?" I ask, not wanting to take away his time with his teammates.

"It just finished. What's up?" he asks, more worried than curious.

"I wanted to tell you something, but it can wait. I don't have to tell you right now," I stammer. I want to tell him, I do, but I don't know how he will react, especially in a locker room.

"Chloe. What's going on?" When his voice is low like that, memories from our nights together start flooding back in.

I push away all thoughts of us having sex and concentrate on the task at hand.

"Do you think that you can come over tonight? I have something I want to tell you."

There is no hesitation with his response.

"I will be there in half an hour."

CHAPTER FOURTEEN

LIAM

I WOULD BE LYING if I said I haven't been on pins and needles all week.

These last seven days have been so damn excruciatingly long. There were more than a handful of times that I wanted to run over to Chloe's apartment and beg her to give me an answer.

Am I going to be a dad?

Am I not?

I needed something.

Every time she would call or text to ask me a question, I would think that this was it, that that was the day I would finally get an answer. And every time, a bit of me died inside when I didn't.

But even if I didn't get an answer, I would have continued to wait it out. I wasn't about to force her to make a decision that she wasn't ready to make. I would continue to wait until she said otherwise.

The whole thing has even affected my game. Instead of concentrating on what was happening on the ice, especially during the season opener, I was dreaming up scenarios that would probably never happen.

I've been completely out of it.

So, when I got out of practice, and I saw that Chloe had texted to call her when I got the chance, I left the locker room as quickly as possible.

Now the leather in my car reeks of sweaty balls because I didn't shower before leaving the locker room, but I'll deal with that later.

The only thing that matters right now is getting to Chloe and finally finding out if our lives are going to look different after today.

My head is spiraling with ideas of what she wants to talk about, and I don't know how I feel about any one of them.

When she tells me, will I be excited? Mad? Indifferent?

The only way to find out is for it to happen.

Getting to Chloe's is the easy part, finding parking is a bitch and a half. It takes me a whole ten minutes to find a small ass spot that I could slide my car into.

As soon as the car is parked, I don't waste any time running up to Chloe's apartment.

I knock on her door the second I make it to her fourth-floor walk-up, feeling like I spent the whole morning doing speed training.

I'm able to catch my breath before Chloe opens the door, but as soon as she does, it's as if I'm breathless all over again.

She is always stunning, but for some reason, she looks like

she's on a completely different level today. My cock seems to like it a little too much.

Because I'm too busy taking in how damn beautiful she looks, it takes me a second to realize that she's covering her nose.

"What?" I ask instead of a greeting.

"Why do you smell like that?" she mutters behind her hand.

"Like what?" I take a whiff of my shirt, and it's the same smell that is currently penetrating my car. Ball sweat, but out of the confines of my car, it doesn't smell that bad.

"Like you cooked yourself in rotten cheese," Chloe tells me, stepping back from the door and putting space between us.

Rotten cheese?

I smell bad but not that bad.

And she wasn't that close to me, how did she get a whiff so fast?

The heightened smell.

I read a few blog posts over the last few days, and a lot of them said that women tend to have their sense of smell heightened when they are pregnant.

A part of me didn't believe it, but now that I have Chloe in front of me looking like she is going to puke, I have to.

"Sorry, I skipped the shower after practice to come straight here."

"You didn't have to come right away," she says, gagging a little. "I can't have this conversation with you when you smell like rotten cheese. Go shower."

She points behind her, down her hallway.

She wants me to shower *here?*

"You're serious?" I ask, trying to keep my laugh in.

"Yes."

"I have no clothes," I tell her, walking into the apartment and closing the door behind me.

"Stay in a towel for all I care, just go shower before I puke." She continues to back away from me like I have the plague or something.

Shaking my head, I throw a smirk in her direction and make my way down the hallway to her bathroom.

I don't wait for the water to heat up before jumping in. Even though we're about to have a serious conversation, my cock still remembers all the stuff that we did the last time I was here. Every single memory is still as fresh as if it happened yesterday. So, the colder and quicker the shower I take, the better for me.

It doesn't help that I'm using Chloe's body wash. Her scent all over me is going to make a certain body part a lot harder than it should be.

Ignoring what smelling Chloe's shampoo is doing to my dick, I finish my quick shower, and I am out within five minutes with a towel wrapped around my waist.

The second Chloe sees me bare-chested I know she regrets telling me she doesn't care if I stay in a towel.

The woman cares and by the blush creeping up her cheeks, she cares a lot.

"You seriously don't have any clothes? Not even in your car?" she asks, trying hard to not look at my torso.

I give her a smirk. "I thought you didn't care."

"I don't," she says, her blush getting deeper.

As much as I would love to tease her some more, I drop it.

"The clothes I was wearing were what I wore to the arena. I didn't think to grab my extras." If I knew that my sweat and bad body odor affected her so much, I would have grabbed them.

Chloe's eyes travel down my body quickly before they settle back on my face. She looks almost embarrassed that I caught her looking, but I don't give a shit.

This woman can look at me all she wants. I just have to keep my dick at bay.

"You might have left a shirt the last time you were here I think. Let me go check," she says, rushing out of the living room and heading to her bedroom.

The fact that I left a shirt here should have been my first clue that I would have Chloe in my life a lot longer than just a few nights. I never leave clothes behind.

Chloe comes back a minute later and hands me a worn-out Knights T-shirt that I indeed left behind.

"I've been looking for this," I say, taking the shirt from her and slipping it on.

Memories from the last time I wore it try to sneak into my mind, but I stop them.

No need for me to think about eating sushi off Chloe's body while I'm in a towel.

"I found it under the couch and figured I would give it to you whenever I saw you next." She's blushing again, so she might have worn it once or twice since then.

Something that I'm more than okay with.

I give her a smile.

When I'm half dressed, we stand in awkward silence, something that we haven't experienced in the brief time that we have known each other. Chloe is pulling at her fingers, and I'm the dumbfuck wearing a towel in the middle of her living room.

We have to talk, so we might as well get on with it.

"Should we take a seat?" I ask, waving toward the couch, trying to break the awkwardness.

She nod, and we both take a seat, more than a cushion between us.

"So," I start.

"So," Chloe repeats, shifting in her seat.

"I'm guessing you made a decision." It's not a question but a statement. If she hadn't, I wouldn't be sitting here waiting for her to say something.

She gives me a nod.

"I did."

I've been waiting for this moment. I've been waiting for her to say something for the last week, and now that she has made a decision, I don't know if I should be relieved or nervous.

I let out a sigh, preparing myself for what I am about to ask.

"What did you decide?" I ask my question carefully, trying hard not to say the wrong thing. I've never been in this type of situation before, and I want to handle it right.

I turn my body toward her.

She sits with her arms folded on her lap and her eyes looking anywhere but up. I want to reach over and make her look at me, but what she's about to say is probably hard for her.

After a long minute she looks up, and I notice that she has tears in her eyes.

Every inch of me wants to know what type of tears they are.

Good? Bad? Angry tears? Tears of hate toward me for putting her in this position?

She looks at me for what feels like forever, but it's only thirty seconds. Chloe takes a deep breath before answering my question.

"I-I decided to keep the baby," she finally says, her shoulders sagging as if a weight has been taken away.

So many things run through my body and mind all at once. Two of the major things I feel are excitement and uncertainty. Excitement over the fact that I'm going to be a dad, something that I didn't know I would be excited about, and uncertainty because I have no idea how the hell we're going to do this.

"You're going to keep the baby." It's a statement not a question.

I might have to repeat that sentence a few times for it to stick in my mind that in a few months, there's going to be a tiny life that is going to depend on me.

"I'm going to keep the baby," Chloe says with a nod, wiping her tears away.

I take a few minutes to digest everything.

When she told me she was pregnant, I tried to hold back all the emotions that came rushing in with the news. I wanted to be excited, but at the same time, I knew I couldn't be. Especially if I wanted to stand by her in whatever decision she made. Keeping the baby or not, it was her choice to make, not mine, even if she did include me in it.

I told myself that I would be ok with whatever decision she made and that was the truth, even though a small part of me did hope that she would keep the baby. It was a small part, but I have to admit that it was there.

Now that I know what she is doing, my body wants to jump up in excitement in a way that I didn't expect.

While I'm trying to digest everything, Chloe takes my silence as something negative.

"It's okay if you don't like my decision," she starts, her voice shaking, all the while more tears escape from her hazel eyes. "It's also okay if you do not want to be involved either. I know I sprung this on you, and it was a lot all at once. We don't know each other. We're not together, and you sure as hell don't owe me anything. So, if you do not want to be involved, that's okay. Just tell me so I can mentally prepare myself for it. I would love for you to be a dad to our child, but if you don't want to, I'm not going to force you."

She's giving me an out.

She's letting me know that she doesn't need me and that she can do this on her own.

She probably thought that I wanted her to go in the opposite direction.

Not giving a shit anymore about not touching her, I break the distance between us and take her hand in mine.

"I'm just trying to digest everything," I say, explaining my silence. I give her hand a reassuring squeeze before I continue. "I told you that I will be there for you for whatever choices you make. Yes, we don't know each other. Yes, this was all so sudden, but just because it is, doesn't mean that I won't be there for you. Or that I wouldn't want to be a part of my child's life. I do. I want to be a part of every single moment. If that's okay with you. I don't want to go anywhere. I just have to wrap my head around it. I'm going to be a dad and that feels weird saying out loud."

Saying it out loud feels more than weird, but I'm sure with time, I'll get used to it.

I'm going to have a fucking kid.

"Yeah, it felt weird for me, too," she says, giving my hand a squeeze back.

Against my better judgment, I wrap my free arm around her shoulders and bring her closer to my body.

Chloe doesn't push me away, she follows the motions and places her head against my chest, taking in my comfort.

"I have something else that I want to talk to you about," she says, her voice just above a whisper.

"Okay, and what's that?" I ask, looking down at her but not letting her put any space between us.

"Us being romantically involved," she says, pushing herself away from me just a bit to look at my face.

Not a topic I was expecting her to want to talk about.

Have I thought about me and Chloe being together? Sure. Up until last week, it was all I could think about.

Now though, jumping into a relationship doesn't seem right. Especially if we're only doing it because she's pregnant.

I want to be with this woman, but I want to be with her when the time is right, not when we are forcing it.

But maybe Chloe does want to force it and see what happens.

"Do you want to be romantically involved?" I ask, feeling my eyebrows rise.

She shakes her head. "I was going to tell you last week that we should pause whatever was happening between us until after the new year. That I wanted to concentrate on dance for the time being. Then this happened, and it cemented that thought process. There are other things we have to concentrate on."

I guess that's confirmation that I was getting friend-zoned.

But I'm one hundred percent on board with it now, even if I wasn't last week.

"I agree. There are things right now that need our attention, and a relationship isn't one of them." I want to add at least not right now to the end, but I keep those words on the tip of my tongue.

"So, you're okay with us not jumping into a relationship together?" she asks, like it's hard to believe.

I give her a nod. "Yeah, I'm okay with it."

She gives me a smile, like she appreciates me beyond belief.

"Thank you, Liam. For understanding," she says, her head landing back on my chest.

"You're welcome," I say, placing a kiss against her curls. Something I have to put a stop to. "So, we are really doing this? We are really having a baby?"

Chloe nods against me. "We really are."

We really are.

Holy shit.

Things just got a lot more real.

CHAPTER FIFTEEN

CHLOE

DECEMBER

I THINK that I've finally wrapped my head around everything.

It only took me close to two months, but I finally got there and am okay with that.

A lot has happened since I found out I was pregnant and decided that I was keeping the baby. Well, maybe not a whole lot, but because of the short time frame, it feels like it.

After letting Liam know I was going to keep the baby and him telling me he was going to be involved, we came up with a plan. Nothing concrete but something to help us get through the next few months.

When we get closer to the baby's arrival, we'll make another plan.

For now, we are going through life as if everything were

the same, as if I hadn't gotten pregnant. Well, relatively the same.

There are calls between Liam and me that weren't there before, with him checking in on me almost every day, even when he's traveling for games. He has even gone to my last two doctors' appointments with me, so that's another difference.

I'm still dancing, though, so that has stayed the same.

After Liam and I talked, I called Dr. Long's office to schedule my next appointment, letting them know which direction I was going in. In the process, I got the okay to continue dancing. As long as I don't overwork my body, get enough rest, keep myself hydrated, and eat right, I'm good to go for the rest of the winter shows.

I was planning on taking a small break for a few months anyway, so everything is working out.

As the days go on, my body is feeling the effects of being pregnant. I'm more tired and hungry every day, and the boobs that I had hoped for as a teenager have started to show up.

But I'm feeling good about my choice, and in a few months, I will get to meet my little surprise gummy bear.

I didn't think that I would be this excited about this, especially with how much I over-thought about everything and my situation with the father, but I am.

So damn excited.

That excitement extends to my dancing, too.

For the last month or so, the rest of the dance company and I have been dancing our asses off to give people the best ballet experience they could have.

And so far, everything has been going off without a hitch, and every single person in the audience has been loving it.

After each performance, all of us dancers feel as if we are on cloud nine and are excited for the next one.

It honestly feels like the best winter season we've had in a long time, and I'm here for it.

Today the excitement of everything is hitting me strong as I walk into my morning rehearsal.

I have a big smile is on my face, and I feel light on my toes, ready to conquer whatever the day throws at me.

"Look at you," Betty exclaims as soon as I walk into our shared dressing room. "You look like you're glowing."

I can't help but beam at her, the smile on my face growing even more. "I feel really good today."

"No more morning sickness?" she asks, raising an eyebrow in my direction.

I hold in a groan.

I've been excited about a lot of things these last two months. Morning sickness, though, has not been one of them.

The nausea has hit me hard. Every little thing makes me want to puke. No matter the smell or the taste, something always makes me nauseous.

Liam has even made sure to tell me that he has showered the few times I have seen him so I don't gag just thinking about smelling his sweat again.

There was a week or two where I was just living off sourdough bread and apple juice. It also didn't help that I spent most of my days twirling and dancing around a stage.

It was bad. Really bad.

These last three days, though, I haven't smelled or tasted anything that had my stomach turning, so I see that as a good sign. I did wake up a little light-headed this morning, but as soon as I ate something, it went away.

"Not in a few days," I say, silently hoping that it stays that way.

"You're sixteen weeks, right?" Betty asks, and I give her a nod. "It's probably starting to fade."

"It better. I'm tired of not being able to look at food without wanting to throw it across the room." I shudder just thinking about looking at a hot dog again.

"I hate morning sickness so much, it makes me want to not get pregnant ever again," Betty chimes right before slamming her pointe shoes against the floor.

"Trust me, I've thought about that, too," I say to her grabbing my makeup bag.

One thing that sucks about doing ballet is all the work you need to do for your shoes to fit properly and look right.

Not only do you have to break them in, but if you have a darker skin tone like I do, you have to douse them in makeup in order to get them the right color.

And you have to do it to every single pair.

So, while Betty breaks in her shoes, I cake mine to be at least a decent color.

Thank God I thought to glue and sew the box of my shoes last night otherwise I would be sitting here all of rehearsal.

"How are things going with you and Liam?" Betty asks as soon as she is done slamming her shoes against the floor.

"Okay, I guess. Nothing new," I say, giving her a shrug.

"I still can't believe that you friend-zoned a professional hockey player," she says, giving me a shake of her head. She's teasing me, I know, but that still doesn't stop me from still feeling bad about my decision.

"We have other things to concentrate on right now. I have to spend the next five months thinking how to be a good mom, not how to be a good girlfriend," I tell her, and by the way Betty looks up at me, I know there's a bite to my tone.

"You're right. I'm sorry I brought it up," she says, giving me a smile and holding up her shoes in surrender.

I let out a sigh. "Do you think I shouldn't have friend-zoned him?"

This is something that has been nagging at me for a while.

Should we give a relationship a try?

It's not like we were doing so before all of this, but maybe us being together would be good for the baby.

But then wouldn't it mean that we are only together for the baby and the baby alone?

Who knows.

I may have doubts occasionally about *that*, but I'm holding my ground on it.

"Oh, not at all," Betty says, getting up from her place on the floor. "I think it's smart not to jump into a relationship. More so now. Is it shocking, especially since the man got you pregnant? A little, but it's not mind blowing. Although—" She stops abruptly, biting down on her lip.

"Although, what?" I ask her, waving my hand for her to go on.

"Having him around can become useful when urges start to arise," she tells me, her perfectly sculpted eyebrows dancing up and down.

"Urges?" I ask.

She's not saying what I think she's saying, is she?

"Yes, urges. You know those of the sexual variety. In a few weeks, you're going to be so uncomfortable that the only way to get through it is to have an orgasm." The way she smiles at me, I can't tell if she's telling the truth or full of shit.

I did read that a woman's sex drive does heighten, but it can't be that bad. Can it?

"You're serious?"

She gives me a nod. "During the last few weeks of my first pregnancy, all I wanted to do was to jump onto Cole's lap and have him fuck me six ways to Sunday."

Not the mental picture I needed.

I try to clear my head as best as I can. "Do those urges happen to everyone?"

I try to remember everything I read, but I'm coming up blank on that question.

My friend gives me a shrug. "I don't think so, but from what I've heard, it happens the majority of the time."

That is not helpful whatsoever.

"Well, if they do happen, I have toys that can keep me company. I don't need my baby daddy."

Maybe if I repeat that in my head a million times, I'll

believe it and won't go seeking him out if the urges I may have.

Even though he did give me the best orgasms ever and had me begging all the while as he praised me.

"I'll buy you some batteries to help you get through," Betty says with a laugh before sliding into her shoes and leaving the room.

Damn, Betty. Now the only thing that I can think about as I finish up my shoes, is sex. Specifically, sex with Liam.

I try to push all sexual thoughts out of my head, for my own sanity, and concentrate on what today is going to look like.

We are two weeks away from Christmas and the company's biggest performance of the year.

So today is going to be jam-packed with minimal time for breaks.

That's what I should be thinking about and not sex, especially sex with Liam.

Once I'm happy with the way my shoes look, I grab everything I need and head out to the stage where we are practicing.

For the next four hours, we rehearse until we're all sweating messes, and the lights on the stage start to feel like heat lamps. We take maybe one or two breaks, but because our performance is so close, we get right back to it.

Eventually, sometime around four in the afternoon, our choreographer decided to call it for the day. A collective sigh of relief sounds through the theater as soon as she makes the announcement.

Before she leaves the room, she instructs us to stay hydrated and have a good dinner and a good night's sleep so that we can get back into it tomorrow.

My guess is tomorrow's rehearsal is going to be ten times longer than today's was.

The theater starts to clear out with only a few dancers left on the stage, me and Betty included.

Everyone is taking off their shoes, all the while I just sit there trying to force my body to move even an inch.

I haven't been this tired after a rehearsal in a long time. It feels like little ants are crawling all up and down my arms and legs. On top of that, I feel like I might puke if I try to stand up.

So much for me thinking that my morning sickness was gone.

Wishful thinking.

I'm finally able to move my body enough to reach over and start to untie my pointe shoes. But even doing something so small feels like a lot of work.

My body probably needs sugar. I'll make sure to pack a candy bar in my bag for all future rehearsals.

Once my shoes are officially off my feet, I try to push myself off the floor and stand up, but the second that I do, I start seeing little black spots.

Okay, maybe I should have taken a longer break.

This is just my body telling me I need to take things a lot easier and not push myself so hard.

Tomorrow, I will talk to the choreographer and ask for more breaks that are a bit longer.

Today, I just went a little too hard, too fast.

I try to stand up again, and this time I'm able to stand to my full height, but the second I do, my head starts to spin.

For what feels like forever, the whole room starts to spin, and it feels like I'm on a ride at Six Flags or something.

Water. I just need water and maybe some sugar, and I will be fine.

"Chlo, are you okay?" I hear Betty ask and for some reason she sounds like she's across the room.

Wasn't she sitting next to me? When did she move?

I don't ask. I just give her a nod.

At least I think I give her a nod, but all the black spots take over my vision, and I feel so dizzy that the next thing I hear is something hitting the stage and someone yelling to call an ambulance.

Why are they calling an ambulance?

CHAPTER SIXTEEN

LIAM

I DON'T KNOW what is more tiring.

Playing three away games back-to-back and not sleeping in your own bed for a whole damn week, or listening to Blake and Christian argue about who might be the fastest.

I'm putting all my money on the second one because I would rather get on fifty flights and play a hundred games instead of hearing these two assholes argue.

Whoever suggested that these two race across the ice is getting my stick up their ass.

Practice ended about ten minutes ago, and the only people left on the ice are the two idiots, me, Logan, and our head coach.

While the two princesses argue, the other two men and I watch them as if they were a car about to burst into flames.

"I'm surprised that Rodriguez hasn't thrown a punch in Jacobi's direction," Logan muses, speaking for the first time since practice ended.

The dude is a man of few words, but sometimes I can't help but to agree with him.

"He won't. He's going to antagonize Jacobi until the kid storms off," Coach answers.

Another man that I tend to agree with.

Well, when it comes to hockey. There's some personal shit that he can work on.

"I'm breaking them up. It's the same shit every single time," I say, shaking my head.

Today is an off day, so thank God we don't have a game, or these two would be embarrassing the whole team in front of the fans.

We don't need that shit. We're currently not only at the top of our division, but we are a game away from being at the top of our conference. If these two continue to argue like a bunch of babies over stupid shit, it could come and bite us in the ass.

Leaving Coach and Logan behind, I skate over to Tweedle Dum and Tweedle Dee and get between them.

"You two done?" I ask, looking between the two of them.

"Not until he admits that I beat him in that race," Blake argues, crossing his arms across his chest.

"You didn't beat me. I won by a literal strand," Christian throws back. From the smirk on his face, I know that he knows that Blake won, but he's going to continue to gaslight him probably until he makes him cry.

Children. I'm dealing with fucking children.

Is this what being a dad is going to be like?

Getting in the middle of arguments about who is faster?

God, I hope Chloe has a girl because no way in hell am I going to be able to handle boys and their damn competitiveness. Especially if the kid takes after me. My competitiveness has only gotten worse since I was a kid, but at least it's not at the level of these two.

I sigh.

There is one way to settle this, and the second that the suggestion leaves my mouth, I know I'm going to regret it.

"Just have another race and end this shit. I don't want to hear you two whine all day."

Both men turn to look at me and give a smirk.

Yup. I instantly regret what I just said.

"I like the sound of that," Christian says, his smirk turning into a sadistic grin.

"Fine, but we are making this interesting. One time around the ice. You have to pass Coach and Logan and Crawford times it. Winner gets bragging rights," Blake declares, holding out a hand to Christian.

Bragging rights.

All of this for damn bragging rights.

I fucking hate my friends.

Since they're annoying the hell out of me, I decided to make this whole thing a little more interesting than just bragging rights.

"Bragging rights and the loser comes over to my place once the baby is born and changes diapers for a day."

They want to act like little bitches, I might as well add something that will be for my own benefit.

Both Christian and Blake look over to me with wide eyes.

They both know that Chloe is pregnant and that we are having a baby together in a few months. I had to tell them and the team what was going on just in case something happened, and I had to miss a few games.

I got some surprised looks, but for the most part, people were accepting of it. So far, the news hasn't made it out of the arena, which I'm happy about and hoping to keep it that way.

I don't need or want people that call themselves my fans to go after Chloe.

My parents were also excited when I told them the news. Shocked but still excited. So damn excited that my mom started to plan a wedding for Chloe and I. Thankfully, she understood when I told her that we aren't together and nipped the wedding planning in the bud. Both call me every few days to ask how Chloe is doing, which I find sweet.

"I've never changed a diaper before," Blake admits, scratching his head. It's like he already knows he's going to lose.

"Think of it as practice for when you have nieces and nephews. Are we going to do this or not?"

I skate to center ice and hold out the stopwatch that was used during the first race.

The two idiots look at each other like they are asking the other if they are really doing this. Neither of them wants to change dirty diapers, so they are either going to race and hope that they win or call it off, altogether.

To my surprise, they both nod and skate over to the edge of the ice to the starting position.

So much for calling the race.

I look back to where Coach Anderson and Logan stand and nod for them to get into position.

Logan doesn't argue, he just keeps his stoic expression and skates over to where he's supposed to be.

Coach, on the other hand, grumbles the whole way across the ice.

"I can't believe I go along with this shit. You four owe me for this," he mutters as he skates past me.

He talks shit now, but he's the first one to sign up whenever one of us starts horsing around. The dude is just as much of a little kid as Christian and Blake.

"Alright. One lap around the ice. You have to pass both Coach and Logan to win. I will let you know who was the fastest. Winner gets bragging rights, and the loser gets to change dirty diapers for a day," I yell out, getting nods from idiot one and two.

"On three," I announce.

"One."

"Two."

"Three."

The second that Coach yells out three, arms go flying everywhere. Christian shoves Blake, and Blake shoves him back before they both find their balance and speed off.

Blake, being one of the team's right wingers, has natural speed that most men wish they had. Christian, on the other hand, does speed drills like no other. He's one of the best skaters I have ever seen and will be fast when you least expect it.

They pass Logan at the same time and continue to move

down the ice to where Anderson is. From where I'm standing, it looks like Christian is in the lead by an inch or two.

Chris is about to win his bragging rights when I see him pull back a tiny bit and let Blake pass him and pass Coach a second before he does.

The grumpy bastard let the kid beat him.

Looks like he does have a heart after all.

"Hell yeah," Blake yells out, pumping his fist in the air.

I look over at my best friend and find him shaking his head acting in disbelief that he was beaten out.

"You better not feed your kid any gross shit, Crawford. No way am I changing diapers that smell like my gym bag," Chris says, skating over to me.

He's putting on a show, and Blake is none the wiser.

"I'll talk to Chloe and see what I can do," I say, raising an eyebrow at him in question.

I just get a shrug in return.

"He was never going to shut up about it," he whispers, wiping his face on his practice jersey.

"He's not going to shut up about it no matter what," I say back, turning to look at Blake taking a victory lap.

I can't help but wonder if his brother is just as competitive. A childhood where two siblings became professional athletes had to be interesting.

Blake finally calms down after his second lap, coming over to where the four of us are standing with a huge smile on his face.

"That was awesome. Anyone want to do it again?"

"No," Coach, Logan, Christian, and I all answer together.

"Damn. Way to burst a guy's bubble," he says, shaking his head.

I'm about to say something, but my reply is cut off when I hear my name and Coach's name being called from the tunnel.

Both of us skate over to the team doctor, who has a worried look on his face.

"Everything alright?" Coach asks, getting the same feeling that I am.

"I just got a call from Chicago Medical. They admitted a Chloe Vega. They have Liam down as the emergency contact."

I don't get off the ice fast enough.

CHLOE

I OVERWORKED MY BODY.

That's what the doctors told me at Chicago Med after I was rushed to the hospital, and they did every single test in the book to make sure that the baby and I were okay.

I went too long without the proper amount of hydration and food that my body needs to function, and having a four-hour rehearsal was no help either. Those were the ER doctor's exact words.

A part of me wanted to argue with him. I wanted to tell him that I was drinking enough liquids and eating right but given how wiped out I was after rehearsal today, I know that I hadn't.

I should have taken more breaks to eat and drink. I should have told our choreographer that I needed to sit down for longer than a minute.

But because I was able to do those things every other day and came out of it okay, I didn't.

Now I have to slow down and rest before it starts affecting the baby.

According to the doctor, slowing down means no more dancing. No rehearsals, heavy or not, and definitely no performances. Nothing that will put strain on my body or put me at risk of falling.

Not only was my body exhausted, but it's also showing early signs of dehydration, and my blood pressure was a little higher than normal. If I fall, I can hurt the baby even more than I already am.

As soon as he told me all that, I saw the rest of my winter performances go out the window.

The doctor told me that I should be out for only a few weeks, but a few weeks is all that's left in the winter season.

I'm done dancing for the year.

And it's all because I didn't take care of myself like I promised Dr. Long I would.

"Are you okay?" Liam's voice breaks through the mental cloud I'm in as we make our way to my apartment.

When I decided to keep the pregnancy, and Liam told me that he was going to be involved, I added him as my emergency contact on my medical forms.

It was a decision made with the baby in mind. If something were to happen, and I couldn't reach the phone or Betty wasn't available, they could call him.

I guess as soon as I got to the hospital, they pulled up my file and gave him a call. Or at least called the number for the team to contact him.

He arrived at the emergency room in a panic. I was

already awake after fainting back at the theater, so I saw the distraught look on his face.

The second he saw that I was okay, and we were able to hear the baby's heartbeat, we both relaxed.

Now he's driving me home, and I don't even care that he smells like sweat.

I give him a nod, keeping my eyes directed at the window, watching all the buildings pass by.

"Yeah. I should have taken better care of myself, though," I say, pulling at my ballet wrap that I'm still wearing.

"Don't be so hard on yourself. You are both okay. That's all that matters," he says, reaching over and giving my thigh a reassuring squeeze.

I want to find comfort in his touch, I do, but I don't let myself.

"Thanks, but it's a little hard not to be. What if I hadn't fainted today and continued to push myself tomorrow? Things could have been worse," I say to him, still not looking over in his direction.

"But it wasn't. You're both fine and once you let your body rest, you will be even better."

I can see why the Knights made him their captain. The man knows a thing or two about pep talks, but right now, they aren't working for me.

"Yeah," is all I say and just continue to look out the window as we drive through the city over to Lakeview.

Liam doesn't say anything for the rest of the trip, and when we reach my apartment and he parks, I about jump out of the car without a word.

It's not his fault I'm in this situation. It was my mistakes that brought me here, so I'm trying to not take my anger out on him, but I'm failing.

And I know I am I'm frustrated that he gets out of the car and follows me into the building.

I'm two seconds away from telling him to leave me alone when he calls after me.

"Chloe, wait," he says as soon as I step onto the first step to head upstairs.

Slowly, I turn to look at him, just wanting to sleep and get this day over with.

"I'm tired, Liam. Whatever it is you want to say, can you please save it for tomorrow?" I don't mind begging if I have to.

Liam opens his mouth to say something but then quickly closes it. He lets out a sigh, and I watch as he slides his hands into his sweatpant pockets like he is debating how to say whatever is on his mind.

He better not lecture me about overworking myself. I already feel like shit, and I don't need him adding to it.

"I want you to move in with me," is what comes out of his mouth, and the second I hear it, I feel my jaw go slack.

Did I hear him correctly? My body has to be way more exhausted than I thought.

"I'm sorry, what?" I ask, dumbfounded.

"I want you to move in with me," he repeats clearly.

He's joking. He has to be.

No way in hell did this man, who I met only four months ago, whose baby I'm currently carrying, asked me to move in with him.

No fucking way.

"I'm sorry," I say, shaking my head. "You're asking me to move in with you? Are you joking?"

Now he's the one who is shaking his head. "I'm one hundred percent serious. Move in with me."

"Why the hell would I do that? I have a perfectly fine apartment here." I don't mean to raise my voice at him, but I can't handle this right now. The day has been way too long already, and he's asking me this? I can't.

I can tell Liam is getting a little irritated, too.

"Because your perfectly fine apartment is a walk-up. You can't be going up and down four floors every single day. The doctor told you to rest and to not do things that put you at risk of falling. Going up and down stairs every day is putting you at risk," he tells me, his face getting stern in the process.

"I will be fine," I say to him, turning to head up to my apartment.

"Chloe," Liam says, his voice sounding angry.

I roll my eyes before turning back to face him. "I said I will be fine, Liam. The only reason you want me to live with you is because I'm carrying your baby, and you want to make sure I don't do anything stupid again. I promise you that I learned my lesson today. You don't have to worry about me." I can feel my anger rising, but I try to keep it at bay as much as I can.

"It's not just the baby I care about, you know?" he tells me, his voice rising, and he closes the distance between us. "I care about you, too. I would care about you with or without the baby."

"You don't have to," I throw out there. "We're not together."

Liam lets out a scoff that makes me tense up my hand into a fist. "We don't have to be together for me to care about you. Hell, if I had my way, we would be together right now, but we're not because I agree it isn't the right move for us at the time. Even then, it's not wrong for me to care about a friend. It's not wrong for me to care about the woman who is carrying my child, together or not."

He says the last few words through his teeth. I can see the anger flowing through his eyes, and as much as I want to throw in my rebuttal, I don't.

I stay silent and let him continue.

"Getting told that you were in the hospital today sucked so fucking much. The whole way there, I didn't know if you were okay or not. So fucking forgive me for wanting you to move in with me and not wanting to worry about you falling every single damn day."

I see his reasoning, and the more I think about it, the more my irritation starts to vanish.

The ER doctor did tell me to avoid anything that could cause me to fall and to take it easy.

Taking four flights of stairs every single day is not easy. Something could happen when I lug groceries up or when my dryer isn't working, and I have to go to the laundromat down the street and carry my hamper up and down. And when my bump starts to grow, it will become even more dangerous.

Even though I hate to admit this, Liam does have a point.

Moving in with him is ridiculous, but if keeps me from falling and him from worrying, it could be a win-win situation.

Crap, why do I want to say yes to him?

I should be wanting to say no.

I can't move in with a guy I barely know. I'm already pregnant with his kid, so I should draw the line there.

But all I keep thinking about is how it's a logical choice.

Stupid logic.

"If we were to step into this arrangement," I start, choosing my words carefully. "How long would I live with you?"

"Until the baby is born," he says with no hesitation whatsoever.

"Excuse me? The doctor told me to rest for only a few weeks."

"So?" he says, so damn unbothered. "I don't care how long the doctor told you, I want you at my place at the very least until the baby is born."

"'At the very least'?" I feel my eyebrows rise to my hairline.

The bastard gives me a shrug. "I'm leaving the door open for renegotiation."

"There will not be any renegotiation. It's going to be just until the baby is born, and that is it."

"Whatever you say. I can be a very persuasive man when I want to be," he says, giving me a smirk.

"I highly doubt that."

"You just agreed to move in with me, so I say otherwise."
He lifts in eyebrow in my direction.

No way did I just agree to…

Then everything I just said comes rushing back.

I did just agree to move with him.

Holy shit.

What the fuck is wrong with me?

First, I got pregnant by the guy, and now I'm moving in with him. What's next? Getting married and falling in love?

Nope, not going to happen.

"Fine. I'll move in with you, but I better not wake up one day with a ring on my finger," I say, shoving him slightly.

"Who the hell said anything about a ring?" he asks through a chuckle.

"And no crawling into my bed. Or walking around in just a towel. Your super sperm already went through two forms of protection, I don't need to end up pregnant with another one of your babies before this one is even born."

He looks like he wants to laugh, but he holds it in, and gives me an affirmative nod.

"Whatever rules you put in place, I will stand by them," he says through a smile.

I narrow my eyes at him.

He's using his charm on me and that pretty smile that got us here in the first place.

Living with him is going to be hard.

Extremely hard.

Even more so when my feelings for him, and everything I felt for him in our time together, haven't fully disappeared. I will be living with secret feelings and reliving the hot memories of the two of us together.

But it gives us both one less thing to worry about, and if anything, I will have help getting ready for the birth and everything that follows it.

If I keep my feelings at bay, we can make this work.

"Okay, then, Mr. Crawford. You just gained a roommate."

"Pleased to hear it, Ms. Vega."

I'm fucking moving in with my baby daddy.

CHAPTER EIGHTEEN

LIAM

I'VE LIVED with two women in my entire life. My mom and my grandma when she came to live with us for a year before moving down to Florida.

That's it.

Never a girlfriend, or a buddy's girlfriend when I lived with a few teammates in college.

So, living with Chloe is one hell of an adjustment.

We know each other well enough to be able to not make things awkward, but we are learning more and more about each other as the days go on.

Every day it's something new, and just a week in, I'm looking forward to learning any little snippet I can about this woman.

Getting to know each other better is not the only thing that is happening in terms of adjustment.

She gave me the rule of not walking around the apartment in only a towel, and like the dumbass I am, I didn't give her the same rule.

I should have, because then I wouldn't be suffering with blue balls whenever I see her. Every night before bed she's in shorts that barely cover her ass and a tank top that looks like it can come apart with one simple tug. Her choice of pajamas also doesn't hide the fact that her body is changing more every day thanks to her pregnancy and in a spectacular way.

She looks fucking amazing, and my dick is taking notice.

Too much notice.

We've only lived together for a damn week, and I've already jerked off to images of her more times than I can count.

I'm going to hell, especially since I told her I was okay with us not exploring our attraction to each other further.

I've been trying to keep myself distracted, but Chloe is everywhere, and like I said before, it's been a hell of an adjustment. Even with me traveling a few times for away games.

Thankfully, today I have the distraction of all distractions.

Something that will keep my mind off Chloe's mouthwatering body and something that will keep her mind off not being able to dance right now.

Christmas decorating.

Usually when December hits, we're in the middle of the hockey season and traveling all over the place, so I don't bother to decorate. I can't even remember the last time I bought a Christmas tree.

This year, because Chloe is here, I decided to change that. She can't visit her family because she doesn't want to risk flying, so I thought I would embrace the Christmas spirit and bring the celebration to her.

First things first, though. I have to convince her to come out of the spare room that's hers temporarily.

Chloe has spent the majority of the last week cooped up, only coming out to eat, grab a drink, or to torture me with her little shorts.

Other than that, she's been in her room.

I haven't asked her why, but if I had to guess, she blames herself for her health scare last week and is not happy with not being able to dance in the remaining shows of her season.

So hopefully this cheers her up, and possibly have a smile on her face before Christian, Blake and Blake's friend Sophia come over and help decorate.

I'm also a bad host and have no idea how to entertain anybody besides Christian the grump, so I need her help in that department.

Taking my chances, I knock on her door. "Hey, Chlo. Do you want to help me with something?"

I hear movement on the other side of the door, and a few seconds later, the door swings open.

She looks at me with wide eyes. "Is everything okay?" she asks, looking me up and down.

I nod. "Yeah, I just need your help with something."

"Okay," she says, following me into the living room, where all the Christmas decorations I had delivered, cover about ninety percent of it.

"Wow," she says, taking in everything. "I didn't know that you were so into Christmas."

I scratch the back of my head. "I'm not."

"Then why does it look like it exploded all over your living room?" she asks, a small smile playing on her full lips.

"I wanted you to be able to celebrate, you know, since you aren't going to see your family."

Chloe looks at me and then looks over at the living room covered in decorations again.

A minute passes before she says anything.

"Did you just buy all of this?" she asks, picking up a stuffed dove I picked out from a computer screen.

I nod, even though her back is facing me. "I did. I don't decorate since I'm not usually home during this time of year, so I bought everything that I thought we needed."

She turns to look at me, that smile of hers growing. "You didn't have to do that."

I give her a shrug. "I wanted to. Besides, if it wasn't for me, you would be dancing right about now or on your way to Texas to be with your family.

"It takes two people to make a baby, and I'm the one who didn't rest when she needed to," she argues, putting down the dove and picking up a dancing Santa.

She's still beating herself up about her trip to the hospital.

I quickly move the conversation back to Christmas.

"I still wanted to do this. Bring some color into the place even if it is only for a bit."

And if it has Chloe's touch, it will look great and possibly convince me to decorate next year. Baby's first Christmas and all.

Will the baby even be here for Christmas, or will Chloe take them with her out of state to visit her family for the holiday?

I guess I should add that to the list of things we need to talk about when the baby gets here.

"If you don't decorate, does that mean that you don't celebrate Christmas?" she asks, walking over to the couch to pick up the garland I had the people at the store pick out.

"I celebrate. I just usually go to my parents' house for a few days. I'm an only child, so I try to go home whenever I get the chance. Usually, I have three days off before I have to get back for a game," I say to her.

My eyes follow her as she moves through the room picking up random Christmas decorations. I try hard to keep my eyes from traveling down to her ass but it's becoming hard.

"Do you celebrate Christmas?" I ask, trying to get back into the conversation before I do something stupid, like go across the room and sit her down on my lap.

"I do, but I don't celebrate on Christmas Day. We celebrate on Christmas Eve and then spend all of Christmas Day sleeping and eating leftovers." She turns to me, giving me another smile.

"Noch Buena, right?"

Chloe looks at me like she is shocked that I know that, and her smile gets bigger.

Points for Liam.

"Yeah, how did you know that?"

"Christian, one of my teammates, he's Mexican, and his family celebrates on Christmas Eve. I've gone with him a few times."

"Did you enjoy yourself?"

I give her a nod. "It was a fun time. Lots of good food, so I can see why you would spend an entire day eating leftovers."

"The leftovers are the best part." She beams.

"Maybe I can ask him to get us his mom's tamale recipe and we can make some this year," I suggest.

"Oh, we don't need a recipe, I know my mom's by heart. We just need to take a trip to the grocery store, and we will be eating tamales until New Year's." I can see her already making a list in her head and I fucking love it.

Just as much as I love seeing her happy.

"We can go tomorrow if you'd like," I offer, wanting to live in excitement as much as I can.

"Okay, it's a date, but first I think we need to figure out what to do with all these decorations. And get a tree. Shockingly, that is the one thing that you missed." She surveys everything again, making sure she didn't miss the tree.

She didn't because she's right. I didn't get the tree. At least not at the store where I got everything else.

"I have it covered. Why don't you get dressed, and we can get started?"

"Why would I get dressed?" she asks.

Why indeed.

If it were up to me, she would stay dressed like this, and I would gladly suffer through blue balls for the rest of the day.

I would do that if Christian and Blake weren't coming over. I would shove a skate up my ass before I let them see Chloe like this.

This is for my eyes, and my eyes only. She may not be mine, but I don't give a shit.

"Because some of my teammates are coming over with the tree," I say, not lying.

"Oh, okay. Yeah, let me go get dressed."

I shouldn't, but I watch her ass sway as she heads down the hallway.

Until this point, I thought my apartment was big enough for two people, but now that Chloe is here, I don't think it is. She's going to take over every single inch of the place, and I won't be able to think about anything but her while I'm at home.

Both a good and bad thing.

Ten minutes later, Chloe comes out wearing a pair of leggings that I can't decide if they are worse than the shorts or better.

I still haven't decided when there's a knock at the front door. I embrace the distraction and answer the door, going to let my teammates in.

But when I open the door, the only person there is Sophia, Blake's best friend, that apparently goes everywhere he goes.

She's a sweet girl and cool to hang out with. The girl is a talker and doesn't take any shit. I'm honestly surprised that Blake hasn't fallen head over heels for her. Or admitted to the fact that he already has.

"Hi," she says, giving me a nod, the blonde bun on top of her head bobs up and down. "You might want to go down and rescue your stupid friends. When you told them to get a tree, they both decided that bigger and fluffier was the way to go, and now they can't figure out how to get it up here."

"There's an elevator," I say to her, opening the door wider and letting her in.

"Yeah, that thing is not going to fit in the elevator. Not even if they stand it up," she says, walking in and taking off her jacket. Sophia wastes no time going over to Chloe. "Hi, I'm Sophia."

"Chloe. It's nice to meet you."

I leave the girls to get to know each other, and head downstairs. Sure enough, Sophia was right. My friends are stupid and probably got the biggest tree that the lot offered. If I were them, I would have chosen the same tree, so I can't fault them for that. It's a beautiful tree.

I don't even want to know how they got it here.

With more than a few head shakes, frustrated signs, and so many curse words getting thrown out, we eventually get the tree up to my apartment. How?

Stairs. So many fucking stairs up to the twentieth floor.

By the time we reach my place, I'm sure the three of us want to watch the tree burn, but the second that I see Chloe's face, that feeling goes away.

She is happy, and that is all that matters.

We spend the evening decorating the massive tree and the apartment. I honestly didn't think I would enjoy myself doing all this Christmas shit, but I did.

Christian, Blake, and Sophia all welcomed Chloe and treated her as if she has been a friend of theirs for as long as I have.

She and Sophia shared their love of some designer that apparently makes amazing dresses. She and Blake talked about different Mexican foods that he was introduced to by with his sister-in-law, Selena.

And Christian, Sophia and she bonded over their shared experiences of growing up in a Latino household. It was in that conversation that I learned Chloe comes from a mixed family.

I learned so much about her in such a short time that I didn't know if I should be pissed or glad that she was sharing all this information with my friends and not with me.

I'm going with glad.

No matter what, I'm still learning about this woman, and it shouldn't matter how I am doing it.

Somewhere around to nine at night, my teammates and Sophia head home, and it's just me and Chloe left sitting on the couch, eating a pizza we had ordered.

I'm about to grab another slice, my cheat meal of the week, when Chloe leans over and presses a kiss against my cheek.

For a solid second, I sit there frozen trying to comprehend what just happened.

I eventually unfreeze and turn to the woman next to me.

"What was that for?" I ask, a smile playing on my lips.

"A thank you," she answers shyly. I raise an eyebrow at her in question. "For today. You didn't have to pull out all the stops, but I appreciate it. It's like a little piece of home."

She looks around the room in awe, like she has a love for Christmas, and I knocked it out of the park.

"You're welcome," I say, reaching over and giving her knee a squeeze.

If she likes what we did today, she will love my mom's house.

Which gives me an idea.

"You don't have to say yes to this, but do you want to go with me to my parents' for Christmas?"

She looks at me a little shocked. "Would that be a good idea? Do they know?" Her hand falling to her stomach.

I don't think I have seen her do that before.

"They know, and I know they would love to meet you, no matter what our situation. So, if you would like to, we can go down for a few days and celebrate Christmas with them."

I'm not the one who came up with the idea. My mom called and asked me to bring Chloe for the holiday when I talked to her earlier in the week.

Honestly, I was going to turn her suggestion down, not wanting to throw Chloe into something unknown. Now that I think of it, though, it might be a good idea.

"You wouldn't mind? I don't want to intrude on your family time. Besides, I was going to ask Betty if I could cele-brate with her family."

A part of my heart breaks at knowing that I wasn't going to be her number one option.

I give her a nod. "No, I wouldn't mind at all. I want you to come."

I should let her go with Betty. I should let her stay here and celebrate with her friend, but a selfish part of me wants her near me and within arm's reach.

Chloe thinks about it for a moment, and I'm almost positive she is about to say no, when she gives me a smile.

"I would love to go with you. But you can't be overbearing when I do things." She throws an accusatory finger at me.

"When have I been overbearing?" I haven't been too bad, have I?

"Every time I cook, clean, or even try to do my own laundry. The doctor told me to rest. He didn't put me on bedrest."

Okay, maybe I have been a little overbearing. But only because I want her to be healthy.

"Fine, I won't be overbearing. At least not while we're with my parents. Inside these four walls it is fair game."

She narrows her eyes at me, but eventually she lets out a sigh.

"Fine, but at least take it down a notch."

"No promise."

She lets out a sweet chuckle, and instead of heading to our respective rooms, we stay on the couch, put on a Christmas movie, and finish our pizza.

We might have just moved in together, and for only a short period of time, but I think we will get the hang of it.

Especially if every night ends with Chloe falling asleep

and me being able to carry her to her bed and place a small kiss against her forehead.

If every night is like tonight, I'll take it.

CHAPTER NINETEEN

CHLOE

LIAM IS a whole different person when he's around his parents.

From the second we walked into his childhood home, he seemed a bit more relaxed and a lot more open.

Not that he isn't that way back in Chicago, but back home, it's as if he has to be the big shot hockey player all the time who has his face plastered all over the city. The few times we've gone out in public, whether to the grocery store or to pick up food, it's as if he puts on this persona that some-times stays on within the four walls of his home.

With his parents, though, it's as if he's still the kid who grew up in Missouri and doesn't have anything to worry about but making his parents happy.

I was a little worried about making the trip down to St. Louis, but from the second that I stepped through the door, I was happy with my decision to come here.

Not only am I getting to see a side of Liam I have never

seen before, but his parents are so warm and welcoming that I feel like I'm a part of their family.

His mom, Lynnette, is one of the sweetest women that I have ever met, and Liam's dad, Lawrence, is just an older version of his son.

Also, the fact that they all have L names is the most adorable thing ever.

Both Liam's parents have welcomed me with open arms and haven't judged me one bit about being pregnant with their son's child with us not being together.

And Lynnette's food is so delicious. I'm tempted to pack up some of it to freeze and keep at home.

I've only been here not even a full day, and I'm already planning on coming back.

It's currently a little bit after midnight, and three out of the four people in the house are off to sleep. The fourth person, me, is lying wide awake suddenly craving some of Lynnette's boysenberry pie.

I've been staring at the ceiling of Liam's childhood bedroom debating, if I should get up, but my craving is becoming too much for me to avoid.

"One slice would not hurt," I tell myself as I throw the covers off my body.

Quietly, I open the bedroom door and start to tiptoe out to the kitchen, making sure that I don't wake Liam who is sleeping in the living room.

When I reach the kitchen, though, I see that my efforts aren't necessary. The man who is supposed to be sleeping is sitting at the table eating a piece of pie.

"Is that the last piece?" I ask a little too loudly, making him jump in his chair. "Sorry," I say through a laugh.

He shakes his head at me, but there's a smile forming on his face. "I thought you were sleeping," he says, taking another bite of his pie, not answering my question.

"I got a strong craving for some pie, so I thought that I would come get a slice before it was gone."

"Have you gotten a lot of those?" he asks, not looking up at me. The man is deflecting.

"Not yet. I think this is one of the first ones. Now answer my question," I say, narrowing my eyes at the man.

If I ever wanted to have daggers shoot out my eyes, this would be the moment.

"What question?" Another deflection.

"Is that the last piece of pie?" I ask, saying all the words as slowly as possible.

Eventually he lets out a sigh and gives me a nervous smile.

I have my answer.

"I hate you."

"How was I supposed to know that you wanted a piece?" he says, defensively, that smile of his growing.

He does have a point, but still.

"You could have come to your room and asked," I point out.

"I thought you were asleep," he argues and the bastard has the audacity to take another bite.

"You can at least let me have the last few bites." I walk

over to the table and take a seat across from him, reaching for his plate.

"And why would I do that?" He raises a perfect eyebrow and pulls the plate back away from me.

"Because if you don't, then I'm going to tell your mom that you took the last piece of pie from her grandchild. See whose side she takes."

Now it's Liam who is narrowing his eyes at me. "You play dirty, Vega. You really do, but I like it, and that's the only reason I'm going to give in."

The boysenberry goodness slides in front of me, and I don't even have to take a bite of the berry-filled crust for my mouth to water.

A moan escapes my mouth the second that the piece of deliciousness meets my tongue.

"Oh my god, this is so good," I say, my eyes literally closing with how good this is.

"Is the baby now satisfied with their mom stealing their daddy's pie?" Liam asks, the grin on his face causing butter-flies to flutter in me.

Like when we first met.

"Very satisfied. If the baby was here and was able to talk, they would thank you," I say right before taking another bite.

I wonder how Liam would feel if his mom would come live with us just so that I could have this pie whenever I want.

"What are you doing up?" I ask, scraping up the delicious goo off the plate.

"I couldn't get comfortable," he says, giving me a shrug.

"Is the couch hard?" I ask.

He shakes his head. "Nah, it's fine. It's just that the couch isn't made for someone over six feet tall to sleep on."

Instantly, I feel bad.

If I wasn't here, he would be sleeping in his own bed and not suffering on the couch. No doubt he needs a good night's sleep since he had a game the night before where he was slammed against the boards more than once. I didn't go to the game, but I did watch it on TV. Those hits were not pretty, even if the Knights won in the end.

"Why don't you sleep in your bed? I can take the couch. You don't have to be uncomfortable."

I don't even finish what I'm saying before Liam is already shaking his head.

"It's fine. It's only for two nights. I can manage."

"You have a game in three days. You won't be able to play if you have a kink in your neck. I'm smaller, so I'll take the couch," I say to him, finishing up the last of the pie.

"It's fine, Chlo. I don't mind sleeping on the couch. You need a bed way more than I do."

That's the second time he has called me Chlo. Not that I'm counting or anything, but I'm so used to him calling me by my full name. Hearing him call me Chlo is odd and in a good way.

I like it way more than I should.

"If you say so, but if you want the bed. Just tell me. I'm happy to take the couch."

"I will keep that in mind," he says, throwing another smile in my direction. This time a lazy one.

Damn.

Why are his smiles affecting me so much tonight? I don't know, but whatever it is, I have to squash it. I can't be falling for my baby daddy right now.

It has to be all the new hormones.

I shift the subject.

"Your parents are amazing," I tell him, giving him my own smile.

"They are," he agrees, picking up the empty plate and getting up to wash it.

"Were they supportive when you told him you were going to be a professional hockey player?" I ask.

There are a lot of pictures of Liam from when he was a kid all over the house, and his room is like a shrine to his high school and college career. I did notice that they don't have a whole lot of pictures of his professional career, and I can't help but wonder why.

"At first they weren't," he says, coming back to the table. "I think a part of them always thought that I would give up hockey after college. They thought that me going professional was a fever dream and that I was going to get my degree and after graduation, and go work with my dad."

"When did they realize that it wasn't a fever dream?"

"When I played in my first NHL game."

"They still had their doubts before that?" I ask. Both Lynette and Lawrence seem like the type of people who would support the child no matter what. I can't help but wonder why they would have had reservations about Liam going the professional route.

Liam gives me a nod. "About a week or two before I officially signed with the Knights, my mom asked me if I really wanted to continue to play. She told me that she was worried that I would get hurt, and everything I worked so hard for would be for nothing."

Wow. "What did you tell her?"

"That the Knights didn't draft me at nineteen because they wanted to pity me. They drafted me because they saw something in me. That would I make the team all that much better. I told her I didn't want to give it up. That I love the sport, but if she wanted me to quit then I would quit. I wasn't going to be happy about it, but I would do it for her."

I can picture Liam and Lynette sitting at this very table having that conversation. I can't imagine the type of man Liam would be if he had quit and hadn't become the star that he is today.

"I'm guessing that they eventually came around to the idea," I say, because no way did the woman I met earlier tell her son to quit the very sport that made him *him*.

"Eventually. There were times during my first year where I could see the battle in their eyes whenever they saw me playing. The fear of the possibility that I would get hurt was there all the time, but eventually they came around to the idea, and now they love it. They brag about me all the time."

"Because they are proud."

"Yeah," Liam says, shaking his head looking very much lost in thought.

"Well, I'm glad that you didn't quit," I say, reaching out and placing a hand over his.

"Yeah, I am too." Liam places a hand over mine and gives it a gentle squeeze, and for the next minute or so, that's how we stay.

Us sitting like this should feel way too intimate, but it doesn't. I could sit like this with him for a long time, and that right there should be why I need to pull my hand away, but I don't.

"What about you? Were your parents always supportive of you becoming a dancer?" Liam asks, breaking the silence between us and shifting the conversation to me.

But he never let's go of my hand.

"Definitely not at first. They wanted me to do something different with my life. But they continued to support me through every single audition. I think they had hoped I would find something that I loved just as much as dancing, but nothing ever came. I enjoyed my undergrad in visual and performing arts, and when I decided to pursue professional dancing, I think that's finally when it clicked for them that this was what I wanted to do and was serious about it."

I remember my mom calling me one day after I told her I was auditioning for my current dance company. She had asked me like five times if I was sure I wanted to do it. She told me that she didn't want it to be a small fish in a big pond type of situation.

When I called and told her that I got a spot, she cheered and cried with how happy she was.

Sometimes it's hard for parents to accept what their kids want to do with their lives, and when they see everything work out, that's when they finally accept it.

From the looks of things, both me and Liam went through the same thing.

"Does your family come and watch you perform?" he asks, his thumb sliding against the back of my arm. It feels too nice to pull away.

I give him a nod. "Usually during my winter performance."

It sucks that it's not happening this year.

Liam's face falls a little at my statement. "I'm sorry."

"It's not your fault," I say as I apply pressure to his hand. "They were going to come since I don't want to fly, but I just told them to save the money for when the baby comes since it's not that far away."

"Is that what you want?" Liam asks.

I shrug. "I don't know if they can afford both trips. They should be here for what's most important. The holidays can wait."

I would love to have my family come to visit me for a few days, but travel, even travel within the United States, is getting more expensive with every passing day. I can't with good conscience let them spend a whole bunch of money to come to Chicago two times in one year.

"I can take care of it," Liam tells me giving me a small smile.

"As much as I appreciate you offering, it's really okay. I'll just see them this summer."

He gives me a look that tells me that he knows I'm full of shit, but he doesn't say anything else.

"If you change your mind, let me know. They could come

for New Year's and stay at the apartment. It's not like we don't have the room. I can even get you tickets for the game on New Year's Eve and make a day out of it."

It's so damn tempting to take him up on his offer, but I can't. My pride is too strong to let him take care of something like that.

"You've already done so much for me, I can't let you do this," I say, patting his hand and finally pulling away from him. The second that I'm no longer touching him, I miss it. "It's okay. Really."

Again, he gives a look that tells me that tells me he knows I'm full of shit, but he drops it. "Okay, but if you change your mind, tell me, and I will make things happen."

I get up from my seat and walk over to his chair and wrap my arms around his shoulders before placing a kiss on his cheek.

"Thank you, Liam."

"Anything for you," he says, leaning into my touch.

I have to get it through my head that he is only saying that because I'm the mother of his child, and I'm currently an incubator.

I untangle myself from him and start heading back to his bedroom.

"Good night, Liam."

"Good night, Chlo."

A part of me wants to ask him to come to bed with me, to forget about the couch and come sleep in the bed with me.

The question is on the tip of my tongue, but I'm too much of a chicken to ask it.

So, I just give him a closed-lip smile and head down the hall.

The whole night, instead of sleeping soundly, I dream about Liam sleeping right next to me and what it would be like if I caved into my feelings.

It would be good, but I can't seem to do it in real life.

CHAPTER TWENTY

LIAM

"I LIKE HER," my father states as he helps me pack up my truck, the one I only use in the winter and should probably trade in for a family car, to head home.

I don't have to look up to know that he is talking about Chloe.

My mom told me the same thing this morning after breakfast.

"Yeah, she's something special," I say, sliding the last bag into the covered bed.

"You sure you two aren't together?" my old man asks, shutting the tailgate.

I go through the last two days in my head and try to remember if Chloe and I had acted like anything other than just friends who are about to have a baby.

Nothing comes to mind.

Sure, I placed my hand on the small of her back a time or two, and she gave me a kiss on the cheek when I gave her her

Christmas present, a necklace with a pointe shoe charm, but nothing comes to mind that would have my dad asking that.

It's not like I snuck into her room late at night and got caught.

"Yup, I'm sure," I say, giving him a nod. "Why?"

"No reason. I just thought you two look cute together is all."

"Look cute together?" I repeat. I have never heard my dad say the word cute. Ever.

"Yeah, cute," he says again, and it feels weird as hell.

"This is Mom's doing, isn't it?" I ask, nodding over to the woman that is currently showing Chloe all the poinsettias that fill the front porch.

My dad lets out a sigh, like he couldn't keep it a secret much longer. "She was talking about it last night. Told me to talk to you about making an honest woman out of Chloe, you know, before the baby comes."

Honest woman?

Who the hell even says that anymore?

I resist the urge to roll my eyes. I guess even though I had told her a number of times, my mom hasn't dropped the whole getting married thing.

"Chloe and I have talked about this, and we both think it's not a good idea to jump into anything. We are concentrating on the baby. That's it."

I don't know how much clearer I can get.

"Have you told your mom that?" he asks, but he already knows the answer.

"A handful of times," I say with a nod.

"Then all I can say is that I talked to you and that I tried."

"Thanks, Dad. I really appreciate this talk," I say with a little too much sarcasm.

"Of course, son. Anything for your mother." He claps me on the shoulder and walks over to where Mom and Chloe are.

When Chloe notices that I'm not with my dad, she turns until she meets my gaze and gives me a sweet smile that I want to spend the rest of the day looking at.

If I wasn't the man that I am, I would go against what Chloe and I agreed on and make her mine in every single way that I could.

She would be living with me permanently and not thinking about moving out when the baby comes.

I want her with me at all times until she grows tired of me.

But we did agree and I'm an idiot who can't get his emotions for a woman in check.

And it's not like she feels the same way.

Ever since she's moved in, things have become increasingly platonic. She is even calling me one of her best friends a lot more often.

I just don't know if the increase of the word friend in her vocabulary is for my sake or hers.

Given the circumstances, I'm fairly sure it's for mine and so that I don't forget where we stand.

I was friend-zoned and hard.

But I can live with it, for now at least.

After another minute of listening to my mother talk about her plants, Chloe finally makes her way over to me.

"Ready to go?" she asks me, her pregnancy glow all that more vibrant.

"Ready if you are," I say to her. Very much wanting to pull her in so that I can kiss her.

If I didn't have ice time later today in preparation for our game tomorrow, we would be staying another night, but unfortunately work duties call.

Chloe gives me a nod before walking back to my parents and giving them both a hug goodbye.

"Did your dad talk to you?" my mom whispers in my ear when it's my turn to say goodbye.

God, this woman will never let it go.

"He did," I say, pulling away from her.

"And?" she asks, the excitement in her eyes dancing.

I hate to disappoint my mom, I really do, but what she wants is not something I can give her. Not right now.

"And nothing has changed, Ma. Chloe and I are still just friends. The baby is our number one priority right now," I say to her, glad that Chloe isn't within hearing distance.

"Such a bummer. She would make an honest man out of you," she says, shaking her head at me.

Again, with the honest crap.

"Dad told me that I should make an honest woman out of her."

My mom lets out a snort and continues to shake her head. "Honey, Chloe does not need you to make her into anything. She's a strong, independent woman, she doesn't need a man.

On the other hand, you need a woman to show you how to live life and realize that you can't survive with just hockey. Chloe is that woman."

I don't know if I should be offended that my mom thinks I need a woman in my life or not. It's not like I only live and breathe hockey.

Maybe during the season but not all year long.

Take this season for example. Sure, I'm concentrating on getting the team to the playoffs and winning the Cup, but I'm also thinking about Chloe and the baby.

My life isn't *just* hockey. I don't *need* it to survive.

But apparently Mom doesn't see it that way.

"I'm fine, Ma."

"Whatever you say." She pats my cheek a little too hard. "Now, go take care of the mother of my grandchild and make sure they both get home safely."

"Yes, ma'am." I give my mom one last kiss on the cheek and make my way over to Chloe to help her into the truck.

As I pull out of the driveway, Chloe waves excitedly at my parents.

Seeing her this excited makes me happy that I invited her in the first place. Even though she couldn't spend it with her parents, it was still a good Christmas, and I am glad I was able to give that to her.

"You had a good time," I state rather than question, as I pull onto the main road of town.

"I did." I don't have to look at her to know that she is smiling. "Thank you so much for inviting me. It was awesome getting to know you a lot better and meeting your parents. They're both so excited about the baby."

"They are," I say, turning onto the expressway. "Did my mom show you that blanket she's working on?"

I was told a while ago that she was working on it, but I didn't see it while I was home. I'm hoping Chloe did too and I didn't ruin the surprise or something.

"Oh my god, yes! She showed it to me yesterday after breakfast. It's so pretty already. I told her that as soon as we find out what we're having, I will let her know so that she can add color if she wants."

I never thought that someone could be so excited about a blanket.

"Are we finding out?" I ask.

I've gone to her last three appointments with her. I've gotten to see the little gummy bear on screen and hear its heartbeat. But during those visits it never came up if we were finding out the sex. I honestly didn't think about it until now.

"I would like to. Would you?" she asks, and when I quickly turn to look at her, she is looking at me with excitement in her eyes.

"Yeah, I would like to know. Mentally prepare myself," I say to her, throwing a smile her way.

She lets out a snort. "Are you afraid of having a girl?"

"Nah, I can handle raising a girl. It's the boys that I'm worried about. Spending time with my teammates has made me realize just how much a pain in the ass boys can be."

Chloe lets out a sweet laugh. "And here I thought it was the other way around."

"Spend a whole day with Christian and Blake, and you will be thinking the same thing as me." There have been three more races since the last one.

"Maybe it's time I go to another one of your games and see for myself."

"Whenever you want. There will always be tickets at the box office for you." And there are. Every game I leave at least one ticket available for Chloe just in case she wants to attend. She hasn't since the first game she went to, but that doesn't stop me from leaving them nonetheless.

"Really?" she asks, sounding surprised.

I nod, keeping my eyes on the road. "Really. You don't even have to ask. There will always be a ticket for you."

"And you wouldn't mind if people see me there?" she asks, and I quickly turn to look at her and see that she is chewing on her bottom lip.

"Why would I mind?"

Does she think I'm embarrassed by her?

"Because people might start to question why you have a pregnant woman attending your games."

"They can ask all the questions that they want. It doesn't mean we're going to answer them," I tell her, but then something clicks in my head. "Is that why you haven't gone to any other game this season?"

"Well, yeah," she answers. "I don't know what you're telling people. For all I know, you're telling them that I'm your girlfriend and that we are expecting a baby. I didn't want to go to one of your games and lie to their faces."

And here I thought that she didn't want to go to any

games because she really didn't want to do anything with me.

I let out a sigh. "The only people who know about the pregnancy are Blake, Christian, Logan, my coach and the team doctor, and they all know our situation. That's it. The only WAG who knows is Sophia and she's not even a WAG."

Chloe shifts in her seat and I turn to see that she has turned her whole body to me. "You mean you haven't told anyone that I'm your girlfriend?"

"No." Why would I? Sure, it would look better in the public eye, but I don't honestly see the point in lying.

"Huh," she says, slumping in her seat.

"Now will you come to another game?" I ask just as we are getting on I-57 toward Chicago, completely ignoring her 'huh'.

She's silent for a few seconds, probably thinking about if it's a good idea or not to attend a game.

"I would love to, if that's okay?" she asks like I haven't been hoping for this moment since October.

"More than okay."

"And you won't get sick of me if I attend all the home games for the rest of the season? I didn't really enjoy the first one much because, you know, things."

I don't know how that game went for her, but I do know how it went for me, and it wasn't good.

"We live together, of course I won't get sick of you." And it's the truth. If I could have her in my space forever, I would be a happy man.

I honestly need to get my feelings for this woman under control. I can't keep thinking like that.

Maybe I should go on a date or something.

"You say that now," Chloe says, bringing me back to the present. "But we've only lived together for two weeks. Things can change."

I take a quick second to give her a look that says give me a break.

"I won't get sick of you after living with you for six months, and I won't get sick of you if you want to attend every one of my games."

"If you say so," she chimes, a giggle following quickly after.

"I do."

"Then get me tickets for tomorrow night. I'm going to cheer on my baby daddy."

I like her calling me her baby daddy a little bit too much.

CHAPTER TWENTY-ONE

CHLOE

MID-JANUARY

FOR THE FIRST time since I told him that I was pregnant, Liam is missing one of my appointments.

He gave me the team's practice and game schedule a while ago. That way I can schedule my appointments around the times that he was available or in town.

It's worked out so far.

Today, though, is the exception. The Knights are at a rescheduled away game and won't be back in Chicago until later tonight, so today is the first appointment I will be going to alone.

Today is also the appointment where we find out the sex of the baby, so him not being here sucks even more.

I can't even FaceTime him during the appointment because he has practice.

But I will make do, and I will find out the sex of the baby, and then when he gets home tonight, I will surprise him.

I'm a bit nervous about the appointment as I get off the train and walk the remaining distance to the doctor's office.

I don't know why, but the appointments always freak me out. I always feel like the doctor is going to tell me that something is wrong, so I keep my fingers crossed until I hear the heartbeat and Dr. Long tells me that everything seems to be going just how it's supposed to be going.

Liam usually helps calm my nerves a bit, but today I have to put my big girl pants on and do it myself.

"Hi Miss Chloe, how are you feeling today?" the receptionist asks me as soon as I walk into the doctor's office, a bright smile on her face.

I gave her a smile back. "Hello, I'm good. I think my bump has finally started to pop out a bit," I say proudly.

"Oh, you will pop out even more in no time," she tells me. "Let's get you checked in and see how our baby is doing."

"Thank you."

Shawna, the receptionist, checks me in, and within five minutes she is bringing me to the back. She gets my weight, takes my blood pressure and has me peeing into a cup to test that everything is normal before taking me into the room to wait for the doctor.

After about twenty minutes of waiting, Dr. Long finally comes into the room with another nurse at her side.

"Hi Chloe, how are you feeling today?" Dr. Long asks with a smile on her face.

"I'm feeling good. The morning sickness has finally

stopped, so I see that as a good sign," I say, never wanting to experience morning sickness ever again.

"A very good sign. Daddy couldn't make it today?" She asks as she goes over to the sink to wash your hands.

I shake my head. "No, he's traveling today."

"Okay, and since he's not here, do you want to wait on getting the gender of the baby?"

I shake my head again. "No, we agreed that I will get it today and that I will let him know when he gets home."

"Okay, great. Then let's get started. This is our ultrasound technician. She will be taking care of you today, but let me check you out first. Make sure everything is good, and then we can see if you are having a boy or a girl."

"Let's do it," I say, all the nerves starting to disappear.

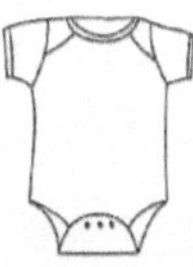

With the ultrasound in hand, I make my way over to the Dark Knight arena.

The team has a fan store outside that I know is open today, and without a doubt, that's the only place I will be able to find exactly what I'm looking for.

It helps that I made numerous trips to the store during the last few games I attended, to make sure.

Hopping off the brown line and taking the bus to the United Center has become a routine since we came back to Chicago after Christmas.

Liam has offered to get me a car for the handful of games I've been to these last few weeks, but I always decline. At least with getting there.

I like moving through the city. It's not something I get to do very often, so now that I have time, I want to take advantage of it. Also, it helps my pregnant self move with all the walking.

He doesn't like it but still lets me do it. It's times like these that I don't know if he is worried about me and the baby or just the baby.

My heart wants to believe it's both, but my head tells me that it's only the baby he cares about. Even if he has told me otherwise.

I shouldn't care, and a lot of the time, I try not to, but it's hard. No matter how hard I try to push down my attraction to him, it keeps coming back up. And worse yet, as the days continue, and I get to know him better outside of our initial time together, that attraction has transformed to be full-on feelings.

I have feelings for my baby's father, and there is nothing platonic about them.

Liam is charming but also so damn caring and loving that I'm not shocked at all that it only took a short time for my attraction to him to evolve into more.

But I have to keep pushing my feelings down. I have to continue to stand my ground and not fall any deeper. I have to concentrate on the baby. We both do.

Setting my feelings for my baby's father aside, I walk into

the Dark Knights fan shop and head straight to the baby section that they have.

It's small, but it has exactly what I'm looking for.

I grab a onesie with Liam's number and name on the back and head to the cash register.

A smile, one that makes me look like an absolute lunatic, stays plastered on my face the whole way back to Liam's place.

I have been planning for this surprise for about a week now, even getting two different colors of wrapping paper. So, the second I get back to the apartment, I head straight to my room and start getting everything ready.

Telling someone the gender of their baby is a special occasion.

So special that I even decided to make dinner to go with the news.

All the stops are being pulled out tonight. Nothing is getting held back.

Sometime around ten, I take out the enchiladas that I made, out of the oven and head to my room to change.

Like I said, I've been planning this all week, so I had time to order a dress in advance that makes my little bump a lot more noticeable.

Once I'm all set, I grab my gift and head back to the kitchen to set the table.

Maybe I'm doing a little too much, but I'm excited. I have to do something that will keep my hands busy.

Right at eleven ten, the door of the apartment opens, signaling that Liam is home.

I'm like a ball of excitement ready to burst out with the news, but I take a few deep breaths to keep myself calm.

I might be failing at the staying calm part because when Liam turns the corner, he stops dead in his tracks the second that he sees me, and his face goes from relaxed to confused.

"Hi," he says, putting down the duffel bag that he uses for short trips and doesn't move from his spot.

He's still wearing his suit, and I have to keep myself from drooling. Seeing him in a suit always takes me back to the night that we met.

God, how I wish we could get a repeat of that night.

Stop it.

"Hi," I say to him, giving him a big smile.

"Everything okay?" he asks suspiciously.

I nod. "Of course, it is. Why wouldn't it be?" I'm pretty sure I'm bouncing up and down, but I don't know if it's just in my head or if I'm actually doing it.

"Because I texted you earlier about your appointment, and you didn't respond," he says, crossing his arms.

I saw his text, and it took everything in me not to respond. If I did, I was for sure going to tell him what we were having. I wanted to wait.

"My phone died, and I forgot to charge it when I got home. I was a little busy," I say, my smile growing even more.

"Busy?" He asks, coming closer to me.

What's with all the small little questions? He should just get to asking the most important one.

"Yup, busy. I made dinner." I wave for him to follow me

into the dining room that he doesn't use, so he could take in all my hard work.

"You made dinner at ten o'clock at night?" he asks, following behind me.

I give a nod as I cross the threshold into the dining room.

The food I made is at the center of the table and the gift that I wrapped is sitting on top of his plate with a little note that says "open me" on top.

I was going to wait until we had eaten to give it to him, but I didn't know if I was going to even make it that far. So, I decided to do it at the beginning of dinner.

"You got me a gift?" he asks, walking over to the side of the table with the gift.

"I did," I tell him, all the while I nervously play with my fingers.

He looks up at me with so many questions in his eyes.

"Okay," he says slowly, picking up the box.

"Open it," I order a little too eagerly.

Liam let's out a chuckle but does as I say.

His mission must be to torture me because he opens the small box so damn slowly. Can he not see that I'm anxious over here?

After a million years, he finally finishes taking off the very light pink wrapping paper that I picked out and starts opening the white box with the onesie in it.

Did I go a little overboard with the tissue? Maybe, but I wanted him to dig for it.

He digs through the tissue for a solid second before taking out the onesie that I bought earlier today.

"That's why I didn't text you back. If I did, I would have let it slip and I wanted it to be a surprise. Surprise!"

Liam looks from me to the onesie, not saying a single word.

After a minute or two, I grow anxious and break into whatever he is thinking.

"Say something," I say, feeling like the night I told him I was pregnant.

Liam drops the box, but keeps the onesie in his hand, and comes over to me, closing the distance between us.

When he's about a foot or two away from me, I see a glint in his eyes that looks almost like tears.

I have no clue if they are happy tears or sad tears. Did everything just suddenly become so much more real to him?

After another long moment, Liam's hands land on my cheek, and he breaks the silence. "We're having a girl?"

His voice cracks a little bit at the end, and it takes everything in me not to break with him.

I give him a nod. "Yeah, we're having a girl."

Everything that happens next becomes a blur.

One minute I have Liam's hands on my cheek. The next I'm in his arms, being lifted up off the ground, and we're both giggling with happiness, and before I know it, I am back on my feet with Liam's hands back on my face, and his lips are pressed against mine.

He's kissing me. For the first time in almost six months, Liam Crawford is kissing me, and all I can do is kiss him back.

One of his hands slides into my loose curls, all the while both of mine go into his dark strands. We both pull at each other like we can't get close enough to the other person. Like we can't get enough, and we need more.

I feel his tongue sliding against my bottom lip asking for permission, and I don't hesitate to open for him and let my tongue dance along his.

I am vaguely aware of the fact that his other hand is sliding against my body in the most delicious way possible.

Feeling his lips against mine, and his hands on my body, has me singing in a way that I haven't sung in five long ass months. Liam certainly knows how to work my body, and I am already on the verge of explosion with just a kiss.

A hungry, aggressive kiss.

Somehow, we both realize what we are doing and pull apart, but just enough for Liam to press his forehead against mine and for our breaths to become one.

"I'm sorry. I shouldn't have—"

"No, it's fine. Please don't be sorry. We both got caught up in the moment," I interrupt him.

He shouldn't be sorry for what just happened. I'm not.

I feel his head nod against mine and watch as his eyes close. He takes a deep breath as if to calm himself down.

I can feel his body against mine, but I don't dare admit that I'm able to feel each hard and long part of him.

The kiss affected him just as much as it did me, but we can't do anything about it.

Still not pulling away, Liam opens his eyes. There is an intensity that wasn't there before, and the second I see it, I know what it is.

It's love.

It's his love for his baby and his next words confirm it.

"We're having a girl. Our baby is a girl."

I can't help but to smile at him with the same type of intensity that fills his eyes.

"We are having a baby girl."

And I hope that she feels all the love that her father will give her, because he will. Liam will love his little girl beyond belief, and I know that he will do anything for her.

I just have to hope that I can at least witness it for a brief period before I move back to my own place.

Because this little bubble that Liam and I are in won't last forever.

No matter how much my heart wants it to.

Priorities. We have priorities.

CHAPTER TWENTY-TWO

LIAM

MARCH

A GIRL.

Chloe and I are having a girl.

Holy shit.

It's been close to a month since we found out, and I feel like I've been on a cloud ever since. And if she had told me that we were having a boy, I would be feeling the same way.

It's not only the high from the baby that has me flying. It's also from everything else happening in my life, more specifically from the Dark Knights being the number one team in our conference.

Yup, after so much hard work, the team is not only at the top of the division but of the whole damn conference. Everyone has been on fucking fire, playing as if every single game has depended on it. At the rate that we are going we'll have a spot in the playoffs and have a chance at the Cup.

This year feels different. This year feels like it is ours for the taking, and we are not going to hold anything back.

And I'm not the only one feeling it. Everyone in the locker room feels it, too.

Take tonight for example.

We're about ten minutes away from the puck drop, and the whole damn room is electric.

It's as if we all took a hit of something during warm-ups, and all we want to do is hit the ice and show the other team what we are made of.

Music is blaring, people are getting in the zone. Tonight is one of those nights that feels like it's going to be talked about by sports fans for years to come.

But because superstitions are very much real, I'll keep that thought process to myself.

"You ready for tonight?" Christian comes over to me in full gear, ready to go. He looks like an absolute beast with his skates on.

"Yup. Are you?" I ask, throwing on my game jersey.

"Feel like slamming a body against the boards tonight," he says, letting out a grunt in the process.

Christian Rodriguez is a goon on the ice, right next to Logan and if anyone messes with our team, he's there to put them in their place.

If he's feeling like fighting already, I know it's going to be a good game.

"Just don't do anything dirty," I say, giving the bastard a shove.

"Do I ever?" he says, giving me a smirk.

I roll my eyes at him. He very much does, especially when he's had a bad day. I just have to hope that today is not one of those days.

After a talk from Coach Anderson and some motivational stuff from me, we make our way to the tunnel to get this game started.

Even before hitting the ice, we can feel the energy of the fans vibrate through the arena.

It's as if we are projecting our energy to the fans without even knowing it.

"Alright, boys, let's go kick some Shark ass and get one step closer to the end game," I yell out to the men behind me and pat our goalie, who's in front of me, on the back.

Grunts sound around me, and the louder they get, the more I feel like this game is going to be one for the books.

The doors open, and the team makes its entrance.

Music blares from the speakers. Fans are chanting out our names, and skating to center ice feels fucking amazing.

Before getting into position, I look over to the seats right next to our bench and spot a beauty with curls on the top of her head and my name on her back.

I would never admit this to her, but ever since she started coming to every one of my home games, I play ten times better. She's my good luck charm, and as long as she's in the stands cheering us on, this team will go places. I can feel it.

I throw a smile in her direction, and she gives me one back right before I get into position and wait for the puck to drop.

The second that the whistle sounds and the puck hits the

ice, I'm in the zone. And I stay in the zone until the Knights win the game, four to one. One game closer to getting a chance to play for the Cup.

Hopefully in a few months time, I will have two things to celebrate.

My daughter and the Knights winning the Stanley Cup.

The second that I get home, I drop my bag, and I start untying my tie. I should really start going without them, I hate the stupid things. But they are a part of the outfits I get every week from the Archwell stylist, so according to my contract, I have to wear them.

Dropping the offensive material on the table by the door, I walk deeper into the apartment, looking for Chloe.

She left the after-game celebration early. She said that she felt tired and wanted to put her feet up. I offered to come home with her, but she kept telling me to stay. After the tenth time, I finally listened to her and called her a car.

My eyes stayed glued to the app, watching her car move every block until she was back home. That was over an hour ago, so she might be sleeping already.

I'm about to go to bed myself when I hear a sniffling sound coming from Chloe's room.

Is she crying?

There is no hesitation in opening her bedroom door to check what is going on.

As soon as I step into the room, I find Chloe sitting on the middle of her bed with tears in her eyes and clothes surrounding her.

It looks like her closet exploded.

"Hey," I say, closing the door behind me and walking over to her bed, taking a seat next to her.

Chloe sniffles some more, wiping her nose on the back of her hand.

"Hi," she says, a tear rolling down her cheek.

"You want to tell me why you're crying?" I ask, reaching out and brushing away some hair strands and tucking them behind her ear.

She shakes her head. "No, because you're going to judge me."

"I won't judge you," I state.

Chloe gives me an eye roll, and I think she's about to tell me to go fuck myself when she gives in and tells me.

"None of my clothes fit," she says, this time wiping her nose with the sleeve of the jersey she still has on. "When I got out of the Uber tonight, my pants ripped. I thought they were just old, and I had been wearing them a lot. That they were about to rip anyway. So, what do I do? I come up here and decide to try on all the other pairs of pants that I have here, to find my next favorite and guess what? Not a single pair fit. The only things that fit are my leggings and even those feel tight."

Pants.

She's crying about pants.

I was prepared for a lot of things, but this wasn't one of them.

In a few hours, I went from being on the highest of highs to sitting with the woman who isn't my girlfriend while she cries about her pants not fitting her.

"We can go to the store and buy you new pants tomorrow," I suggest.

"I don't want to buy new ones. I want the ones that I already have."

Of course, she does.

"Sweetheart, your body is going to keep changing, so the ones you already have aren't going to fit for a while. We can save those for after the baby comes."

Daggers. All I get are daggers directed right at me and if they were real, I wouldn't have any eyes, maybe even lose my tongue.

"You know if it wasn't for your pretty smile, charming personality, and your magic dick, I wouldn't be here crying about pants," she spits out.

Damn, she's feisty when she wants to be and I'm not going to lie, I like it more than I should.

"Me and my magic dick apologize." I try to say it with a straight face, but I can't. A laugh that I try to hold in leaves my mouth and more daggers get thrown at me.

"Get out and let me wallow with my pants," she says, shoving me off the bed and out of the room.

The more I laugh, the more I get cursed out by hazel eyes.

Eventually there is a door between us, and even though I'm laughing at the whole situation, I can't help but feel bad.

"Chloe, I'm sorry," I say to the door and all I get is a grunt in return.

Great. Instead of consoling her, I pissed her off. Over pants.

I rake my hand through my hair, knowing that I messed up and start making my way over to my bedroom.

It's when I'm taking my second shower of the night, that I'm thinking of ways to apologize to Chloe when an idea hits me.

An idea that will have her feeling like a queen. Hopefully.

As soon as I'm out of the shower, I pull out my phone and scroll through my contacts until I find the one I need. I don't even bother looking at the time before pressing the call button and waiting as the phone starts to ring.

It takes a total of thirty seconds for someone to answer.

"Hey, I'm going to need a favor from you."

CHAPTER TWENTY-THREE

LIAM

I KNOCK on Chloe's door early the next morning, hoping that she is in a better mood than she was in last night.

And if she's not, I'm hoping that my surprise will get her there. And if that doesn't work, I'll make her pancakes. That usually seems to work.

"Chlo? Are you up?" I say against the wooden door, knocking again.

"Yeah." I hear her say from the other side.

She sounds calm.

Taking my chances, I open the door to her room and step inside.

In the time that she has lived here, she has really made this space her own and the second that I walk in, I'm surrounded by her scent. I keep my nose from taking a big whiff and do what I came here to do.

"You doing okay?" I ask the woman who has captivated my thoughts since I first laid eyes on her.

She gives me a nod and sits up. Her bump is a lot more prominent than it was a few weeks ago. But I guess that's what happens when you're close to being seven months pregnant.

"I'm fine," she says, leaning her head against the headboard. "Sorry, I freaked out on you over pants."

"It's okay. I'm sorry that I was such an asshole to you," I say to her, meaning every word. "You mind if I sit?"

She shakes her head, and I make my way over to her side of the bed, taking a seat on the edge.

I fight with myself to not lean over and brush away the few strands of hair that block her eyes, but I keep control. I don't need us crossing the line again and suffering from blue balls for another two months.

Instead, I place the gift bag that I walked in with on the bed in front of her.

"You got me a gift?" she asks, not taking her eyes off the pastel pink bag.

"I did. I thought it would be fun if we did something today."

"Something?" she asks, looking back at me. "Like the two of us?"

Why does that sound so shocking?

We do stuff together.

Right?

I try to think of something that we did together that doesn't involve food, going to her appointments or even attending one of my games, and I can't think of anything.

The only thing that comes to mind is the night we met

and how we went for pizza and then back to her place, but even then, that involved food.

So, I guess Chloe and I haven't done anything much together outside of this apartment.

Time to change that.

"Yes, do something. The two of us. If you're up for it." I give her my best charming smile, hoping that she falls for it.

"Don't you have practice today?" she asks, reaching for the bag.

I shake my head. "It's Sunday. Coach decided to be nice and give us the day off, but it just means doubles tomorrow."

"That doesn't mean you will come home smelling like sweat, does it?"

I don't shower one time, and I get reminded to always do so if I even want to step foot into my house.

But whatever keeps the mother of my child happy.

"I'll make sure to take an extra shower before coming home."

"Please do," she says, finally reaching inside the pink bag and pulling out the light pink coat that I put on top.

She looks up at me, shocked that I bought her clothes. Without a doubt, she's probably thinking I have a death wish, and maybe I do.

"Just go with it, okay? I promise by the end of the day, you won't be thinking about clothes whatsoever," I say to her, standing up from the bed and starting to making my way out of the room. "There's more in the bag. Wear everything. I have a car picking us up in an hour. So be ready."

I throw one more smile in her direction and leave the

room. Hoping that she does as I say, and my surprise goes as planned.

"What are we doing here?" Chloe asks in a curious tone, a little over an hour later as we sit on a park bench inside Lincoln Park.

We've been sitting here for about five minutes, watching people pass by and enjoying the sun that decided to bless Chicago on this Sunday in March.

I give the woman sitting next to me a smile. "Don't worry, you'll find out soon enough."

She looks at me like she doesn't believe me but after a second, she gives me a nod and goes back to people watching.

As she watches people enjoy the park, I watch her.

She looks absolutely beautiful, and it has nothing to do with the fact that she is wearing the clothes that I bought her. The beauty is all her, and if I could sit here all day and watch her, I would. Just like I would spend hours with no end watching her dance.

"That dress looks really good on you," I say, proud of myself and my early morning shopping spree.

Chloe looks down at the dress in question, running a hand along the fabric that stretches over her stomach and gives me a smile.

"Thank you. And thank you for the dress. It's beautiful," she says, her cheeks turning a shade of pink. "You didn't need to buy me anything, let alone a whole outfit."

"I wanted to, besides, I wanted today to be special, and that dress fit the bill," I say, reaching over slightly and sliding my thumb against the back of her hand.

"And why is that? What's so special about today?" she asks.

Before answering her question, I look around the park, hoping I'm able to spot my surprise and sure enough, she is walking toward us.

She's late but at least she's here.

"Because, my sweet Chloe, today, we are having a photo-shoot," I say nodding toward the woman who is approaching us with a camera wrapped around her neck.

Chloe follows my line of sight and I see her mouth pop open a bit when she sees our photographer for the day.

"Photoshoot?" she asks, turning to look back at me with a confused look.

"Yeah, I thought that it would be nice if you got some maternity pictures done. You know, to look back on and maybe show our daughter just how beautiful her mom looked while she was pregnant with her."

After what happened last night, I wanted to give Chloe a confidence boost and to show her just how beautiful she looks while pregnant. I wanted to show her that even though her body was changing, it was changing for a good reason.

So, I called Eliana, an old friend who happens to not only be a photographer but owes me a favor or two.

"I can't believe that you would do that for me," Chloe says, giving me a look of disbelief.

"I'd give you the world if you'd let me." I tell her with every ounce of honesty in me.

Chloe doesn't get a chance to respond because soon we are being joined by Eliana.

"Sorry, I'm late. I had to go pick up one of my cameras across town," our photographer tells us, not even aware that she interrupted a moment between me and Chloe.

I break my gaze from Chloe and stand up from the bench and introduce the two women.

"Chloe, this is Eliana, our photographer, who apparently doesn't know how to use her phone to send a quick text message," I say, narrowing my eyes at the woman with the camera. "And Eliana, this is Chloe."

"It's nice to meet you, Chloe," Eliana says, holding out a hand for Chloe to shake. "I apologize in advance if I try to strangle your baby daddy once or twice during our session today."

Chloe lets out a laugh at our photographer possibly torturing me. "It's nice to meet you, too. How do you two know each other?" she asks, looking between the two of us.

"We met a few years ago at a team function," I say, giving her the simplest answer.

Chloe nods, and soon Eliana is talking to her about what she wants from the shoot.

The smile that takes over Chloe's face at hearing every single detail is one that I want Eliana to capture just so that I can have it framed.

It doesn't take long for the shoot itself to start. The two women are laughing, and Chloe is having the time of her life.

All the tears from last night about her clothes not fitting have been forgotten.

Somewhere around the halfway point of the shoot, Chloe goes to the bathroom, and I'm left with Eliana, who is looking at me like a kid at a museum wanting to ask too many questions.

"What?" I ask, tired of getting stared at.

"How did you two meet?" She finally asks the question that I'm sure she wanted to ask from the beginning.

"At the ballet that you decided to skip," I say, giving her a pointed look.

Eliana was supposed to be my date for the ballet all those months ago. In the last few years, we have gotten close and have almost a brother and sister relationship. So, when I heard that she was going to be in town that night, I asked to come with me.

Thinking about it now, I can't help thinking about how different my life would be if she hadn't canceled on me.

I would have probably spent the majority of the time talking to Eliana and not been enthralled with Chloe as much as I had been or even at all.

I probably would have never met her, and there for sure wouldn't be any baby two months away from arriving.

It's a mind to think that so much would have not happened had I had a date that night.

"Damn. I shouldn't have canceled. I could have been the one pregnant with your kid," she says sarcastically.

Sarcastically or not, that would have never happened.

"Why did you cancel that night, anyway?" I ask.

Eliana is a flake, has been for as long as I have known her, so her canceling on me isn't surprising. I had gotten my hopes up that that night would have been different, but it wasn't surprising.

I thought that she was going to cancel today, but here she is.

"My dad found out that I was in town and forced me to go to dinner with him," she says with a tinge of anger in her voice.

Eliana and her dad have an interesting relationship, one that I've been privy to since her dad is Coach Anderson. I've only gotten bits and pieces of both sides of the story, and the only thing that I can say is that they are both so damn stubborn, it's no wonder that they bump heads.

Not only does Anderson have to get his personal shit together, so does his daughter.

"Does he know that you're in town this time?" I ask curiously. Coach didn't say anything.

Coach's daughter shakes her head. "Nope, but he will tomorrow. I have a meeting with the Knight's marketing team. You're looking at the team's new head photographer. Possibly."

Great.

Coach is going to be pissed all the time if his daughter is around day in and day out. I can feel it already. And there is no 'possibly' about it. Eliana is a good photographer and will for sure get the job.

And that little statement is on the tip of my tongue, but thankfully Chloe comes back and puts the focus back on her photoshoot.

"Chloe, would it be okay if Liam stood in on some of the pictures with you? I would love to get a few of the two of you together," Eliana suggests, as Chloe comes closer to where we are standing.

I made a really good choice with the dress that I picked out. Just looking at her makes me forget how to breathe. The pink and soft tones of it make her glow all that more prominent.

"No, I don't mind. I was going to ask if you could include him," Chloe says, giving her a smile.

I'm about to interject and say that this day is about Chloe and Chloe only, but before I can say anything, Eliana is pushing me over to where Chloe's standing.

The woman gives me a bright smile, and I give her one right back as I go stand next to her.

I turn to face the camera, only to find our lovely photographer shaking her head at us.

"What?" I ask.

"Do something," she says, bringing the camera up and waving her hand.

"What exactly do you want me to do?"

"Oh, I don't know, get close to her, or maybe even touch her. I can't take pictures of you looking all awkward."

The last time I was called awkward, I was a thirteen-year-old boy trying to find a pair of jeans that would fit the length of my legs.

I stand closer to Chloe but apparently that's not good enough because Eliana stalks over and starts positioning me.

"You would think that as a professional athlete, you would know how to pose," she says as she yanks my body in different directions.

"You would think that as a photographer, you would be nicer to your subjects," I throw back.

She legit scoffs at my comment. "Chloe, I have no idea how you could reproduce with this guy."

"I'm a peach, and she knows it," I say to Eliana, narrowing my eyes at her.

Chloe just laughs. "He's sweet and caring when he wants to be."

Eliana just shakes her head and continues moving my body in different directions until she is happy with something.

In the end, Chloe and I end up standing right next to each other, no space in between us with both of our hands on her stomach.

"Great. Now stand there, look at each other, and act like you are, oh I don't know, about to have a baby."

Eliana goes back to her spot, and I let out a small growl.

"If she wasn't a friend, I would fire her," I say, which causes Chloe to let out a laugh.

"Be nice. She said that she was doing this as a favor to you."

"Want to know why she owes me that said favor?" I ask her, trying my hardest not to get lost in her eyes.

Or worse yet, lean down and repeat my slip-up from a few weeks ago and kiss her.

Fuck, that kiss was good. So damn good, that I jerked off in the shower afterward.

A sweet giggle sings into my ear. "Sure."

"The night of the ballet, Ms. Sour over there was supposed to be my date. She bailed on me right before I left the apartment. Looking at it now, I'm glad that she did, because otherwise I wouldn't have met you, and we wouldn't be having a baby soon. But I didn't know that then, so I asked her for a future favor in return of not disowning her as a friend for ditching me."

The look on Chloe's face is priceless. "Seriously?"

I nod. "I'm perfectly fine with blaming her for that night if you are."

When she laughs at my suggestion, I can't help but smile at her.

For the next few minutes, I stand next to Chloe, not saying a word and getting mesmerized by her hazel eyes, just like I've done more than a handful of times in the seven months we have known each other.

Never will I tire of getting lost in them. No matter what our relationship status is.

"Thank you for doing this," Chloe tells me as we hear the shutter of the camera go off.

"You don't have to thank me for anything."

"But I do. I don't know why, but yesterday I was feeling so self-conscious about the changes happening to my body that it hit me hard. Who would have thought that I could cry over a pair of pants? My body is changing, and I should have expected it. You went out of your way to make me feel beautiful today, and for that I can't thank you enough."

I slide a hand off her bump, up until I'm cupping her cheek.

"Don't just let yourself just feel it today. You not only look beautiful today, but you've also looked so damn beautiful every day since I've met you. So fucking beautiful that I want to take every single picture that Eliana takes today and have them all framed so I can look at them whenever I want."

A blush creeps up her cheeks at my words, but they are the truth.

"You know, you have to stop saying things like that," she says, even though she leans into my touch.

"And why would I do that?"

"Because I'm going to start to think that maybe we made the wrong decision in not jumping into anything."

"No, we made the right decision," I say because we did.

We weren't in a place to jump into anything serious when she found that she was pregnant. We had a lot of things going on. Dance, hockey, the baby, finding common ground.

But I feel like things between us have changed since then. We've gotten to know each other, spent time together without the pressure of being perfect. We know how to work together, something that we didn't know how to do seven months ago. If we were to revisit the subject now, I feel like we would be able to make it work.

"But I will say this," I continue. "Things change. We've

changed, and if that was something that you wanted to revisit, I'm game if you are."

The blush that coated her cheeks a bit ago, now deepens, and I can see it go down to her chest.

"You're just saying that because I'm having your baby," she says as if she is trying to convince herself of those words.

"I'm saying that because I'm attracted to the woman in front of me, and my feelings for her have grown in the last few months. Do I find it hot seeing your body change because of my baby inside of you? Of course, I do. But my attraction to you has been present since the night we met. The baby has nothing to do with it."

I'm laying everything out there. I don't care to hide anymore what I feel for this woman. And I feel a lot.

These last few months have taught me so damn much about Chloe. So many things outside of what I was initially attracted to.

She's kind and warm-hearted. She's exactly who I would choose to be by my side for as long as I live.

But if she wants to stay just friends for all our lives, then I would. For her.

Chloe and I look at each other the remainder of the shoot, not saying a single word, just letting Eliana get all the pictures that she needs.

Eventually, Eliana yells out that she got everything that she wanted to get. She tells Chloe that she will send her the link to all the pictures in a few days.

We say bye, and Chloe and I make our way over to where our car is waiting for us.

When we get to the car, I open the back door for her to get in, but before she gets in, she turns to me and places a small kiss on the corner of my mouth.

It takes me by surprise, and my face must have shown it because Chloe lets out a little laugh before she gives me a smile.

"I'm really glad that Eliana bailed on you seven months ago. I couldn't have asked for a better father for our daughter."

I don't know where that leaves us, but that kiss I'm going to store it away with all of the other small kisses she has given me through the last few months.

If all I get is small kisses, I'll take it.

CHAPTER TWENTY-FOUR

CHLOE

A PICTURE SHOWS up on my phone screen, and the second I see it; I fall in love with it.

Eliana sent me the link to the pictures from the photoshoot a few hours ago. And since the Dark Knight away game against Detroit just ended, and I'm no longer spending my time drooling at the TV whenever my baby daddy skated by, I decided to scroll through them.

Every single picture that I've seen so far has been absolutely beautiful. Eliana has an amazing talent, and I can see why the Knights hired her to be their head photographer.

The one picture that has me falling in love, is one of Liam and me.

We both have a hand on my stomach, with one of mine overlapping just a bit and sitting on top of his. Like I was holding it there, not wanting him to move an inch.

If I remember correctly his other hand was on my hip,

and while mine was playing with the edge of the black sweater that he was wearing.

How we are standing, though, isn't what made me love the picture instantly. It's the way we are both looking at each other.

I'm looking at him as if I'm mesmerized, and he's looking at me as if I'm the most beautiful thing in the world.

If I were to show the picture to a stranger and have them describe what they saw, they without a doubt would say that it was two people in love.

The picture even has *me* questioning if what I'm looking at is just for the camera or very much real.

Even after what Liam told me as we were taking the picture, I'm still leaning toward it being for the camera. At least on his part.

I've been mesmerized by the man since I met him, and now seven and a half months later, that hasn't changed. It's gotten stronger if anything.

But I'm still in the mindset that I have to protect my heart, and I'm going to stick with that because my daughter needs my undivided attention, now and when she comes. I can't concentrate on anyone else.

Even if that person is her father.

Her very handsome and sexy father.

Nope.

I'm not going to think like that, especially not right after thinking about my daughter. The same daughter who is a direct result of me falling for that handsome and sexy smile that is owned by her father.

Nope, not going to think about it whatsoever.

Because if I start thinking about how sexy Liam is, I'll start thinking about certain urges that Betty warned me about months ago and so far, I've been good. I haven't caved, and I'm not going to start now.

I swipe my finger along the screen to change the photo but again, I'm met with another photo of me and Liam and the second I see it my thoughts are back to the way he's looking at me.

And how good he looks in that tailored sweater and those pants that leave very little to the imagination.

"Don't think about his dick. Don't think about it, it's what got you into this situation in the first place. Just don't look at him, and you will be good." I try to give myself a pep talk, but it's not helping.

The more I look at the picture, the more I see everything that my brain has pointed out. Not only that, but my thoughts also start to shift even without me wanting them to.

Shift to what exactly?

Oh I don't know, just thoughts of how good that handsome face would look between my legs right about now.

Dammit.

I was doing so well.

So far in my pregnancy, I haven't thought about sex. I mean, I thought about it but never like this. Never while looking at a picture of me and my baby daddy and feeling like I'm in heat just looking at him.

No way in hell that is normal.

Remember what Betty said. Fuck me six ways to Sunday.

"Damn you, Betty and your stupid talk of urges." I lock my phone and slam it a little too hard against the couch cushion.

Maybe if I walk around the apartment, stretch out my legs a bit, that will take my mind off wanting to jump Liam the second he gets home.

I have never been more happy that he's at an away game than I am right now. But it's a Detroit game, which means he will be back tonight which doesn't help any. My thoughts just shift to him getting home and me asking him to help me find some relief.

"Nope. Not happening."

I make a loop around the living room and then to the kitchen and then back to the living room. My legs and back are thankful for the movement.

When I head down the hallway, I feel like my sexual thoughts have dissipated, but then I pass Liam's room, and they come back stronger than ever before.

It was just a small whiff of his cologne or aftershave, and suddenly, the little bud between my legs is pulsating and asking for relief.

"Just think about his nasty sweat and how he made you gag when you first smelled it," I say to myself as I make my way back down the hallway. "Yeah, that's a good idea. Think about sweat. Think about Liam sweating and smelling like rotten cooked cheese."

I keep repeating the same thing over and over in my head, and as much as I try to think about Liam sweating and smelling like cheese, nothing seems to work. The only thing that I can think about is his cologne and taking a sniff of it as he's hovering over me about to slide into my pussy.

"Fuck it."

I need to remedy this right now before he gets home, and I do something stupid. And the only way to do that is to take out my arsenal of vibrating toys.

I've been holding off using them this long, but I can't take it anymore.

I quickly check the time and see that I have another two hours until Liam comes home. That should be enough time to do what I need to do.

Urges are no fucking joke.

Heading straight into my room, I go directly to my closet where the box of toys is hidden out of plain sight.

Thank God I thought about bringing them when I first moved in here, because no way in hell was I going to be able to make it back to my apartment just to grab a toy.

I need relief right now, and I sure as hell know that my fingers won't be able to handle it.

Opening the box, I reach for one of my favorites that I know will give me the orgasm that my body is so desperately asking for.

As soon as I have the toy in hand, I check it quickly for a charge. As soon as it turns on, I feel relieved because there is no way I would be able to wait for it to charge and come to life.

I get up from the floor as quickly as I possibly can, what with my bump being in the way, and then climb up on my bed.

Right away, all my clothes start coming off, and as soon as I am under the covers, I move the toy down to my core and press the 'on' button. The second that the vibration meets my clit, I feel an instant relief.

"Holy shit," I breathe out.

The vibrations feel so damn good that my legs are shaking right away. Everything feels absolutely amazing.

I don't know why I did not think about this sooner. It's like I'm in heaven.

Images of Liam and me together all those months ago start rushing into my mind.

How feeling all his weight on me made me quiver.

How full he made me feel when slid into my pussy and how I missed it when he slid out.

The things he said in my ear, the way that he called me a good girl. Everything from our five nights together is front and center, and I'm loving every little bit of it.

I circle my vibrator along my entrance and then up to my clit, coating the silicone in my arousal.

A hum escapes me as I move it down to my entrance again, teasing myself by sliding it in and out.

I slide the toy all the way inside of me, or as much as my bump will let me, and I slide it back out, imagining that it's Liam and not a piece of silicone.

I'm about to push the button to put it on the highest speed when suddenly, all the vibration stops completely.

"No!" I practically yell out, pushing the button repeatedly for it to turn on, but nothing happens.

"No, you were supposed to be charged," I whine, throwing my head back against my pillows.

My skin feels hot, and I'm out of breath but the urge to orgasm is right there. I can feel it and it was taken from me. I try the button a few more times, but still I'm left on the edge.

"Crap, so much for it being charged," I grumble, throwing the blankets off my body and going back to the closet.

I don't even bother looking for the charger. That will take too long. Instead, I try out all the other toys I have just to see which one will turn on, and after sifting through five or six toys, I find my battery-operated one and try it out.

"Fuck, yes," I say when it turns on, and the small bullet starts vibrating in my hand.

It's not as powerful as the one that I was using but will do for now.

I just need one orgasm and I will charge every toy that I have so that I don't have to go through this torture again.

Instead of going back to the bed, I place the toy against my clit right here in the closet. I'm so damn desperate for a release, I don't want to wait to get comfortable.

The vibration against my clit feels good, and I'm about to start circling it around when the vibration starts to slow down and a second later, it stops completely.

"Why are you doing this to me?" I say into my closet.

This honestly can't be happening.

I'm so on edge right now that if I don't get what I need soon, I'm going to start crying.

The good thing about the toy that's currently betraying me is that all I need is a battery, and I will be good to go.

Liam must have some somewhere. I think I might have seen some in the kitchen.

Gripping the battery-operated toy that is on my shit list at the moment, I get up on my feet and leave the walk-in closet.

I don't even bother putting on clothes. Liam isn't home. Nobody is going to see me.

The second that I open the door to my bedroom and step into the hallway, though, I regret that thought process.

Why, may you ask?

Because the man in question is currently standing at the end of the hallway.

What the hell is he doing here?

I let out a yelp, and instead of running back into the safety of my room, I cover my not so bitty bits and turn.

"What the hell are you doing at home?" I yell out in a panic.

"Um, I..." Liam starts to say but then stops.

I turn slightly, and I see that he's still standing where he just was but this time his eyes are focused on my ass and his mouth is opening to say something but nothing comes out.

"You weren't supposed to be here until later," I say, trying hard not to freak out any more than what I already am. I finally come to my senses and run to my room, quickly closing the door behind me.

"We were able to leave early," Liam says, his voice sounding closer. He must have finally found the will to move.

"It was a two-hour flight. How early did you leave?"

"It's only an hour flight from Detroit, Chloe," he says, his voice coming from just outside my door.

"Your flight information said two." I have no idea why I'm arguing with him about this.

Maybe because he saw you naked for the first time in seven and a half months.

"We were in a different time zone, Chlo," he says.

Of course, I would forget about stupid time zones when I'm trapped in an orgasm obsessed state of mind.

"Chloe, open the door," he says a few seconds later.

"I'm good, thank you," I say, thinking that it might be a good idea to hide under my covers.

"I have something that you may want," his voice is low, and my body is liking it a little bit too much.

"Oh yeah? And what is that? A black hole to suck me into and erase my embarrassment?" I will never live this night down.

"Why don't you open the door and find out, sweetheart?"

It's the sweetheart that does it for me. With a resigned sigh, I open the door just a smidge, enough to peek my head out and cover my body.

"What?"

He gives me a smirk to end all smirks. "Did you lose something?"

I don't know what I'm more mortified about. The fact that he saw me naked when I was on the hunt for batteries for my toy. Or the fact that I dropped said toy, and he found it and is now showing it to me?

Both are equally as embarrassing.

I try to reach for it, but the man has height on me, so he quickly takes it out of reach.

"Uh-huh. You're going to have to come out here and get it."

I don't move. I can't believe that he would do this to the mother of his child. Asshole.

"You're seriously going to torture the woman who is carrying your baby?" I throw out, very much wanting to stick my tongue out at him and act like a child.

Even more so when the asshole starts to grin.

"If she wants an orgasm, I will. With my tongue, fingers, or cock, she can take her pick," he tells me, his eyes gleaming when I let out a gasp.

No way.

This isn't happening. I must be dreaming because there is no way in hell that Liam is saying what I think he's saying.

I watch as he comes closer to the door, the toy I was using on myself a few minutes ago in his hand, taunting me.

Liam is looking like he's the predator, and I'm his prey. And I'm liking it. I'm liking it so damn much.

And the second that he says his next few words, I'm an absolute goner. The desperation taking over.

"Do you want one, sweetheart? Do you want to come?" he asks, in that low voice of his that has me holding my legs together a little tighter.

I give him a nod, not being able to speak.

"Then be the good girl that I know that you are and come and get it."

CHAPTER TWENTY-FIVE

LIAM

THIS WOMAN KEEPS SURPRISING ME. This is the third time that I've come home, and the night has gone the complete opposite from what I thought it would.

First, it was the night when she told me that we were having a girl. I kissed her for the first time in five months, and it felt good to have not only my mouth on her but also my hands. It took everything in me to pull away and not suggest anything sexual.

The second time the night didn't go as planned was when I found her crying in her room over her ripped pants and everything else not fitting. The very same night where I acted like an asshole instead of consoling her.

Then there's tonight.

Our game against Detroit ended a little bit ahead of schedule so we were able to make it to DTW in record time and head home early. My plan for tonight was to head home and maybe convince Chloe to watch a movie with me and possibly go over that list of baby names she's been sending me.

It was going to be a quiet night, nothing too crazy.

Then I walked in.

The apartment was quiet and from the looks of the living room, that was where she was before heading to her room. I thought that she had fallen asleep on the couch and then went to her bed.

No big deal.

Then I get to the hallway.

I heard the footsteps hitting the hardwood and the door opening before I saw her and when I did, my jaw fucking dropped.

Chloe was naked as naked as can be. My eyes took in every single delicious inch of her, all the while my mouth watered. I wanted to close the distance between us and take her in my arms and have my way with her.

Her tits were full, and her belly looked absolutely breath-taking. I knew she had gained a few curves since the last time we were together, and now I knew exactly where they were. For a solid minute, I just stood there, not being able to think about anything, but Chloe.

I couldn't even talk.

When she went back into her room, I was finally able to compose myself.

That only lasted for a second or two, because instantly my mind went somewhere else.

Why was she naked?

Did she have a guy over?

And if she did, why did she think it was appropriate to bring him here where he would get killed for even looking at her?

She's carrying my child; no other man has the right to touch her. Nobody but me.

I was getting ready to barge into the room and punch the shit out of whoever was in there with her when I noticed something on the floor.

A little bullet.

The second that I saw it, I calmed down.

She didn't have a guy over, but she was having some fun by herself.

I pick up the small toy and press the on button to test it out.

But nothing happened.

The batteries must have died, and she ran out to look for some.

And since she thought I wasn't supposed to come home for a while, she ran out here naked to get to her release quicker.

But I was home.

I did see her naked.

And right now, the only thing that I want to do is give her that orgasm she so desperately wants. An orgasm that won't be coming from a shitty little toy.

Chloe steps out from behind her door, into the hallway,

and this time when she steps in front of me, she doesn't cover herself up.

She stands in front of me with shoulders back and with all the fucking confidence in the world.

The woman can't get any sexier.

"Is it okay if I touch you like this?" I close the distance between us and let the back of my hand graze her cheek.

This is the first time I've touching her like this in months. I've been wanting to touch her like this so damn badly, but I never crossed the line. Now that it's happening, I want to savor it, because I don't know if it will ever happen again.

But even though she is standing in front of me, without an ounce of clothing on, I still need her permission to do what I want.

"More than okay," she answers, her chest rising a bit.

"Do you want me to touch you somewhere else?" I let my finger slide down her neck to her collarbone before moving back up.

"Yes," she says, a little bit breathless.

"Where?" I will touch her wherever she wants me to.

"Everywhere," she says, not taking her eyes off me.

Fucking hell.

I want to say fuck it to savoring her and just have my way with her right now, but I hold back.

"I will," I say, lowering my finger back down, this time not stopping at the base of her neck. "I just have one question."

"And what is that?" she asks a little too quickly, like she's eager to see what I have planned.

I'm eager, too, baby. I'm eager, too.

"Tell me, sweet Chloe. Were you playing with yourself before you came out here?" The words leave my mouth, and my finger travels down her chest.

Her tits are so fucking full that each of them deserves my undivided attention. Every part of me wants to mark them as mine. I want to mark every single inch of her as mine.

"I was," she answers, her head getting slightly thrown back when my hand grazes her nipple.

"And why did you stop?" I ask, taking her nipple between my fingers and giving it a tug.

The way she lets out a moan tells me that she is a lot more sensitive than she was before.

"Because my toy had to recharge," she groans as if remembering the fact.

"Hmm, I'm going to take a wild guess that you weren't able to get where you wanted to before it died."

My hand leaves her chest and travels down to her stomach.

In all the time that she has been pregnant, I have never touched her stomach. Don't get me wrong, I have wanted to.

I wanted to sit on the couch and talk to the baby, maybe even let her listen to music, or just sit there until I felt her kick. But I had it in my head that it would be way too intimate and not something that I should do.

Now I'm taking advantage of it while I can.

Chloe shakes her head. "No, I wasn't able to."

"Do you want to now?" My hand slides down from her stomach to the top of her pussy. I guide my fingers through her folds once and when she lets out a shover, I pull away just slightly.

She's sensitive everywhere.

"Yes, please," she says, letting out a moan in the process.

"How were you touching yourself? Like this?" I circle her clit just enough to cause her back to arch. "Or were you just letting the toy rest against your clit?"

A whimper escapes from between her lips. "No. I wasn't touching myself like this."

"What were you doing?" I continue my motions against her clit, and I'm trying to control myself and not give a lot too quickly.

"I was sliding it inside of me."

"Like this?" I ask sliding my fingers down to her entrance and teasing her with one finger and then two. She's so wet already, my cock is going to slide in so easily.

Chloe lets out a gasp as one of my fingers slides into her. "Oh my god."

"Is this how you were touching yourself, sweetheart?" I ask, letting the palm of my hand rub against her clit to give her more friction.

"Yes."

"Do you want me to keep touching you?"

"Yes, please," she pants out.

I give her a nod, closing the distance between us even more if that's even possible and placing my lips an inch away from her ear. "Tell me that you're mine tonight. Tell me that any rule that we put in place is void, at least for tonight. Tell me that I can have you in any way that I can, and come morning, you won't regret a single thing. Tell me that you will be a good girl and beg."

A hand lands on my face, and it pulls me back just a bit. Just enough for me to look at her in the eyes as she responds.

"I'm yours tonight. All rules are void. You can have your way with me, and I won't regret it in the morning. And I promise you that you will have me begging for every little thing."

There is no hesitation as I slam my mouth against hers and kiss her.

There is nothing simple or sweet about the way my mouth dances with hers. It's all hunger and desperation, and no matter how long my tongue dances with hers, I want more.

So much fucking more. I've been wanting to kiss her like this for months, and it's finally happening.

I won't be holding back tonight.

Not a single fucking bit.

Even though I don't want to pull away from her, I do. I have plans, and those plans don't include fucking her in the hallway. This woman deserves a bed. Even more so when she's carrying my baby.

"Let's get you more comfortable," I state, moving my hands off her body, only for a few seconds and bending down to pick her up and cradle her.

The second that I have her in my arms, Chloe doesn't waste any time getting comfortable, laying her head against my shoulder, and wrapping her arms around my neck.

"Such a gentleman," she says through a giggle.

"Always," I say, placing a kiss against the corner of her lips. "I've fucking dreamed of having you in my bed," I say to her as I walk us over to my bedroom, letting my hands dig into her naked body.

She feels so damn good.

"I don't believe you," she says against my neck.

"Believe it, sweetheart," I say, walking into the room.

The second that I set her down and she lies against the light gray sheets, I know that whatever image I had in my head regarding this moment did not do the real thing justice.

Months.

For fucking months, I have wanted this woman in my bed, in my personal space, and now she is finally here.

Naked and waiting for me to make her body sing.

"I could look at you like this forever and never get tired of it," I say, unbuttoning my dress shirt, having gotten rid of my jacket and tie at the airport.

A sweet blush creeps up her chest, painting her full tits a nice shade of pink.

But she doesn't respond to my words. Instead, she watches me undress just like she did the night that we met.

Unlike that night, though, I don't take my time getting rid of the material covering my body. All my movements are hurried, not wanting to take any more time away from being able to explore every single square inch of Chloe.

The second that the last article of clothing is off me, I grab one of Chloe's legs and drag her to the edge of the mattress.

Her legs fall open and the second I see her pussy glistening with arousal, my mouth starts to water. I haven't forgotten how she tastes. I have that embedded into my mind. But when you have been wanting to taste something again, you act like a starved man. And in a way, I am.

I'm a starving man, and I'm about to have my meal.

That meal being Chloe.

I fall to my knees in front of her and without warning, I place my mouth on her pussy and show her just how beautiful I think she is with just my mouth.

"Oh, my god, Liam," Chloe pants out, one of her hands landing in my hair.

I don't stop my attack on her pussy. I tease and suck on every single inch of her as if this will be the last time that I ever taste her.

Her panting fills the room, and it takes everything in me to not take my cock in my hand and give myself a few heavy-handed strokes.

Right now, it's all about Chloe and Chloe alone. I could give two shits about my own needs right now.

And for the rest of the night, that's what I do. I concentrate on Chloe and what she wants.

I give her the orgasm that she couldn't get from her toy earlier and then give her three more to show her just how fucking sexy I find her.

I use everything I have in my arsenal to show her that she is everything, and that she has me to worship her body whenever she wants.

In the end when we are both satiated and ready to give in

to sleep, I get a feeling that this one night isn't going to be enough.

One night wasn't enough seven and a half months ago, and it sure as hell won't be enough tonight.

I want her not only tonight and tomorrow but next week, next year and every single day after that.

I want it to be just the three of us. No one else.

And if I have it my way, it will be.

CHAPTER TWENTY-SIX

CHLOE

THINGS HAVE SHIFTED between Liam and me. Ever since our night together a month ago, things have definitely shifted.

And I think that they shifted in a good way.

I won't lie and say that we haven't repeated that night because we have. Almost every night, I wind up in his bed, and he makes me feel so damn good that I sleep all through the night, which helps when you have a watermelon attached to your body.

Not only am I sleeping in his bed and letting him take care of every single urge that my body has, we've also been a lot more affectionate toward each other.

We hold hands when we go to the grocery store.

He wraps his arms around me when we sit on the couch and watch Knight game replays or a movie.

And we've been kissing each other whenever we want.

That one right there has taken me some time to get used to but now, I look forward to every single kiss that Liam gives me. No matter how small.

The big question though is, are we together?

And all I can say is, I don't know.

We're acting like a couple. We have sex like two individuals who are in a relationship. Hell, I only step into my room to grab a change of clothes.

But we haven't talked about it.

There hasn't been any conversation regarding our relationship status, and I don't know if there ever will be.

I made myself clear from the beginning, even before I found out that I was pregnant, that I wasn't going to jump into a relationship. That I had priorities to take care of.

But now I might unknowingly be in a relationship with someone.

Liam and I should really talk about that.

It's been something that I've been wanting to bring up, but something always gets in the way.

But today, has to be the day because I'm tired of being unsure.

Being unsure of my relationship status isn't the only thing that has been taking over my mind this morning.

Another thing has been homesickness, something that hit me like a pound of rocks this morning.

In all my adult life, I can't remember a time when I was so homesick that just the thought of seeing my mom brought tears to my eyes.

Usually before I got to this point, I would book the first flight to Austin and spend enough time with my family to hold myself over until the next time I got homesick.

But since I put myself on the no-fly list because I didn't want to risk anything, I haven't been home. Now that I want to go, I really can't because I'm so far along in my pregnancy that Dr. Long says it's a risk.

I should have taken Liam up on his offer to fly my family here for New Years', but I couldn't do it, given everything he's already done for me and the baby.

Letting me live at his place without paying a dime.

Silently paying for all my doctor visits and blood work. I found out about this one because I called my insurance one day after being told that I didn't have a copay when I was sure I did. They told me that they haven't received a single thing from my doctor. So, I asked Shawna, and she told me.

He was doing so much already. I didn't want to add another thousand-dollar bill to it.

I should have pushed pride aside and let him do what he wanted because now it's hitting me so hard that I'm sobbing just looking at my mom's contact on my phone.

Thank God Liam isn't home.

Him seeing this meltdown would scar me. He's already seen one meltdown. He doesn't need to see another.

I do my best to push down my tears and press my mom's name on the screen.

Maybe talking to her for a little bit will help me stop being such a mess.

"Hola, mi niña." My mom's voice sounds through, filling my ears.

The second I hear her voice, a sob escapes me.

So much for not being a mess. These hormones are kicking my ass and taking any prisoners. I hate them so much.

"Hi, Mami," I say, hiccupping through my sobs.

"Chloe, what's wrong?" Instantly my mom's voice is filled with worry.

I would be worried, too, if my pregnant daughter called me sobbing.

"Nada, I just miss you," I say, sniffling and wiping away my tears.

"I miss you too, honey," she says, and even by hearing her voice I know that she is smiling. "You know that we'll see each other soon."

"I know, but I still wish you were close by," I admit through another sniffle.

"Me, too, mija, me, too," she sighs.

Being pregnant and living in a different state is not only hard for me but also hard for my mom.

She has always been a nurturing person, so me being pregnant and her not being able to be her by my side the whole time hurts her.

Growing up, she always told me that she had wished that her mom had been alive during her pregnancies. That way she would have someone there to guide her who wasn't my dad or a doctor.

That's how I feel. I have Liam and Betty, but I really wish

I could have my mom here, too. I can text her and call her every single day, but it's not the same.

I would love to get a hug from her right now and eat some of her flautas. I've been craving my mom's food so much these past two weeks. I'm so tempted to ignore my doctor's orders and get on a plane just to have her coffee and maybe some tacos de papa.

Or maybe if my desperation reaches to the level it was at a few weeks ago, I can try to convince Liam to take a road trip down to Texas with me.

He would spend countless hours in the car with me and drive across the country to satisfy my cravings, right?

Not with them finishing up the season and possibly going to the playoffs.

"Maybe I can move things around and I can head to Chicago sooner or maybe even stay for longer," my mom suggests taking me out of my thoughts.

A small smile forms on my lips.

We already talked about this in January, and we have decided, Liam included, that my mom would come stay with us for a little bit leading up to the birth and staying after.

That way she didn't miss anything, I had my mom in the room while my insides were getting ripped open, and Liam and I had help figuring things out afterward.

I would love to have my mom come here sooner, but she's a school counselor, and her school year isn't over yet. So, her coming sooner means that her kids won't have her if they need anything.

With my due date being at the end of May it works out

perfectly for her. I just have to hope that our little surprise doesn't decide to pull a fast one on us and come early.

As for the longer part, I will take her up on that.

Liam and I haven't talked about it yet, but me moving in was only until the baby was born. So, when that happens, it would be nice to have my mom here when he's a few neighborhoods away.

Besides, I don't know what the hockey offseason is like. For all I know, he could be gone for weeks.

"You don't have to come early. It's okay," I say, wiping my nose with my sleeve. "But if you want to stay longer, I'm okay with that."

"Liam wouldn't mind?" she asks.

I told my parents back in December that I was moving in with Liam. Surprisingly, they thought that it was a good idea after a FaceTime call with him.

Even though my parents are traditional as hell, or at least I thought that they were, they were completely okay with me living with the man who had gotten me pregnant.

My mom said that it would put her at ease knowing that someone was there looking out for me and taking care of me. My dad agreed.

I just didn't tell them the small little tidbit about me moving out after the baby is born.

"No, he won't mind," I say to her, not mentioning a single thing.

"Okay, then we will plan for that."

My mom and I talk for a few more minutes, and as much as I want to say that talking to her helped the whole homesickness thing, I can't. The second the call ends, I miss her more than I did when I first called her.

The tears are constant for the next few hours. By two o'clock, they are no longer tears from being homesick but tears of feeling lonely.

A feeling that I haven't felt these last few months but suddenly is hitting me.

Why?

I see Liam every day.

I see Betty a few times a week since she has more time now that she officially hung up her tutu after the last winter show.

So, I interact with people. I talk to them and spend time with them, so I shouldn't feel like I don't have anyone in my corner, but I do.

I have people. People who care about me, who love me, who want what's best for me, and who will do anything to help.

But once the baby is here, that might change. I'll have Betty and my family, but maybe not Liam.

After I leave the hospital, he doesn't have to worry about me. I will move out, go back to my apartment, and only see Liam whenever the baby is concerned.

I think that's what is making me feel this way.

I'm gaining a kid, but I'm losing someone in return.

Someone that has been a pivotal part of my life for the last eight months. Someone who has seen me at my worst and best and was even there for me through the tears over ripped pants.

Liam became my anchor through it all, has become one of the most important people in my life, and in four to six weeks that will disappear.

I didn't want to get attached, but I did.

Wiping at the tears that have escaped my eyes, I start folding the baby clothes that I had washed before calling my mom.

We had a small baby shower last weekend with Betty, a few of our dancer friends, and a few of Liam's teammates, and his parents. We got a lot of baby clothes, tutus, hockey jerseys, and most importantly, diapers.

Which we will have for years since Christian and Blake decided that two pallets of diapers and wipes would be the best gift in the world.

I can't even tell you where the diapers are stored. They're everywhere.

So, I thought I would keep myself busy by washing all the little clothes.

As I fold, I separate everything into two piles.

One pile for Liam's apartment. One pile for mine. Might as well start planning the move now.

My emotions are really trying to knock me out today because even that little thought has me crying.

I try to calm myself down, but nothing helps so I just let the tears flow.

That's how Liam finds me an hour later as he walks into the apartment after going to a team charity event this morning. Folding clothes and crying.

I'm tired of him finding me in such emotional situations.

"Everything okay?" he asks. He's always asking if I'm okay. Always, and I hate it when my emotions betray me and show him that I'm not.

No matter how hard I try to keep the tears away, they always betray me.

I give him a nod, trying to push down all the emotions from today so that he won't see the full extent of them.

"Are you sure?" he asks, coming in deeper into the living room.

"Yeah, I'm sure," I say, my voice breaking only a little bit. I might be able to get through this without adding any more tears to my day.

I can see it on his face that he doesn't believe me, but either way, he gives me a nod, and comes to sit next to me on the couch.

He gives me a small smile before turning to look over at the piles of clothes that I have going.

"Is there a reason why you're separating everything into two piles?" he asks, leaning his elbows against his knees.

"One pile for my apartment, one pile for here," I say, trying not to look at him. If I do, I might cry.

"Are we using your apartment for storage or something?" he asks, giving me a confused look.

"No, the piles are for when I move out." I'm able to get the words out with my voice having some strength behind it.

"Move out?" he asks, his voice full of surprise.

"Yes, we agreed that I would only live here until the baby was born. After that, I am moving back to my place," I tell him while I fold up a onesie and put it in his pile.

"Right," he says, dragging out the word.

"I figured I would get started now because later I won't be able to get anything done. So, this pile is for me, and this pile for you," I inform him, putting at each pile. "We should also figure out the whole diaper situation since we have way too many."

My voice is getting stronger by the minute.

I can do this.

Liam doesn't say anything. He just sits there still with a confused look on his face, and all the while he scratches his head like he is trying to figure something out.

A lump starts forming in my throat, but I'm able to push it down. "I should also start packing up my room. That way when the day comes, I can just grab a bag and head home."

I can't believe how calm I sound right now. Talking to my mom seemed like so much work with all the tears and emotions rushing out.

I was literally wiping away tears seconds before he walked in, and now there's not even one in sight.

"So that's it then? The baby comes, and you're out of here?" Liam asks, his voice has something to it that I can't pinpoint.

I nod. "That's what we agreed on."

"I know that's what we agreed on. I was there. I was the one that said until the baby was born. I just thought that after everything that's been going on for the last month, things would change. I thought that you and the baby would stay here for longer."

"How much longer?" I ask, keeping my eyes down in the tiny clothes.

"I don't know. Forever?"

I finally look up at the word forever.

No way he wants that.

"I can't stay here forever, Liam."

"Why the fuck not?" he asks, sounding almost mad about it.

"Because," I tell him, not knowing what else to say.

"Because isn't a fucking answer, Chloe. Why the hell can't you live here?"

"Because! What happens when you meet someone, and you want to bring them over and have them spend the night? Where am I going to go? I don't want to hear you sexing up another woman, and I sure as hell don't want a stranger coming around my kid while she flirts with my baby daddy."

I don't know where that came from. Never have I thought about Liam with anyone else or what it would mean if he brought someone home. It was never a thought, because Liam has never shown anything but fidelity to me even without a relationship holding him to me.

Its devotion to his daughter not to you.

"Who said anything about me meeting anybody else?" he asks angrily, standing up from the couch and putting some distance between us.

"We're not together, Liam. You can meet and date and sex up whoever you want,"

"How did we get here? How the hell did we get from you telling me that you want to move out to saying that I can date and sex up whoever I want? I don't want to be with someone else. I don't know if you've noticed, but for the last six months, I've been with you or with the team, that's it. I went to a bar once, and that was to celebrate winning a game, and you started out the night with me. I'm only interested in one person, and I thought we were going in the right direction, but now she's telling me that she wants to move out and that I should date other people that aren't her."

"You only think that you're interested in me because I'm pregnant with your baby," I say, dropping my eyes from his.

"You've said that before. You said it at the park, and you are saying it now. But have ever I told you that?" he asks, no longer yelling. "Have you heard those words come out of my mouth? Because if I remember correctly, I've told you before that you are way more than just my kid's mother. I've told you that I would care about you with or without the baby."

"What happens when the baby comes, and all that disappears?" I ask, finally feeling the tears again.

"It won't," he says through his teeth.

"You don't know that. We're not a couple. We're not in a relationship. We're not tied to each other. You're saying all these words, but what happens when the baby comes, and they all disappear?" I say, letting a tear escape.

"We're not together because you said it was best," he answers back.

"You agreed to it," I argue.

"Yes, I did. Because it was the best decision at the time, but that doesn't mean I stand by it now."

"What does that even mean?" I ask, wiping at my face.

"It means that if I could go back, I would make you mine. It means that I don't give a flying fuck if we didn't know each other for all that long, or that we were going to be parents. I would have made you mine, and you wouldn't be having doubts about how I feel about you."

He goes silent, not even moving, just waiting for me to give him some sort of response. He stands in front of me, his whole body radiating all the anger he is feeling, waiting for me to say something.

I don't say anything because I don't know what to say.

Do I believe him and take his word for everything that he just told me? That he only wants me and still will when the baby comes?

What if he's wrong? What if I take him for his word and become his, but the second we leave the hospital everything he told me disappears?

What would I do then?

I don't want my daughter to start off her life with a heart-broken mother.

Loving Liam wouldn't be hard. Hell, I'm basically there already. So, I can see myself spending the next four weeks falling even harder for him and then getting everything ripped away.

I can't do that to myself.

"We can't go back, though," I say, letting the tears roll out.

Liam's posture doesn't change. If anything, he gets a lot more rigid.

Our gazes lock for what feels like an eternity with Liam eventually breaking it.

Without a word, he leaves the apartment, the door slamming behind him.

I don't run behind him. I just sit there and let out yet another sob and cry into my daughter's clothes.

I was feeling lonely earlier, but this is on a whole different level.

CHAPTER TWENTY-SEVEN

LIAM

I SHOULDN'T HAVE WALKED out. I shouldn't have left her while she was crying. I shouldn't have raised my voice at her.

I should have stayed and talked everything through with her, but I didn't.

I was so damn pissed that I needed to leave before I said something that I was going to regret.

After everything that I told her, after telling her repeatedly that she was more than just the baby's mother, she still doesn't believe me.

I don't know how many other ways I can say the same words to finally get it through her head. That I want to be with her because of who she is and not because she's the mother of my child.

I know we're not together. I know that we never made anything official after spending a whole damn month in the same bed. It might be my own fault for not broaching the subject sooner, but it fucking hurts hearing the woman who owns your whole damn heart tell you that she doesn't believe you. It hurts that she hears all the proclamations about your feelings toward her, yet she still thinks that in a few short weeks, she'll mean nothing.

Chloe can never mean nothing because she's fucking everything to me. She's more than just the mother of my child, she's more than just a roommate, more than just a one-night stand. She is so much fucking more to me and she doesn't see it.

I've been falling in love with this woman for the past seven months, and she doesn't see it.

This may be such a petty thing to get pissed off about, but I don't give a shit anymore.

I want her, but she doesn't want me.

I should walk away. I should put everything that has happened between us, behind me and walk away so we can concentrate on raising our daughter together.

That's what I should do, and maybe eventually I will be able to, but for right now, the woman who I met less than a year ago owns too much of my heart to walk away from her. Maybe with time. A lot of fucking time.

Right now, I'll drink my body weight in alcohol and worry about the consequences tomorrow morning when I hit the ice.

"You want another one, Cap?" the bartender asks, knocking a knuckle against the bar.

"Yeah," I say, giving him a small nod.

"Celebrating something?" he asks as he pours some whiskey into my tumbler.

I shake my head. "Not tonight."

"I hear the Knights are getting new owners soon," the guy says, trying to make conversation.

Most nights I would go along with it, but tonight I'm not feeling it.

"Yeah, it should be announced soon," I say, taking a long pull from my drink.

Thankfully, someone calls him to the other side of the bar, and he walks away.

At least that saves me from being an asshole to someone else.

I take another pull and savor the fermented grains scratching at my throat.

Since the team is officially in the playoffs, this is going to be the last drink I will be having until the last game is played.

This is our year. I know it is. We are the best we have ever been and there is no doubt in our minds, in the mind of the fans, that this year the Cup will be heading to Chicago.

I just have to make sure that all this stuff with Chloe stays off the ice, and I will be golden.

Finishing up my drink, I pull out some cash to leave the bartender, and I'm about to start heading out when someone sits on the barstool next to me.

Who it is, takes me by surprise. Never did I expect this guy to ever step foot in a dive bar.

"We got to stop meeting like this, Crawford," Elliot Lane says, waving over the bartender.

"I didn't take you as a dive bar type of guy," I say, getting situated in my seat again.

The guy gives me a shrug. "I had a meeting a block over and really needed a drink to erase the mess that sitting in a room full of morons did to me."

"And it just so happens to be the very one that I was in?" I ask because it's a huge-ass coincidence that this guy would walk in while I was here.

"I guess so," he says right before giving the bartender his order.

The bartender then turns to me and asks if I want another, and I don't hesitate in saying yes. I'm already paying for it tomorrow, might as well make it worth it.

"Why so gloomy, Crawford? I thought you would be at the top of the world right now."

"Oh, yeah? Why is that?" I ask, taking a drink as soon as the bartender places a fresh tumbler in front of me.

"I heard the Knights are going to the playoffs. That should be reason enough right there," he says, taking a drink from his own tumbler.

I let out a snort. "I thought that you were going to tell me because my daughter is going to be born soon."

Soon. So very soon she is going to be here, and we don't even have a name picked out or even a nursery ready to go.

We should get on that.

But I guess we are going to need two nurseries since Chloe is moving out. We need double of everything.

"Damn. Really?" Elliot turns slightly, giving me an eyebrow raise.

I nod. "Yeah, really. She's due to arrive at the end of May, beginning of June."

"That's so close," he says, like he is shocked by the news.

"Yup. Very."

"How did you and the mom meet?" he asks, taking another drink of his amber colored liquid.

Another snort leaves my mouth. "The ballet."

That apparently really takes Elliot by surprise because he starts coughing. As if how I met Chloe is the most shocking thing ever.

"The one in September?" he asks for clarification.

"The one in September," I confirm.

It absolutely blows my mind how much someone's life could change in eight months. It's fucking insane.

"Well, congratulations, man," he says, tapping my tumbler with his.

"Thank you," I say, taking another drink.

Elliot sends a nod in my direction. "Don't take this the wrong way, but you don't seem all that excited about becoming a dad."

I start shaking my head before he has even finished talking. "I am excited. Extremely excited. I can't wait to meet her and hold her and just get to know her. It's just that some things went down tonight that put me in a shit mood."

Elliot may not be the best ear for this, but I need to talk to someone. I could call Christian and talk his ear off, but I feel like he's too close to both me and Chloe so whatever he says is going to be biased one way or the other.

I don't know Elliot all that well. Sure, we've acted

friendly at events and have hung out a time or two, but he's more of an acquaintance than a friend. He might be the best person for this conversation.

"Let me guess, baby mama drama?" he asks, finishing off his drink but waving off another.

"In a way, yeah," I say, twirling my tumbler, the ice hitting the edges.

"She wants full custody?" the billionaire asks and I can't help but roll my eyes.

"She wants to move out after the baby is born and doesn't accept the fact that I want to be with her." God, I sound like I just saw someone kick a puppy or something.

"So you love her and want to be with her, but she is putting every single wall up and not letting you get close to her." He perfectly summarizes Chloe's and my situation.

"Yup, that's pretty much it," I say, finishing up my drink. I'm done with alcohol for the night.

"Sounds intense."

"It is."

For a solid minute, we both sit there, twirling empty glasses not saying a single word.

Elliot is the one that breaks the not so awkward silence.

"Want advice from someone who doesn't do relationships and only has one good example in his life that is definitely not his parents?" Elliot states and it takes me a second to comprehend what the hell he just said.

I give him a nod. "I will take anything you want to give."

"Don't pressure her. Don't push her to make a decision, especially one that has to do with being on the receiving end of heartbreak. I'm sure that you told her how you feel, and that she has heard you, but if you met her in September, and she is having your baby in a few weeks, she's going through a lot. She might not be ready now, but she might be eventually. And when that time comes, she will come to you. If that's what she wants, she will come to you. You just have to let her."

It's as if he dove deep into my brain and pulled this piece of advice out of the deepest crevice that I have.

That is what I've been telling myself all along, but for some reason tonight, I decided to go rogue and forget it.

"Are you sure that you only have one good example of a relationship?" I ask because no way he just pulled that out of his ass.

"Yup, very sure. Did it help?" he asks, giving me a knowing look.

I let out a sigh. "Yeah, it helped."

"Good. You should get out of here then and head back to your lady. She might be worried."

I give him a nod and slap a few bills on the counter and make my way out of the bar.

When I left the apartment earlier, the only things that I grabbed were my wallet and my phone. I didn't remember to grab my keys, which turns out to be a good thing. No way would I be able to drive after three whiskeys.

Walking back to my place helps me clear my head a bit.

What Elliot said helped a lot, and most of my anger from earlier has dissipated. The only thing that still pisses me off is Chloe moving out.

I don't want her to move out. I look forward to walking through the door and seeing her beautiful smile. And adding in the fact that I can see it almost every single day is just icing on the fucking cake.

But like Elliot said, I can't force her.

I can't force her to stay and live with me. And if she does decide to stay, it has to come from her and her alone.

No matter what, though, her moving out still fucking stings.

I continue to make my trek back to the apartment, making it back into the building and up the elevator to the twentieth floor right before midnight.

Walking in, I half expected to see Chloe still in the living room or possibly in the kitchen, but she's in neither. She must have gone to her room.

Heading down the hallway, I think about knocking on her door like I have done countless of times before, but this time I decide against it.

There's a chance that she is still mad. So, giving her more time to calm down might be a good idea.

So instead of knocking, I continue to walk down the hallway and head into my room.

It doesn't take long for me to get ready for bed and to turn off all the lights and just lie there, contemplating every little thing.

Around two in the morning, my bedroom door opens, and Chloe comes in.

She doesn't say a single thing as she closes the door

behind her or even as she moves through the room or climbs into the bed.

All month she has been in my bed, and after everything that has happened tonight, I thought that tonight was going to be different.

I'm glad that it isn't, because the second I feel her body pressed against mine, I relax and open my arms for her.

Her head lands on my chest and one arm stretches across my bare stomach, while the other rests against her baby bump.

Having her lie here with me like this, is as if nothing happened.

Eventually, I break the silence. "Are you really going to move out?" I ask my voice low.

I hate the answer she gives me as soon as it leaves her mouth. "Yes."

One simple word, and it changes everything.

"Okay," I say, feeling defeated.

"I'm sorry," she says, a wetness landing against my chest.

She's crying and I say the only thing that I can say.

"I'm sorry, too."

CHAPTER TWENTY-EIGHT

CHLOE

MAY

"WHAT DO you think about the name Sienna?" I ask as I sit cross-legged on the floor, watching Liam put together a crib for the nursery in his extra bedroom.

After putting it off for so long, we finally decided that it was time to get some baby furniture and start putting everything together since our window for when the baby is arriving, keeps getting smaller and smaller.

"I like it," Liam starts. "But I'm not overly in love with it," he finishes as he screws on one of the wooden legs.

"Okay, so I will be crossing that one out," I say, not feeling the name now that he's said how he feels about it.

Taking my pen, I cross out the name on the list that I have going on.

A list that has been growing since we found out what we are having.

We have officially hit the point in my pregnancy where picking out a name and making sure that the nursery is all set up and ready to go have become a top priority.

We're getting things done, but there is still a lot more waiting for us in the trenches.

One of those is coming up with a plan just in case Liam is out of town when I go into labor.

After an amazing season, the Dark Knights are officially in the Stanley Cup playoffs. Good news for the team, bad news for me because given my due date, there's a slight chance that Liam could be states away when it's time.

Right now, he's not worried, but that could change depending on if the team advances to the conference finals.

I want the Knights to win, but I also want Liam in the room with me when it's time.

We just have to keep our fingers crossed and hope for the best.

For now, we have baby names to think about and baby furniture that needs to be finished.

"What about the name Courtney?" I suggest.

Liam doesn't even answer, he just makes a face and goes back to concentrating on tightening a screw.

"So, crossing out that one, too," I say, dragging the pen across the paper.

I have a feeling that there will be a lot of crossing out before we find the right one.

I'm about to suggest that we should just pick a name out of a hat or something, but then I catch a glimpse of Liam's face and I stop myself.

Things between Liam and me have been okay these past two weeks after our heated conversation but we are still a little rocky.

He says he's not mad whenever I ask him, but he still seems to get agitated whenever I mention the fact that I will be moving out when the baby gets here.

I might not move out right away, but it is still happening.

I've been trying to make the best of the situation, but it's a little hard at times. Especially when he doesn't talk to me, and I feel like I'm pulling words out of him.

Just a little glimpse at what I was afraid of, I guess.

I shake my head, not wanting to think about it and move on to the next name.

"Oh, what about Gabriella?" I toss out there. It's cute but I don't know if I'm sold on it.

"Sounds way too much like that girl's name from *High School Musical*." He throws out.

I'm surprised that he even knows what *High School Musical* even is.

First the Bad Bunny ringtone and now this. If I didn't know it already, I would say that Liam Crawford knows more about pop culture than he lets on.

"It is the girl's name from *High School Musical*," I tell him, trying to hold back a smile.

"Then I would scratch that off, too," he tells me, nodding toward the list.

"Okay, so no Gabriella." Another strike across the paper. "Are there any names that you like? I can't be the only one who put a list together."

Liam just gives me a grunt in response.

A grunt.

Grunts are mostly how Liam has been communicating these last two weeks.

I'm tired of them. So damn tired. I've been avoiding talking about this, but I can't ignore it much longer.

"Liam?" I say, trying to get his attention but he's staring a little bit too hard at the crib in front of him.

"Liam," I say with a little more strength behind it and finally he looks up at me. Annoyance all over his face.

I hate seeing him like this. I hate that he's looking at *me* like this.

That look on his face is very much about me moving out. I know it is, and as much as I want to give in and give him what he wants, I can't. I have to stand behind this. I have to move out. Even if I turn out to be wrong. And if I am, I will be the first to admit it and kick myself in the ass for doing this to him. For denying what he said, and for denying his feelings at all.

But I have to get there myself. If I ever do.

My shoulders slump a little bit, and I say the only words that I can possibly think of. "I'm really sorry."

Liam's expression shifts from being annoyed and irritated to confusion and then finally to caring and worried.

He doesn't need me to explain what I'm apologizing for.

With a shake of his head, he abandons the crib and comes over and sits next to me. One of his heavily-tattooed arms makes its way around my shoulders and I can't help but to lean into his embrace.

He hasn't held me since the night he stormed out, and I miss it.

"You have nothing to be sorry about," he says, letting out a sigh.

"I'm moving out, and you hate it," I say, letting my head fall to his chest.

"I don't hate it," he tells me and I can't help but let out a snort after hearing his lie. "Okay, fine. I hate it but I'll get over it."

I've learned enough about him these last few months that I know he won't.

"I've been taking my anger about this out on you, haven't I?" he asks, already knowing the answer to the question.

"You have. I think this is the most you've talked to me in two weeks. You've been giving me clipped answers and a lot of grunts," I whisper, nodding my head against his chest.

"I'm really sorry, Chloe," he whispers back, tightening his arm around me.

"I know you are," I say, feeling a prickling in my eyes.

I won't cry. I will not cry.

"We can't keep living like this," he says, and I'm about to suggest I move out now before things get worse, when he speaks again. "We need to come up with something that won't have us mad at each other when our little surprise arrives."

He's right.

Me moving out now will just continue the problem. We have to shelve whatever this thing with us is and make sure that this baby comes into this world knowing that her parents can at least get along.

"Let's just put it on the back burner for now. We won't talk about me moving out and I won't continue to pack the baby's or my stuff. It won't even be a thought. We'll wait for her to come, and in the meantime, the only things that we will concentrate on is this nursery, and you playing the best hockey games of your life to get that Cup and bring it home."

"The girl who told me when I first met her that she didn't know much about hockey, is now calling the Stanley Cup just the Cup."

I stab a finger into his side. "I blame you. I was perfectly fine with only knowing that hockey is played with a puck. Now my brain is filled with hockey lingo, statistics, and way more things that I didn't think I needed to know."

"Now you do."

"Now I do."

"Let's do it. Let's put everything on the back burner and just concentrate on what's happening now, and we will think about everything else later," he says with determination in his voice.

I can't help but smile. "Okay."

We don't move from our position, or even say a word for however long, we just sit there in silence, either taking each other in or thinking.

Eventually, it's Liam who breaks the silence.

"Two syllables."

"What?"

"Her name. It should be two syllables like her parents. It should match."

"Okay," I say, a little confused, but still pulling back from him, running through names in my head that are only two syllables.

There are so many.

"Emma," he says, answering my earlier question. "I like the name of Emma."

I run it through my head a few times.

Emma, Chloe, and Liam.

Liam, Chloe, and Emma.

Chloe, Emma, and Liam.

It works, and just thinking about it brings a smile to my face and makes my heart swell in the process.

I like it, too.

"I think Emma is perfect," I tell him.

"Then, Emma it is," he tells me, a smile appearing on his face.

I gave him one back and then look down at the bump that has taken over my body.

"Hi, Emma," I say to her, letting my hand run against my shirt, hoping to feel her kick.

Liam shifts next to me, and he continues to shift until he is lying on the ground and has a hand extended over to my stomach.

Before the blowout, as I'm now calling it, he would talk to the baby every night, rubbing my stomach and telling her all the hockey stories that he could think of.

I didn't know how much I missed it until now.

"Hi, Emma. Daddy can't wait to meet you, my little ballerina," he tells our daughter, kissing my bump.

I try to ignore the kiss and what it does to me as much as possible. "Little ballerina, huh?"

He gives me a nod and looks up at me with a glimmer in his eye.

"Or hockey player. Whatever she decides. That's up to her. All I know is that she is going to be just as beautiful as her mother, and I won't have it any other way."

CHAPTER TWENTY-NINE

LIAM

JUNE

AT THE BEGINNING of the season, I had hoped the team would be able to get through its woes and maybe make it past the first round of playoffs.

That's all that I wanted.

We were good, and even with the rumors of an ownership change, we were going to play the best damn season that we could to get to the top.

As the season started, and we played game after game, I started feeling it in my bones that this year was going to be our year. That we were going to pull out all the stops and show the NHL world that the Knights were worthy of the Cup once again.

We had a few setbacks with an injury or two, a suspension mixed in, but our season turned out to be better than anyone could have hoped.

We've been able to stay at the top of our division all season long. We've been in the top two of our conference since January. And when April hit, we were able to make it to the playoffs.

First round was a fucking breeze, as we beat Arizona four games to one, and for the first time in years, we made it to round two.

The team was electric, and the fans were optimistic that we would be able to beat Dallas.

We got our asses kicked in games one and two but somehow were able to get our momentum back and take the series in six games.

It has taken us almost the whole damn existence of the franchise, but the Chicago Dark Knights were finally able to make it to conference finals.

Was beating out Los Angeles easy? Fuck no. Those assholes made us sweat, cry, and bleed. They tried taking everything that we had, but we hit them harder.

One key point was that Los Angeles lost one of their goalies in game three, so they were functioning with one player in that position, and it hurt them.

We took the series in game seven, and it felt so damn good.

Our next stop was the finals against Florida, and we were fucking ready.

Like LA, those fuckers have not made it easy. Every single game has been a back-and-forth and has ended in a handful of penalties and injuries.

During game four, Blake ended up with a broken nose

and Christian was ejected from the game for going after the player who punched Blake.

It was a fucking shit show, and somehow, we still came out with the win.

But Florida forced a game seven, and now we are minutes away from playing the last game of the season.

Eighty-two regular season games and twenty-five playoff games, have all come down to this.

And the best thing about it is, we're playing on home ice. We just have to make sure we go through every single superstition like we depend on it and play like this is the last game we will ever play.

Are the Knights going to win? I don't know, but I'm doing everything in my power to make it happen. But I'm not going to say the words until I know for sure it's going to happen.

But playing at home is a good thing.

Another good thing about being in Chicago for game seven is Chloe.

Her due date was three days ago, and the baby is still not here.

A part of me was worried that I would miss the birth, but it seems like my baby girl is going to continue to torture her mom until all of this is over.

Chloe has been in the arena for every home playoff game, and while she's not behind the glass in the first row like she was during the regular season, she's still here, and it means the absolute world to me.

She's been very much my good luck charm this season.

Hopefully, her good luck stays with me through tonight because I'm going to really need it.

The whole damn team is going to need it.

"One more game," Christian says, coming over and slapping me on the shoulder. He's been doing it all playoff season and once a hockey player starts something and it continues to go well, he will do it 'til the day he dies.

"One more game," I say, giving my best friend a nod before he walks away.

"Hey, Cap?" Blake calls out, catching me as I go to grab my stick.

"Yeah?" I ask, turning slightly.

"I just talked to my brother. He says Chloe, her parents and your parents, made it up to the box," Blake informs me, giving me a nod.

Since Chloe is so close to going to labor at any minute, I want her to be around as many people as possible. I don't want anything to happen while she's alone.

It's why she moved in with me in the first place, so she can have someone there in case something happened.

Her parents arrived two weeks ago, and they will be here for about a month, something that I arranged without Chloe knowing, so that has been helpful. Especially since I've been gone a lot these last few weeks.

These last few games, I've made sure that the box I put them in was filled with people who would take care of her if something happened.

Family, friends, anybody that she could go to if her water broke, or she had to go to the restroom.

So hearing that Blake's family is also there helps bring my nerves about her, down a notch.

"Thanks, man," I say, clapping him on the back.

"Thank me by kicking Panther ass," he says, that stupid-ass grin of his on full display.

"You already know it. Have to get payment for that busted-up nose and messing up your pretty face," I say, nodding toward his face guard.

"Fucking assholes. We gotta let Logan loose or something tonight," he says through his teeth, lifting his hand to his busted nose.

"We'll see what we can do." I tap him with my stick and head over to the door to get in the zone.

I try to clear my head as best as I can. For a minute, I close my eyes and clear my head of all outside noises. The only thoughts that I let myself have are those that include my stick and the puck.

For a short minute, it's just me on the ice with nothing stopping me from shooting the puck into the net. Just me and the sport that made me the man that I am today.

My team built me into the player that I am, and I will do everything that I can to make sure they end up on top. I owe them that much.

Tonight, doesn't have importance. Tonight, is just any other game and should be treated as such.

We're going to go out there and kick some Panther ass.

One minute is all I need, and I'm fucking ready.

The voices behind me quiet down, just like they have done every playoff game before this one. My teammates are aware of my little ritual, so they know that as soon as I'm ready, off to the ice we go.

"Alright, boys," I start. "We have three periods, twenty minutes each. There's something out there that we want. Let's go get it. There's only one team that's getting their name added to the cup tonight, and it sure as hell isn't going to be a team from Florida. So, let's. Fucking. Go."

Every single person in the room erupts, the vibration can be felt on the floor.

One by one, we start filing out of the locker room and making our way onto the ice.

The crowd was electric during warm-ups, and the second our blades hit the ice for the second time tonight it is a whole different level.

It feels as if no time is wasted from the second we skate onto the ice to when the puck is dropped.

Everything becomes a total blur.

One second we were in the first period trying to get the puck from the Florida forward and the next are in the third period with twenty seconds on the clock and a tied game.

Anderson yells out a call, and we start putting it in motion.

One more goal. That is all we need.

I bring my stick back and pass the puck over to Blake who then passes it to Logan. Volkov handles it for a few seconds while I skate across the ice and get into position. I make eye contact with him, and as soon as he winds back and slaps the puck to me, I'm already feeling in my bones what my next move is going to be.

The black disk hits my stick and not a second later, I'm already moving toward the net.

The only sound that registers is the sound of my stick hitting the ice. It's just me and the goalie.

He thinks he knows which way I'm going to shoot, but he has no idea. He hasn't had a clue all night.

With nobody around to stop me, I wind and slap the blade of my stick against the puck, and I watch it fly.

Fly and fly until it goes over the goalie's left shoulder and into the net for goal number four.

The buzzer blares through the stadium quickly followed by the horn calling it a game.

Four to three.

Four to fucking three.

Holy *shit*.

Holy fucking shit.

We won.

The Dark Knights just fucking won the Cup.

Bodies slam against me and yells and cheers fill my ears, and all I'm trying to do, is comprehend what just happened.

I just scored the final goal in game seven of the Stanley Cup Finals. Who the fuck even does that?

Me. I fucking do that.

The Cup is coming to Chicago.

The whole team crowds together at the boards, everyone with huge-ass smiles on their faces and tears in their eyes.

They can't believe what we just did either.

I have no clue how long the pile-up goes on for, but we eventually pull apart to hug the other people on the ice.

Skating over to center ice, I look up at the box where I know Chloe is supposed to be, expecting her to be cheering and yelling and possibly jumping up and down as much as her bump would let her.

But she's not there.

The box is completely empty.

Not a single person in sight.

Almost immediately, my heart starts to race, and I starts to panic. All at once, I want nothing to do with the celebration that is currently happening on the ice.

I need to find her.

I need to go to her.

A hand lands on my shoulder, and I'm getting turned toward something.

"It's time, dude. She's on the way to the hospital. Jacobi's brother called the team doctor. Let's go." I hear Christian's voice through all the noise, and it takes me a second to comprehend everything.

It's time.

She's on her way to the hospital.

It's happening, it's fucking happening.

And on top of all that, my team just won the Cup.

Holy fucking shit.

Christian must see the panic on my face because he gives me a rare smile.

"Looks like your little girl was waiting for her daddy to finish the season on top. Now let's fucking go."

Nine months ago, I was wanting to stab my eyes out to get myself out of going to the ballet.

Who would have known that that night would have changed everything?

One night at the ballet, one where I would tell myself that I would make sure my team makes it to the Cup Finals, but also where I met Chloe. One night is all it took to change every single thing.

I'm a part of a Stanley Cup championship winning team.

I'm about to be a dad, and even if it's not the right time, I'm going to make Chloe mine.

Once and for all.

CHAPTER THIRTY

CHLOE

I'M SITTING up in the box, watching the game, when I feel a sharp pain in my stomach. I've been having pains since last night, but they weren't anything that I couldn't handle. I've been dealing with Braxton-Hicks contractions for the last two weeks. I was sure it was nothing.

This one, though, this one fucking hurts.

The sharpness of it, has me closing my eyes and trying my hardest to take a deep breath, but it feels as if no air is coming into my body.

"Okay, that's it. We're going to the hospital," My mom says from next to me, getting up from her seat and trying to get me up.

"No, we can't, they still have one more period to play." I whine, turning to look down at the ice where Liam and his teammates are currently trying to get anything past the Florida goalie.

The Knights are ahead by one, but even I know that that score could change in a second. I don't want to miss it.

"Chloe, ándale. You have to go to the hospital," my mom urges, tugging on my arm and trying to get me up.

"But you said that labor takes forever, I can stay and watch the rest of the game," I tell my mom, but then I get hit with another pain so sharp that I almost double over, and I'm sitting down.

Holy shit. Whoever made contractions so damn painful hated women.

"That one was way too close, sweetie. You have to go to the hospital," Lynnette says as she comes and stands next to my mom.

I'm in so much pain that I can't even marvel at how cute she looks wearing Liam's jersey.

"I'm fine," I say through my teeth as I try to give her a smile.

Both women give me a look like that says that they will drag me out of here if it comes down to it. I try to avoid their glares and look around the room for someone to help with this. Labor takes hours. I have time to watch one more period.

I make eye contact with my dad, and he just looks away like he doesn't want anything to do with it. Lawrence does the same thing.

Huffing, I move on to my next victims. Sophia shakes her head and mouths something about being scared of the moms. Blake's mom and stepdad agree with the two grandmas that are about to grab me by an ear each and make me leave. My last hope is Blake's brother and his fiancée.

Their eyes are wide, and they are looking at me like they can't believe that they are my last resort. We have a stare off, and I think that I'm winning with the brother, Hunter, when holds up his hands in surrender.

"I vote hospital. I'll drive you there if you want. I don't think I can deliver a baby at a hockey game," he lets out.

"Who said anything about you delivering the baby?" his fiancée, Selena, or Lennie as he's been calling her all night, asks giving him a 'you're crazy' look.

"Who else is going to do it?"

"Oh, I don't know, how about one of the many EMTs or medical professionals that are in the stadium?" Selena tells him, and I'm on her side. I don't want or need a football player between my legs.

Another sharp pain hits me, and I have a feeling that if they get any closer, I'm going to pass out.

The moms are right. It's time to go to the hospital.

"Okay. Let's go. Let's go to the hospital." I pant out, trying to remember those breathing exercises I learned. "Someone has to call the team doctor so they can tell Liam as soon as the game is over."

"I'll call on the way there," Hunter says as he walks over and both him and my dad help me up and walk me out to the car.

The hospital better have a TV because there is no way am I going to miss Liam and the Knights winning this game.

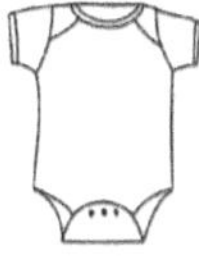

Apparently, you can be five centimeters dilated and not even know it.

When we got here and the nurses brought me back, I thought that they were going to say that I wasn't dilated enough, and that they were going to send me home.

Wrong.

By the time that I got to the hospital, I was already five centimeters and had to be admitted.

Meaning? I was going to miss the last period of the game. Sure, I can check the score on my phone, but it's not the same as in person.

But I still have my dad bring it up on his phone and start it up right where the game was when we left.

Given the cheering I heard from the nurses' station a bit ago, I know the outcome, but I want to see it with my own eyes. I want to see it for the first time and support Liam in every way possible.

Because that's what you do for the man that you love.

The fact that I'm able to even think the words is jaw-dropping, but it's how I fucking feel. And it's not the baby hormones talking.

My parents and I settle in my room, and as nurses come to hook me up to machines and take samples for whatever tests they are conducting, I watch the game.

Who knew that one night with a hockey player could turn you into an obsessive fan?

As the game continues, I bite my nails the whole time in anticipation of whatever is going to happen. Turns out that Florida ended up tying the game right after we left. So, for the majority of the third period, it's a tie game.

When the clock on the screen ticks to under a minute, that is when things start going from exciting to nerve-racking.

My eyes follow the number twenty-one all over the screen, and when he gets the puck in the last twelve seconds, I let out a scream.

I watch as Liam brings back his stick and slaps the puck across the ice and somehow makes it go into the net, right past the goalie's left shoulder.

He scored the winning goal. Instead of letting out another scream, I start to silently cry.

They did it. They won. They won it all.

I hate that I couldn't be there in person.

My eyes stay on the screen, and I continue to cry tears of happiness for the man who has given me so much these last few months, that I almost miss the door opening.

When I turn to see who it is, expecting it to be a nurse coming in to check on me, I cry even more.

Liam comes into the room, looking freshly showered in a pair of sweats with the team logo on them and a T-shirt, and just seeing him makes me cry even more.

Why the hell does this man keep bringing out the crazy emotions out of me?

Instantly, Liam starts to panic and rushes to my side, checking whatever is visible of my body for signs of distress.

"Are you in pain?" he asks, quickly turning to my mom for help.

I let out a few sniffles and reach over to place my hand against his bearded cheek. He hasn't shaved since mid-April.

"You showered?"

He nods. "I didn't want to smell like I cooked myself in rotten cheese."

I let out a teary laugh and glide my thumb along his cheekbone. "I'm so proud of you. You guys did it."

Liam gives me a dazzling smile and turns his head slightly to kiss the inside of my palm.

"I can't believe it either. It hasn't hit me just yet," he tells me.

Every part of me wants to close the distance between us and kiss him, but my parents are here, and things will get embarrassing and awkward fast.

My mom, being my mom, notices my dilemma and pats my dad on the shoulder to get up from the chair he's sitting on.

"We're going to go get something to eat," she says, giving me a smile right before grabbing my dad's hand and leaving the room.

"Are you sure you're not in pain?" Liam asks, placing his hand over mine, and rubbing small circles along my skin.

"I'm sure," I say before doing what I wanted to do earlier and leaning up and brushing my lips against Liam's.

I've been wanting my lips back on his for a long time, and now that it's happening, I can't get enough.

I want more, but there is not much more you can get while in a hospital bed and have wires everywhere.

"Did I tell you that I was proud of you?" I say when I pull away from him.

"You did," he says, dropping our hands and letting them rest on my lap. "Is that what the kiss was for?"

I nod. "That, and I really wanted to do it."

"And why is that?" he asks, a smile playing on his lips and his eyebrows rising.

"Because I realized something earlier," I say, my eyes casting down a bit.

"And what did you realize?" he asks, sitting on the bed, until he's right next to my legs, one of his hands landing on my stomach.

"That I love you," I say with all the conviction that I'm able to muster. Of course, I had to tell him while I was in labor. How cliché of me.

Liam, who was looking down at my hands, looks up with his eyes wide with surprise.

All this time, he's been the one who has expressed his feelings. I was always the one that denied what he was saying, and I never told him that I felt the same way.

I thought it. But I never said it.

Until now. To him and to myself.

"I'm going to need you to repeat that," he orders, his face still looking stunned.

"I realized that I love you," I say again, this time with a lot more strength behind the words. "I know that I'm always pushing your feelings to the side, but I was doing it because I was scared. I was scared that if something happened between us, I would lose you. These last few months, you've become my everything. Friend, lover, father of my child. And while you were my everything, you showed me so much. Kindness, care, love. I kept telling myself that you were only interested in me because of the baby, but even that was getting harder to believe. I'm sorry I pushed your feelings to the side. I'm sorry that my thoughts sometimes got the best of me. I don't want to keep pushing you away. I don't want to move out either. I want to stay with you wherever you live and raise our daughter together. I don't want to figure out holiday arrangements and who gets what weekend. I want us to go to your hockey games and take Emma to her dance recitals and go visit her grandparents in Missouri and Texas. I just want to do this with you, Liam. I want to do this with you and only you. And now I'm a blubbering mess."

I don't know when my tears went from silent to full-on sobs. I swear, there is something about this man that makes my emotions and feelings go haywire.

He did it the first night we met, and he continues to do it now.

Liam shifts, until he's right next to me and taking me in his arms, consoling me.

"I want to do this with you and only you too," he says, into my hair.

"You do?"

"I do. Want to know why?" I nod my head against his

shoulder. "Because I love you, too, sweetheart. I have for a while. You just wouldn't hear it."

"I'm sorry."

"It's okay, you're hearing it now, and that is all that matters."

"Yeah," I say to him.

We stay in that position until a nurse comes in to check in on me.

According to her, we have a long way to go, so we should get comfortable.

So, we do.

For the next five hours, I try to do everything to stay comfortable. I decided to go drug-free for the birth and by the time the nurse tells me that I'm about nine centimeters dilated, I am regretting that decision.

And when I was told that it was time to have this baby, I regretted it even more.

The baby was going to be here very soon, and I was going to feel every single second of it.

My mom and Liam end up staying in the room with me while my dad went out to the waiting room to be with Liam's parents.

Once the doctor gives the go-ahead, everything starts happening so fast.

My mom and Liam each stand at one of my sides, all the while nurses surround them, waiting for something to happen for them to jump right in.

"Okay, Chloe. I'm going to have your mom and Liam hold your legs, and when I say push, you push as hard as you can, okay?" Dr. Long instructs and all I can do is nod.

"You got this, baby. Your mom and I will be here the whole time," Liam tells me, pressing a kiss to my forehead.

"Alright, Chloe. When I say push, you push until I say stop. Got it?"

I give her another nod, not able to find my voice.

"Okay, on three. Push, Chloe. Push."

I do as I'm ordered and push with all that I have. I push until my insides feel like they are getting ripped apart. I push, and I push, and when Dr. Long finally says stop, I feel like I ran a damn marathon while burning alive.

"You are doing so good, baby," Liam says, brushing my hair back.

"One more Chloe. One more and your baby is here."

"She looks like you," Liam says from where he sits next to me on the bed, an arm around me and our daughter.

"My mom said the same thing," I say looking down at the little girl sleeping in my arms.

"I can't believe that a night at the ballet would result in a whole new person coming into our lives," he says, slowly grazing her cheek with the back of his finger.

"I can't believe it either," I say, smiling up at him, remembering what it was like to make eye contact with him from across the room. "I wouldn't change a single thing about it, though."

"Neither would I. Not skipping that night was the best decision that I have ever made. I love the two of you so much."

"And we love you, too. More than you will ever know."

This time last year, I had one thing in mind, and that was dancing.

I was determined to be the best ballerina and dancer that I could be. I was at my peak, and I never wanted to come down.

But now, I still love dancing, and everything that comes with it, but the best decision I made for myself was to keep this pregnancy and give my life a different meaning. I have a little family now, and I may have been at the peak of my career, and I still might be, but being here with Emma and Liam, I'm at the peak of my life, and there is no coming down from it.

Don't get me wrong, I will go back to dancing, but I will do it with my little girl right next to me and Liam, my anchor, in the audience cheering me on. And I will do the same for him with every single hockey game until he retires.

"I never would have put a hockey player and a ballerina together but in our crazy- ass world, it works," Liam says, placing a finger under my chin and tilting my head up to give me a chaste kiss.

"It really does," I say, a smile spreading across my face.

"Thank you for captivating me that night."

"Thank you for giving me *everything*."

EPILOGUE
LIAM

MY EYES POP open the second that I hear something crashing against the floor. If it was any other time, I wouldn't have panicked but since there is now a baby in the house, I'm jumping up to fight off whatever intruder made it into the building and up to my apartment.

It's when I'm on my feet, ready to fight whoever it might be, that the sleep finally clears from my head and my eyes adjust to the minimal light in the living room.

No intruder.

Just Chloe's dad, looking at me like he's trying to hold in a laugh.

"Sorry," he says, leaning down and picking up the vase that he bumped into. Apparently, it's an indestructible vase because it's still intact. "I didn't know you were sleeping on the couch."

I rub at my eyes trying to wake up a little bit more. "The

air mattress that I had in the nursery has a hole in it. I thought that the couch would be better than the floor."

My back hates it but it's only for a few more days, so I can handle it. Besides, the season is officially over, so I don't have to worry about being in pain during practice, at least not for a couple of weeks.

"Is there a reason why you're not sleeping in your own bed?" Saul, Chloe's dad asks, coming over to the couch and taking a seat.

I take a seat a few cushions away and answer his question. "Because Chloe is in there with the baby," I tell him.

"So? You can be in there too," he tells me. "Did you two already have a fight? Do I have to kick your ass for hurting my daughter?"

I shake my head at him, starting to feel a lot more awake. I don't even know what time it is.

"We didn't have a fight and I didn't hurt her." I inform him. "I just thought that since you and your wife were here, it would look bad to share a bed with your daughter."

The Vegas' have been here a little over a month and are set to head back to Austin next week. They've been a big help to both Chloe and I with getting adjusted to being new parents. As for the sleeping arrangements, they've been sleeping in Chloe's room, Chloe in my room and me in the nursery that has yet to be occupied by Emma.

Chloe and I might have said the words "I love you" to each other, after so many months of fucking tension, but I don't want to rush her into anything overly complicated.

Even sharing a bed. Emma should be our top priority, not me taking Chloe on dates or even sexing her up.

Saul lets out a loud snort but then quickly remembers how early in the morning it is and quiets down. "Hijo, we're here because you and my daughter shared a bed already, which resulted in my beautiful granddaughter. I think me and my wife would be completely fine if you sleep in the same bed while we're here."

He does have a point.

We are here because of my shared experiences with his daughter, but that still doesn't make it any less awkward.

"Sleep in your bed tonight. Save your back," Saul says before I can respond to anything.

I just give him a nod. As much as I want to sleep in my own bed, with my girl right next to me and my baby girl sound asleep in her bassinet, it's not up to me. That's Chloe's decision and I'm going to keep it that way.

I'm about to respond when the baby monitor on the coffee table starts to make noise. Even though I'm not sleeping in the same room, I'm still doing my part when it comes to taking care of Emma in the middle of the night. Waking up at odd hours shouldn't just fall on Chloe. It's my responsibility too and since I'm already awake, it's my turn.

Saul throws me a nod and a smile before I get up from the couch and head down the hall to the master bedroom.

I open the door as quietly as I can and find that Chloe is still sleeping and hasn't heard the baby rustling just yet.

A smile can't help but to spread across my face as I see the sight of the two of them.

Walking over to the bassinet, I lean over and find my three-week old daughter tossing and turning and making little noises that tell me that she's about to let out a loud cry.

"Hey baby girl, you okay?" I say, lifting my daughter up, and cradling her against my bare chest, trying to calm her down before her mother wakes up.

With baby in hand, I walk over to the nursery and after checking her diaper, I grab one of the bottles that Chloe placed in the warmer for me last night and go sit on the rocking chair in the corner.

It's crazy to think that not even a year ago, this little girl wasn't even a thought and now watching her eat and having her in my arms is one of the coolest and best things that has ever happened to me.

Above getting drafted at nineteen.

Above winning the Stanley Cup, but not before meeting her mother.

I feed Emma for a bit longer and after burping her, she ends up falling back asleep. I should get up and walk her back to her bassinet in the other room, but since she's only going to be this small for so long, I decide to just stay here and take her in.

Apparently, I stay long enough for Chloe to wake up and come into the room.

She walks in still wearing the short and tank top combo that I have a love hate relationship with. If she was able to, I would be dragging her back to my bedroom and pulling down her choice of sleepwear and having my way with her.

That thought quickly disappears, though, when I remember what I'm holding in my arms.

It doesn't stop me from being captivated by this woman like the first night that we met, though.

"Why didn't you wake me?" Chloe asks, closing the door behind her and giving me a smile.

From where I'm sitting, I can see that her eyes are still filled with sleep and that she could use a couple of more hours in bed.

As much as I want to tell her to get a few more hours of sleep, I don't. I've been chewed out a few times since we came home from the hospital about that very thing, and I don't feel like going there again at five o'clock in the morning.

"It was my turn." I say, giving her a shrug and looking down at the sleeping baby in my arms.

"Did she take the bottle?" she asks, coming closer to me and the baby.

I give her a nod. "Like a champ."

"Good," Chloe says, giving me a smile and coming to sit on the floor next to the rocker.

For a few minutes, we watch the baby sleep. I'm about to suggest to Chloe that she go get ready for the day but when I look up, I see her looking up at me sort of lost in a daze.

"What?" I ask her.

The second I ask the question, her gaze shifts a bit and becomes a lot more heated than I have seen in a few weeks.

"Do you remember when we were taking pictures with Eliana and you said that if you could, you would take every single picture that she took that day and frame them, just so you can look at them every single day?"

I nod. It's the day that I started making my feelings known, of course I remember.

And I get those pictures framed.

One of me and Chloe is currently on the table next to me, and I have another in the living room. If she would have let me, there would be one in my bedroom.

Our bedroom?

I have no fucking clue.

"I do."

"That's what I want to do right now. I want to take a picture of the two of you so I can frame it and look at it every single day." She tells me and the smile she gives me is so damn beautiful that I can't comprehend how the actual fuck I got so damn lucky.

"Take it," I tell her, throwing her a wink. "My phone is on the changing table."

Her smile gets even bigger as she quickly gets to her feet and goes to grab my phone.

"The passcode is 090622," I say, rocking back and forth to keep the baby asleep.

"What's 090622?" she asks, her brows bunching up as she types in the code.

"The night we met." I state, and right away she is looking up at me with a stunned expression.

It takes her a second to say something. "You have the night we met as your passcode?"

I give her a nod. "I do. Did you think I was lying when I said that I loved you?"

I can't help but let an eyebrow raise and throw a smirk in her direction. The blush that I can see coating her cheeks is like a reward.

She shakes her head. "No, I-I," she stutters then stops as if she's trying to collect herself. "I just didn't think you would be that sentimental."

"Sweetheart, when it comes to you and our daughter, I'm very fucking sentimental." I tell her, throwing her a wink that just makes her blush all that deeper.

Chloe bites down on her lip and takes a picture without giving me any warning.

I just chuckle and look down at our daughter in my arms.

"Hear that, Emma? Your mommy didn't think that I could be sentimental. Little does she know, I'm sentimental as shit." I tell the sleeping baby, leaning forward and placing a kiss against her dark curls that are so much like her mother's.

"Shut up. Let me take pictures of the sexy tattooed man holding his baby," she throws out.

Great, now I'm the one blushing.

I hear the camera shutter go off and I look up and throw Chloe another smile.

"Come over here," I say nodding toward the rocking chair, getting an idea.

She doesn't question me; she just walks over.

Shifting Emma, a bit, I grab Chloe's hand and pull her toward me until she's partially sitting on my lap.

"What are you doing?" she asks in a whisper, a small laugh escaping.

"Taking a family picture," I say, grabbing my phone from her hand and positioning it so that all three of us come out on the screen.

Apart from a few pictures at the hospital, there aren't that many pictures of the three of us together. I'm changing that.

Both Chloe and I do our best to change up the poses without moving too much and not waking up the baby. For the most part we succeed, with most pictures of the two of us making silly faces to the camera. It's the last few pictures where my lips are against Chloe's that are my favorite.

Moments between us have been far and between these last three weeks, so any moment I get with her I will make the most of it.

For a second, I get so lost in kissing her that I almost forget that I'm holding the baby. Almost. I pull away from Chloe when I feel Emma squirm against me.

"She doesn't like you kissing her mommy," Chloe says, giving my lips one last kiss before putting some space between us.

I can't help but let out a snort at the statement. "We better fix that then, because when her mommy is ready, I'm going to be doing a lot more than kissing."

A sweet giggle fills my ears and Chloe shifts until her head is leaning against my shoulder and I can feel her breath against my neck.

"Will you? Will you be doing a lot more than kissing?" she says after a few beats of silence.

I nod. "Unless you tell me otherwise."

"Never," she tells me, placing a kiss right against my neck.

Something that sounds very much like a growl moves through my chest and escapes through my lips and I don't hesitate to pull Chloe's body closer to mine. "Keep saying things like that and pretty soon, you will be finding a ring on your finger, and you won't be able to get rid of me until I take my last breath."

"Is that just a promise or a guarantee?" Another kiss lands against my neck and I can't help but to think this woman is going to be the death of me.

Hell, she has been since the first night we met.

"One hundred percent a guarantee," I say, pulling back a tiny bit to place my head against her curls.

"Can't wait," she purrs, curling herself even more into me.

I don't know how long we sit there for, but I don't care. For that little bit, it's just me, Chloe, and our little girl.

So many things have happened in the last ten months, and I wouldn't change anything for the fucking world.

A night at the ballet gave me everything that I didn't know I wanted. Everything that I didn't know that I fucking needed. Absolutely fucking everything.

In ten months, I added a Stanley Cup win under my belt, I was given the title of dad and hopefully in another ten months, I can earn the title of husband, because I wasn't lying when I mentioned a ring.

Chloe and I may have only said I love you three weeks

ago, but I know that this woman is my everything. I knew it a few months ago and sure as hell know it now. I'm not giving her up. I will never let her walk away from me.

Me and her are the forever type of thing and that is how it's going to stay. No matter how long it took her to realize it.

I love her and she loves me.

We're going to build a life together. I'm going to win more cups, and she's going to continue to dance and make sure every single person watching her is captivated and maybe, just maybe we will be able to give Emma a sibling or two.

For now, though, I'm going to enjoy having both of my girls in my arms.

"Hey, Chlo?" I whisper, nudging her hip with my hand.

She lets out a hum telling me that she is falling asleep. "Hmm?"

"Thank you for captivating me that night." I repeat the same words I told her in the hospital after Emma was born.

She pulls back and gives me a smile. "Thank you for being in the audience and giving me the world."

"Always, sweetheart. Always. Just like I told you I would."

EXTENDED EPILOGUE
CHLOE

Three months later

I don't know what I should be more worried about.

The fact that I just got a text from Liam that said Christian and Blake are going to be arriving at our apartment soon to fulfill some bet they made or the fact that his two teammates might ruin my surprise.

I want to go with the second one, I really do, especially given what day it is, but the word bet scares me.

What bet?

And why the hell do they have to go to the apartment to fulfill it?

I sometimes don't understand these three and I live with one of them.

Dios mío, all I can picture is them playing hockey in the living room and Emma being in the middle of it.

Liam won't let anything happen to her.

Sure, but that still doesn't help alleviate the worry.

Shaking my head, I try to calm down while me and my surprise get on the train to head back to the apartment.

It's been a year.

One year since the ballet and one year since Liam and I met. A whole damn year.

It may not be an official anniversary date, even with Liam having the date as his passcode, but I'm still treating it as a special day.

This time last year, the only thing that I was thinking about was dance and now a whole year later, my life is completely different than how I would have imagined it.

And I wouldn't ask for anything else.

Because of my pregnancy, I may have lost the chance to perform for a few weeks, but that's okay. It was for the better and now not only am I slowly getting back into dance, but I also now have my daughter and Liam and that is all I could have asked for.

That and hoping that my surprise doesn't get ruined. I've been planning this for a while now and I really want to make sure that it all comes out perfectly.

Is that too much to ask?

A bark sounds in front of me telling me that yes, it is too much to ask.

"It's fine. Everything will be fine. You will get to the apartment before the boys, you will surprise Liam and everything will be okay."

I honestly don't know why I'm worrying about it so

much, it's not like Liam is going to leave me if something goes wrong. He'll laugh, sure, but he'll still fuck me in our bed tonight and show me all the ways that he loves me.

That right there is still so surreal to me.

Last year I was content being a dancer and it being every inch of my life. Now, I can't see myself without Liam and Emma.

The man loves me in so many ways that I find it crazy and the fact that I can say *our* apartment, and *our* bed is even crazier. I gave up my apartment officially two months ago and moved everything that I own into Liam's. There is no going back, there's no potentially moving out, this shit is one hundred percent real, and I love every single thing about it.

And hopefully my surprise goes well, and he will love it even more.

When the train arrives at my station, I grab the stroller my surprise is in and start making my way home.

Thank god I thought about taking a stroller to my dance class this morning, because no way was I going to be able to walk with this big boy in my arms all the way home.

Getting to our apartment building is the easy part, the hard part comes when I wheel my surprise into the elevator, and it start to freak out.

"It's okay. It's only for a few seconds," I say to it, trying to calm it down so it doesn't pee, and I have to buy Emma a new stroller.

Thankfully, the elevator ride isn't that long and the second that we step on solid ground, the freaking out stops.

I'm sweating, why am I sweating?

Brushing off my panic, I walk us over to the front door and hesitate for a second.

Maybe this is a bad idea.

What if he doesn't like it?

One way to find out.

I open the door and right away I hear the sound of the TV and a few male voices.

Sounds like Christian and Blake are already here. Thank God I didn't decide to buy a sexy outfit and wear it.

Walking into the apartment, my hand firmly on the stroller, I head to the living room and find Blake and Logan, another teammate, sitting on the couch watching a baseball game on the flat screen on top of the fireplace.

No Liam.

I have a little bit of time to calm down.

"Hey, guys," I say, giving them a shaky smile.

"Hey, Chloe," they both say, giving me waves.

"Where's Liam?" I ask, pushing the stroller back and forth so that what's inside doesn't make any noise.

"In the room helping Christian change Emma's diaper. She had an accident," Blake explains, turning back to look at the TV.

"Why is Christian changing her diaper?" I ask, a little confused. I thought that they came over to fulfill a bet.

"Because he lost a race and now, he has to change her diaper for a whole day," Blake answers with a big smile on his face.

How my daughter became a part of this bet, I have no

idea and I really don't want to know. But either way, I should check in on them.

"Can you watch this while I help them?" I ask, pushing the stroller to the middle of the living room between the two men.

Thank god, I thought to put a blanket over it then the surprise would be ruined.

Both Logan and Blake look at each other with confused looks before they give me a nod.

"Sure?"

"Thanks."

Leaving the stroller, I head down the hallway and into the nursery where I find the two huge men looking down at the baby laying on the changing table.

"There's no way you feed her just milk. That smell does not come from only milk," Christian says, waving a diaper around.

"Trust me, it's just milk. Just take off the onesie and change her diaper," Liam instructs his friend.

"And what do I do with the onesie? It has shit all over it." I may be hearing things, but I think Christian gagged a little.

"Put it in the bag and I will throw it away or burn it," Liam suggests, and I can't help but laugh.

Both men turn to look at me. One looks like he wants me to rescue him and the other is amused by the whole thing.

"You two need help?" I ask, trying hard not to smile.

"Nope, Chris has it covered. Don't you?" Liam says giving his friend a hard slap against the shoulder.

"Sure, if you find me in my own puke, you know why," he grumbles and turns back to the baby and starts cleaning her up.

I feel bad for the guy and I'm about to step in and help but Liam shakes his head at me and walks me out of the room into the hallway.

"How was your dance class?" He asks, after placing a chaste kiss against my lips.

I love it when he does that.

"It was fine, we should be getting the schedule for winter rehearsals soon. Why is Christian changing our daughter's diaper?" I ask, even though Blake already gave me the answer.

Liam shrugs. "The idiot lost to the rookie. Figured it was something to make things interesting."

And he calls Christian and Blake children. He's one too.

"When was this race?" I ask.

"I don't remember. December?"

"December and he's finally paying up now? He could have come over two months ago, and I would have gladly passed over my duties," I say to him.

Liam smiles down on me before pushing me against the wall and giving me another kiss. "Have I told you how much I fucking love you?"

"Not today."

Liam opens his mouth to say something, but he's stopped when Blake comes into the hallway pushing the stroller.

"Um, Chloe? Your stroller is whining and moving around," he says looking a little scared.

My eyes go wide as I look from Blake to the stroller back to Liam. This is definitely not how I planned on this going.

"Thanks." I say, sliding under Liam's arm and taking the stroller from Blake. He heads back to the living room and me and Liam are left in the hallway with his surprise right in the middle.

"What is that?" Liam asks, a small smirk forming in his face.

Given the sounds that are filling the hallway, he has an idea of what it is.

"Today is our anniversary," I say, pushing my shoulders back and giving him a bright smile.

"Our anniversary?" He asks, looking at me with a raised eyebrow.

Did he forget?

No way, it's his passcode.

"Yeah, the anniversary of the night we met. Did you forget?"

He scratches his head. "I thought it was tomorrow," he says sheepishly.

Oh my god.

I can say so many things, but I don't.

"Well, it's today and I got you something. A surprise," I say, feeling a little nervous he's not going to like it. Maybe he changed his mind. And if he did, hopefully he changes it back because no way am I returning it.

"A surprise," he says, looking at the stroller.

"Yes, take the blanket off."

He does as I say in the slowest way possible. It reminds

me of the night I told him we were having a girl, and he took all the time in the world opening the present.

The second that the blanket is off, though, the smirk he's wearing turns into a full-blown grin that takes over his face.

"That night you told me that you moved into a bigger apartment because you wanted to get a dog, but you hadn't done it yet. Right away, I started picturing you with a golden retriever puppy that you would spoil rotten. I was planning it for a while and last week I stopped by the shelter and found this little guy. He was a part of a litter that they found by the river. He was the last one. The second I saw him, I thought he would be the perfect addition to our family."

I watch as Liam crunches down to be at eye level with the golden retriever puppy in our daughter's stroller. His smile grows with every swipe at the puppy's fur.

"You got me a dog?" He asks in amazement.

I bite down on my bottom lip. "I did. Is that okay?"

That's what I've been freaking out about. I know we're together and building a life, but I still didn't want to overstep.

Liam stands to full height and walks around the stroller and our new addition and once again cages me against the wall.

"Very okay. Thank you," he says right before his lips land against mine.

The kiss is short, since we have company, but it's enough to leave me panting and wanting so much more of my man. So, so much more.

"The puppy isn't the only surprise," I say pulling my lips away from him just slightly.

"Oh yeah?"

I nod. "I also might have stopped at a toy store before my class this morning." I say, remembering the last time I used my *toys*. That memory is still something I think about every single day. And every urge that I have Liam satisfies every single time.

"Toy store?" he asks, and I can see his smile growing as his forehead rests against mine.

"*Toy* store, yes. I'll show you. After your friends leave," I say, giving him a wink.

Apparently, he doesn't like that because the man legit growls.

"Fuck that," he says pulling away fully and starts heading down the hall. "You two, leave." He orders of Blake and Logan.

"But it's only the sixth inning and Bauer is on fire."

"Go watch it at a bar, or hey, better idea, your apartments."

Both men grumble but nevertheless, they get up and leave.

"What about Christian?" I ask Liam when he comes back to the hallway. I'm trying to hold back a smile but fail.

He throws me a wink and heads into the nursery as if he were on a mission.

"Hey asshole, you're on baby and puppy duty for the next two hours," Liam tells Christian, and I hear him opening drawers and the closet door probably getting a diaper bag ready.

"What the hell? Why? And when the hell did you get a

puppy?" Christian asks as he comes out of the room with Emma in his arms and gives me a confused look. When he sees the puppy in the stroller, he looks even more confused.

I can't help but laugh and take my daughter from him and adjust the new onesie that he put her in.

Liam says that she looks like me, and while she may have my curls and my eyes, she is all Liam.

"Right now," Liam says coming out of the room. "Here is the diaper bag. There are bottles ready with milk all set to go in the kitchen, take all of them plus the baby carrier," he says, handing Christian the diaper bag. "Here is the baby and the puppy, don't come back until I text you."

I hold in a laugh as Liam takes Emma from my arms and hands her over to Christian.

The laugh erupts when Liam picks me up and throws me over his shoulder, leaving his friend in the hallway dumbfounded.

"Liam!" I yell out as we make our way down the hallway.

"You're going to owe me for this!" Christian calls out toward us as we walk into our bedroom and Liam slams the door behind us.

"Leave!" Liam yells toward the door and before I can even comprehend what is happening, I'm back on my feet and he's on me with our lips and tongues playing tonsil hockey.

"So, you said something about a toy," Liam starts, pulling my shirt over my head.

All I can do is laugh and let him have his way with me.

One year. That's all it took.

One year to go from nothing to everything.

Liam gave me everything I never thought I needed.

And in return, I will give him the same.

THE END.

Read the other 2 books in the series!

Read Christian's and Eliana's story!

Grab Passing The Red Line today and start reading!
Read it today!

Read Blake and Sophia's story!

Grab Hitting The Goal Line today and start reading!
Read it today!

WHAT'S COMING UP NEXT?

Are you wondering if Logan Volkov is getting his own book?
He is!
But before we get to Logan, we have to step into the darkness
a bit.
And why not start that by stepping into the world of the Lane
Family?
Book 1 of the Lane Family is coming Fall 2024! I hope you
are ready!
Pre-order now!

PLAYLIST

Get You - Daniel Caesar, Kali Uchis
Happiness is a Butterfly - Lana del Rey
Für Elise - Beethoven Collection
Cherry - Harry Styles
Take Me To Church - Hozier
Still Don't Know My Name - Labrinth
Heather - Conan Gray
Give Me Love - Ed Sheeran
A Drop in the Ocean - Ron Pope
La Santa - Bad Bunny, Daddy Yankee
Mi Coranzoncito - Aventura
Suga Suga - Baby Bash, Frankie K
Nasty - Ariana Grande

Powerful Deception

Fake Love

Salutis Meae

ABOUT THE AUTHOR

Jocelyne Soto is an independent author living in California. She loves reading romance and discovering new authors. She comes from a big Mexican family, and with it comes a love for all things family and food.

Jocelyne has a love for her mom's coffee and writing. In her free time, you can find her reading a romance novel on her kindle while writing heartwarming and chaotic romance stories in between.

Check out her website for ways to connect with Jocelyne!
www.jocelynesoto.com

BB bookbub.com/authors/jocelyne-soto

g goodreads.com/jocelynesotobooks

instagram.com/authorjocelynesoto

tiktok.com/@authorjocelynesoto

facebook.com/authorjocelynesoto

X x.com/authorjocelynes

pinterest.com/authorjocelynesoto

Join my ever-growing Facebook Group. You get first looks,
sneak peeks and giveaways!

NEWSLETTER

Sign up for my Newsletter!
You will get notified when there are new
releases to look out for, giveaways and more!

9 781956 430196